THE
MOMENT BETWEEN
THE PAST AND THE FUTURE

THE
MOMENT BETWEEN
THE PAST AND THE FUTURE

Grigory Baklanov

Translated by
CATHERINE PORTER

faber and faber
LONDON · BOSTON

First published in 1994
by Faber and Faber Limited
3 Queen Square London WC1N 3AU

Typeset in Palatino by Intype, London
Printed in England by Clays Ltd St Ives plc

Translation © Catherine Porter, 1994

Catherine Porter is hereby identified as translator of this
work in accordance with Section 77 of the Copyright,
Designs and Patents Act 1988.

A CIP record for this book is
available from the British Library

ISBN 0–571–16444–7

2 3 4 6 8 10 9 7 5 3 1

ONE

The brick two-storeyed dacha, with its semicircular porch and white pillars, had had three owners by the time Usvatov moved in. Each new arrival had banished the spirit of his predecessor and established his own presence by making alterations to the inside of the house, or building on to the outside, so that from whatever angle one looked at it, no one part resembled another.

Three years before the death of Stalin Academician Elagin had arrived. Elagin was said to be the author of a brilliant work of Stalinist theory which 'opened up new philosophical horizons'. For his anonymous labours he was promoted from associate to full membership of the Academy of Sciences, and was able to buy himself this dacha in a prestigious village near Moscow. He did not live there permanently, since he apparently owned another house in town, on Nikolin Hill; no one knew the exact details, but he paid all his village expenses promptly, and was always on time with his bills.

It was Elagin who added the semicircular porch, knocked through the main entrance and replaced the existing doors with shuttered stable-type doors. Two white pillars, guarding the entrance like sentries, supported a semicircular balcony with white carved balusters and white railings, and on summer evenings, when the sun dipped beneath the branches of the pine-trees, Elagin loved to sit on the balcony, dangling his slippers from his toes. How sweet it was to breathe the evening air in the peace of the country. To think that all this had once been an unimaginably distant dream. He remembered himself as a young man one summer may years ago, when he and his weeping, terrified wife had pushed their

1

vomiting four-month-old son in his pram to the professor's forest dacha. It was a Sunday, and they were far from the town and any help, and they could see their baby dying before their eyes. They had hurried round the high fence timidly knocked and calling out the professor's name – but the mossy wicket-gate of the dacha remained closed to them. When it was finally opened, they stumbled from the gloom of the forest into another world: the warm, dry, sunlit garden with its huge bed of roses – tea roses, crimson roses, black-red roses and roses they had never seen before, whose very smell made their lips sweet; the wooden cottage with its fresh coat of green paint and its white windows; and the old man – the professor himself – sitting framed by two huge blue fir-trees, sunning himself peacefully like a starling in its nest. At the time it had seemed as though they could think of nothing but the baby, yet it all remained in Elagin's memory, and as the years passed he recalled ever more vividly the rose-beds, the dacha, the white windows and a special lightness in the air, unlike any he had ever breathed before.

Elagin's life was almost over before the dream of the balcony and the dangling slipper came true. In the garden below, his dumpy bespectacled daughter dipped fluffy yellow ducklins into a little bath set out in the sun; she should have had babies of her own to bathe by now. At his daughter's happy shrieks his grey-haired wife, her face puffy from bending over, sat back on her wide behind and looked up smiling from the rose-bed; it was many years now since Elagin had slept with her. Deep in thought, talking and gesticulating to himself his son walked along paths lined with nineteen different strains of phlox. In his gait and demeanour he was the very image of a science don. 'He's got everything!' marvelled Feklusha, the domestic help. She was the only one who thought so, though. Elagin remembered someone saying that nature toils to produce its geniuses, then takes a rest with their descendants. By the age of four his son could read fluently; when friends came, he would read out of a book, and everyone thought he was very sweet. By the age of six he had started displaying a talent for science. And now at thirty-three – the age at which Christ had died! – he was as bald as a fifty-year-old and still showed great promise and a talent for science ... Elagin sighed, turned away and sighed again: it was hard to imagine the three of them managing without him. Although he would never have admitted this to himself, there were times when he felt an almost physical revulsion for his son, with his broad, bent back and his shuffling, paw-like feet.

After his anonymous philosophical labours and all that ensued from them Elagin had grown increasingly depressed. His colleagues' flattery did not please him any more than the villagers' obsequiousness; if he shook hands with them, they bowed and scraped and walked away as though he had given them a medal. When he arrived in the village some had hurried over to introduce themselves and invite him to meet their families, little knowing that the slightest hint of his complicity in the mighty Stalinist achievement would make him faint with terror. He knew only too well what had happened to the authors of other brilliant Stalinist works, the ones who had not merely disappeared but had had their names obliterated from living memory. He started waking in the middle of the night and listening in fear for the sound of an approaching car. He also developed the unfortunate habit of looking over his shoulder ... All this was in marked contrast with his imposing appearance.

Throughout a life spent working on abstract issues he had eagerly seized every opportunity to write about the 'people' as creators of language. He always imagined the 'people' to be rather like Klava the dairymaid, who brought the milk each morning on her motor cycle and poured it from her big churn in a thick yellow stream into their can on the porch. 'Drink up, my lovelies, it's all fresh from the cow!' she would say with a bright smile on her round weather-beaten face.

One day when some workers were securing the foundations of his garage – he loved that word, 'secure' – he saw that

3

instead of piling in builders' rubble they were levering a freshly uprooted clay-covered tree-stump into the foundations with their crowbar. Incensed, Elagin rushed out on to the balcony in his heavy camel-hair dressing-gown with the silk cord. 'What the hell do you think you're doing?' he shouted down to them. 'You should be ashamed . . . !'

At that point he heard Klava shrieking, probably unaware that he was there. 'In my day if you had a horse, two cows and a couple of sheep, they called you a kulak and packed you and your kids off to the Urals. This bloody lot have cars and brick houses, but *they're* not kulaks, oh no . . . !'

Hanging her churn and her string bag on the handlebars of her motor cycle, the kindly Klava, who had brought him his milk all these years, did not berate the workers as she should have done but laughed spitefully. Her face at that moment frightened and confused him, and he sheepishly withdrew into his room without saying another word, while the workers went on manoeuvring the stump into the trench. He never told his wife, and when a crack appeared along the garage wall after the first winter, he looked as puzzled as she was as to where it had come from. The men had been such good workers, after all . . . For the first time he felt all the vulnerability and insecurity of his position, should anything – God forbid! – happen. The kinder power was surely that which punished without quarter but defended a select few, and he entrusted his quaking soul to its mercy.

An era had ended, yet the dead man still held sway over the living. People dared not hope that the times they had lived through had been artificially sustained; they seemed natural and eternal, and people could seen no other future for themselves. Who would have imagined that before long the unthinkable would happen, and all secrets would be revealed? That at one party meeting after another lists of those who had recently been beyond criticism would be read out, and that what the powerful and mighty had got up to behind closed doors with little girls and actresses would be disclosed?

4

What was the purpose of all these revelations which undermined the very foundations of society? And so Academician Elagin was forced to make wretched excuses to his inquisitive colleagues (the older ones especially), swearing that yes, he had indeed once licked cream from the naked shoulder of a pretty girl – an actress, the same age as his daughter – but nothing else, mainly because he wasn't up to it any longer, as his wife could testify . . . Here, of course, he was taking liberties with the truth. Those knowing little girls had taught him that he was indeed still up to it. For the first time in a life of ignorance and academic pursuits he had discovered and regretted much, and even started to regard his son with a certain condescending disdain.

When the house was bought by its next owner, Evgeny Stepanovich Usvatov, Elagin was long dead, a massive heart attack having spared him from further interrogations by inquisitive colleagues. Evgeny Stepanovich bought the house before the 1975 currency reform, and afterwards he was visited several times by Elagin junior, slightly seedy now but still with the same donnish manners and demeanour. The foolish fellow had got it in his head that he hadn't been paid enough and that Usvatov owed him money . . . Elagin's son had actually received the money before the reform, but had not had the sense to spend it in time, and now he seemed to think that he was owed some sort of compensation, and that he and his sister should be found alternative accommodation. 'You're one of us, after all . . .' he kept saying. Evgeny Stepanovich would send him packing, but he was forever creeping back to haunt his old home. He had grown up there, and suddenly the door had been slammed in his face. All his old friends had held on to their jobs, new people were making their way in the world; it was only right that they should share some of what they had, not push the others out . . .

Evgeny Stepanovich hated the stupid way Elagin's son had gazed at him, especially since he had indeed underpaid him – he had bought the house for a song and would certainly be able to sell it for three times the price. During one of the man's visits he led him out to the porch, from which the troops of a construction battalion were digging out some rotten foundation blocks. 'See that? Look what you've sold me! It's rubbish!' Evgeny Stepanovich shouted.

He was in his early fifties, and was still fit and strong, and the soldiers, stripped to the waist, crowbars in their gloved hands, laughed happily at the balding little owl at his side. 'They filled it in on the cheap! It's daylight robbery! In Moscow you dig a metre before you reach clay, here it's less than half a metre. And you have the nerve to keep coming back . . . !'

That night Evgeny Stepanovich was suddenly awakened by footsteps prowling through the house. A full moon shone outside the window, and the dark shadow of a fir branch waved against the gleaming blind. Sleep and fear at first prevented him from realizing that the sound was his own heart pounding in his ears. He saw himself once again pushing Elagin's son towards the dark trench and driving him out of the yard, and he saw the bent back and the bald head pass through the wicket-gate for the last time . . . As he lay there, he sensed that this contained some sort of message for him. But in the light of day the fears of the night appear absurd.

Under the veranda, which warped and slipped further away from the house every winter, Evgeny Stepanovich laid new foundations a metre and a half deep. The cracked pillars were repaired, all the floorboards downstairs were taken up, the undersides were painted with two coats of wood-preservative and the boards were relaid. Afterwards Evgeny Stepanovich entered the draughty, empty rooms, their newly painted windows flung open to get rid of the smell. He strode proprietorially over his new floors, he jumped on them (he was alone, so no one could see him), he walked and jumped again; the boards had been fitted perfectly, not one moved or creaked underfoot.

The following year a fence was put up around the garden.

One day when Evgeny Stepanovich was driving past the builders, he went to the foreman and said, 'Now look here, these posts have been laid wrong . . .' And so the fence was laid on concrete blocks.

Several years later Evgeny Stepanovich celebrated both his sixtieth birthday and a recent literary award by throwing a house-warming party at his dacha, in the good clean air of the country.

TWO

It was an illustrious gathering. As well as various people of Evgeny Stepanovich's own rank, there was a cosmonaut and his wife, and a famous chess-player who rolled up in a white Land-Rover, which caused a big stir. There was also the author of a number of much discussed novels, and a man who sang his own songs in a hoarse voice rather like Vysotsky's. Successful, wealthy people who had worked hard to ensure life's many little blessings, they conducted themselves with the modesty appropriate to those who are aware of their power and bask in its privileges. The elegant banquet that afternoon did not go unappreciated, and one of the guests, in a quiet voice which everyone heard, proposed a toast to 'all those who have made it possible'.

The star of the occasion, Evgeny Stepanovich, was congratulated on his medal, even though it had not yet been officially announced. To be frank, Evgeny Stepanovich had been expecting this highly coveted honour. In fact he had spared no efforts to get it, since modesty, as the poet said, is the surest path to oblivion. Evgeny Stepanovich, who also had a gift for imagery, used to say that for a government official to allow people to forget his existence is as fatal as losing speed on water-skis – you sink and drown. He had actually read this somewhere but had found it so pleasing that he had appropriated it for his own use.

The minute the fuss about the award was over he experienced a familiar nagging sense of dissatisfaction. His wife, Elena, who always expressed herself bluntly when they were alone, said, 'If you weren't such a dope, you'd have got something a lot better than that bit of tin. What about old so-

8

and-so? Why do you let everyone grab the best prizes?' She mercilessly reeled off a list of names, but Evgeny Stepanovich did not want to spoil things on this of all days, and refused to be drawn. Besides, she generally supported him loyally in all his ventures, and he valued her advice. At the time when he had been defending his doctoral thesis she had rung round all the people they knew. To those on the 'left' she had said, 'Don't you understand, he's one of you! He can't let it be known, for tactical reasons. You know how they win people over and fill up every niche. Without you behind him, they'll walk all over him . . .' To those on the 'right' she said, 'You know he's one of you, you *must* support him. They're plotting to trample on him, I've heard it on good authority . . .' As a result of all Elena's lobbying he was backed by both camps.

Recently, on returning to the cool of the country one evening after work – it had been a particularly hot day in Moscow – Evgeny Stepanovich had been held up by some roadworks: massive steamrollers trundled through the blue-grey fumes, and the asphalt was black, sticky and of excellent quality. Evgeny Stepanovich had always meant to asphalt the drive to his dacha, and after a few telephone calls to the relevant people he was promised a couple of lorry-loads of asphalt and a gang of students from the Highways Institute – 'construction troops', as they were known during the summer months.

As usual, of course, something went wrong; Soviet spacecraft manage to rendezvous in orbit, but in this sort of thing somebody invariably slips up, and the students arrived not on Thursday but at the weekend, so that the asphalt was being laid just as the guests were arriving. Since it was too late to change anything, Elena Vasilevna told her guests with a disarming smile, 'Please don't mind our little escapades!' 'Escapades' did not sound quite right here, but like all incomprehensible utterances, the meaning was understood.

Outside the massive cast-iron, scroll-topped gates a row of cars stood in the shade of the fence, some with their drivers dozing at the wheel. The students, in their worn jeans, track-suit bottoms, beach caps and home-made paper hats, sat beside the ditch on the other side of the road. All wore the faded orange waistcoats which were compulsory for their third, working semester on the roads. As car after car drew up at the gates, they waited for the next lorry-load of asphalt, swatting the mosquitoes off each other's sweaty backs, swigging cartons of milk and bottles of water and savouring the smell of roasting kebabs and charcoal smoke coming from the garden.

The person in charge of the kebabs was Elena Vasilevna's brother-in-law. A man of drunken habits, he was not normally allowed into the house – or even over the threshold – but his kebabs were unrivalled. Evgeny Stepanovich strictly forbade the others to give him anything to drink, and would run out every so often to see how he was doing. The man's greasy face was scarlet from the heat of the coals, and as he fanned the row of kebabs, sprinkled them with water and pushed back over his ear the lock of hair which fell from his bald patch, Evgeny Stepanovich's chauffeur handed him skewer after skewer of lamb from the two basins of marinade which stood on the grass. The kebabs dripped fat on to the charcoal, wafting their fragrant blue smoke under the pine-trees. Meanwhile dishes were brought to the veranda, the tables were laid and then plump hostess with her huge raven-black beehive hairdo came out to apologize to her guests that Basalaev had not yet arrived – and everyone knew that they could not possibly start without Basalaev.

The guests wandered about the garden and gathered around the chess-player's white Land-Rover, which had left deep tyre-marks in the fresh asphalt by the gates. ('Don't worry, old man, they can smooth it out,' his host assured him.) The chess-player announced, as if people of their circle would find it the most natural thing in the world, that he had picked up the car in England straight from the factory, minus tax, which meant it had cost him just three thousand pounds, rather than four and a half. Sterling. He eagerly climbed inside, fiddled with the controls and made the chassis rise up in the air; 'Very useful over there if you get stuck in the mud on country lanes,' he explained. 'The farmers use them. You should see their roads . . . !'

As Evgeny Stepanovich moved among the guests, the subversive thought suddenly came to him that this kind of conversation would not so long ago have been . . . Well, life moved on, things changed – but was it for the better?

The guests were all from the same world, and the talk was of forthcoming appointments, promotions and various rumours. The only person out of place was a retired colonel, who was said to have served in the army with Evgeny Stepanovich. Whenever anyone addressed him, he smiled the tense, eager smile of the deaf. People did not notice the man himself so much as the five bright rows of medals on his grey jacket. He was small and nondescript, and the medals looked rather ludicrous on someone of his frame and stature.

On his retirement the Colonel had devoted himself to veteran affairs, and he dreamed of setting up a little museum of his army division and publishing a book on its military exploits. He had done quite a bit of research, and in the course of this had discovered that among the now prosperous and distinguished people who had served with them was none other than Evgeny Stepanovich Usvatov.

Clutching a folder of papers, he had shyly rung the bell of Usvatov's Moscow flat, hoping to enlist his support for the museum. But he also had another secret purpose in mind. His elder son wanted to enter the Academy of Foreign Trade (or that's what he thought it was called), and his daughter-in-law was determined to better herself. So the Colonel, who adored his grandsons but had fought in the Finnish War and the Second World War without ever managing to make the right contacts, had finally resolved to make an appointment to see Usvatov. He stood outside the door like a petitioner, gripping his folder and a tempting list of items 'in special demand', available exclusively to veterans. He was received coldly.

Evgeny Stepanovich had no need of a Soviet-made Orpheus partition, price 1,500 roubles, or a Minsk refrigerator, or a Moskvich motor car – he could get hold of such items any time he liked. When Elena Vasilevna later recounted the story to their friends, the part about the Soviet-made Orpheus partition was especially successful. 'Made at night, from skimped materials, I'll be bound!' one of them laughed.

But, as they say, everyone has his uses. And when pushed by his son and daughter-in-law to attempt a second visit, the Colonel was greeted most warmly and even invited out to the country, something he would never have thought possible. Flattered and disarmed, he checked his medals and, on discovering to his chagrin that two were missing, set off for the military store. After finding his name on the list they stuck his five rows of four medals – awarded for various battles during the war and various achievements after it was over – on to a plain bar.

Bearing a copy of their divisional newspaper – a precious gift, since there were only two in his entire archive – the Colonel caught the suburban train and set out on the hot sandy road from the station. He got lost several times, asked the way and, terrified of being late, finally arrived at the house long before anyone else.

Since the asphalt was being laid by the main gates, he was directed to the wicket-gate on the far side of the garden. Usvatov's wife appeared. 'Sorry, I didn't quite catch . . .?' he said, fiddling with the small pink hearing-aid which nestled behind his ear like a dental plate. She repeated her name, but as he had not caught it the first time – Vasilevna? Vlasevna? – the uncertainty remained and, unable to ask her again, he played safe and avoided addressing her directly. He was amazed by the enormous *coiffure* piled on top of her head, but she was extremely friendly. 'He was in Evgeny Stepanovich's regiment,' she explained to the guests as she introduced him to them. 'They fought side by side along the whole front!' He gave a tense smile, forcing himself to remember his mission for his son and glancing distractedly around the table for somebody he might appeal to. They were all influential people, with limitless opportunities – what would it cost them to help? Surely he had only to give them the wink, and everything would fall into his lap. People like this were always clinching deals during fishing trips and parties. Yet he dimly sensed that however such deals were clinched, the outsiders admitted into this select circle were few indeed.

Evgeny Stepanovich waved perfunctorily at him from a distance while Elena Vasilevna explained to the others with an enchanting smile exactly what his role at the party was to be: 'You must tell our guests all about Evgeny Stepanovich's experiences at the front. We shall be *fascinated*!'

The Colonel laughed. 'But we weren't in the same regiment . . .' Elena Vasilevna's large, affectionate, cow-like eyes went cold. 'Come now, I know you have something to tell us!'

The silky touch of her palm left a scent of French perfume on his hand and confusion in his soul. Perhaps this was how things should be? Old and respected former front-line soldiers, festooned with medals, would be wheeled in from all over the country to pay tribute to the war record of Leonid Ilich Brezhnev, fighting for the right to remember every trivial detail and making the Colonel, who really had fought, feel quite ashamed. On 5 May 1975, the thirtieth anniversary of Victory, Brezhnev had been made Hero of the Soviet Union and it was as though all front-line soldiers were also being honoured in his name. The Colonel remembered being on a trolley bus on that day and some drunk, evidently a former trench-soldier, announcing loudly to all the passengers, 'I suppose he's been sitting in his trench all these years! Funny they've only just dug him up . . . !'

The Colonel himself found it most distasteful to claim these privileges when you came to power. But you couldn't go around telling a bus full of people such things about the General Secretary and Supreme Commander . . .

THREE

The guests sat noisily at the rough-hewn pine tables in the large glassed veranda, where the ceiling and walls were lined with bright freshly varnished planks. A fair amount of food and drink had been consumed, and people's faces were sweaty and animated, yet dish after dish was brought out and served. The pies were made by Angelina Matveevna, who was an absolute genius at baking. The family called her Evangelisha and introduced her to their guests as 'our friend', although she was never actually invited to sit down with them. Carrying in and cutting the pies to rapturous cries of delight was the hostess herself.

Evgeny Stepanovich never ceased to marvel at his wife's capacity to organize things so that everything took care of itself, everyone was happy and it only remained for her to pick up the compliments. Historical systems changed, philosophers came and went, yet that simple, eternal combination of horse and rider endured. Ride or be ridden. Master and beast.

'Darling Elena Vasilevna, in all Bolshevik honesty, you're a genius!' puffed Basalaev, the most respected of the guests, weighed down with food. 'I've stuffed myself with onions and mushrooms, and now these pies . . . Where have you been hiding the pickled mushrooms all this time?'

'In a porcelain jar in the fridge – I knew you'd be coming!'

'They're *good*! You'll have to winch me out of here with a crane!'

At this point Elena's brother-in-law ran in from the garden bearing several skewers of kebabs. He was no longer red from

14

the heat of the charcoal but a smouldering blue. The juicy meat, smoking and slightly charred, dripped fat.

'Give this man a drink,' commanded Basalaev, who had the habit of addressing people as though they were not there. Evgeny Stepanovich said nothing, and waited for the brother-in-law to seize some empty skewers and run off with them jangling before murmuring, 'Mustn't do that, old chap.'

Every so often he would survey the people sitting at his table. Each one of them had made his way in life. If his old mother had been alive, he could imagine her saying to him with tears in her eyes, 'What fine friends you have, Zhenya!' Yet in the flow of jokes and laughter the same expression would occasionally flit across their faces, like an inexorable 'No!' He understood that look only too well, he sensed it with every muscle of his face.

Elena Vasilevna walked regally round the table with an enigmatic, prophetic smile until she reached the chair of the Colonel, forgotten amid the talk, and gently laid her broad hands on his shoulders, announcing, 'I think Andrei Fedorovich has something to tell us . . .!'

He flinched. Sergei Fedotovich, he wanted to correct her, but he lacked the courage to draw attention to himself in this brilliant company.

'I'm going to let you all into a little secret: Andrei Fedorovich was in the same regiment as Evgeny Stepanovich! Together they went into battle, together they took Berlin . . .'

The Colonel flinched again. He wanted to say that their Third Ukrainian Front had been many miles further south, but the soft hands dug their cherry-red nails into his shoulders.

'Come now, dear Andrei Fedorovich, I can see you're longing to tell us all about it . . .!'

'Speech, speech!' cried the ladies.

He stood up like a doomed man, feeling very old. Throughout this excruciating party he had found not a single person to talk to. No one had addressed a word to him, apart from 'pass the salt'. He had burdened not one of them with his presence, listening to the toasts and wondering in panic what he would say when his turn came, as it inevitably would . . . He ate almost nothing. If it hadn't been for his army museum and his son and daughter-in-law's insistence that he come, he would never have humiliated himself like this in his old age. Taken Berlin indeed! Look at Berlin on the map – and look where their front had been! Did he really need favours from such people?

'I can't describe it very well, of course – and I'd like to say we were actually much further south, in Budapest . . . They even struck a special medal . . . And Vienna . . . There were heavy battles in Vienna too.'

'Yes, yes, but what about Berlin?' Elena Vasilevna insisted, then addressed the table. 'You know, when I listen to these two reminiscing together . . . Here are the real novels, which never get written!'

She poked a bright fingernail menacingly at the novelist, who acknowledged the rebuke by contritely clasping his hand to his heart and saying, 'Yes indeed, literature is truly in debt to the people . . .'

The Colonel, definitively promoted now from Sergei Fedotovich to Andrei Fedorovich, realized that he was completely cornered, so he told them about the far-off battle for Staroglinskaya; he had been seriously wounded and posthumously awarded the order of the Military Red Star as they had taken him for dead. Had they known he was not, he would probably not have got his medal. They had blocked the German advance, of course, but so many of their men had been slain that he tended to dismiss his own courage and merely blamed himself for their deaths. He now made a gift of this battle to Usvatov, since the other man clearly needed it so much more. As they say, the only reason to invite a horse to the wedding is to haul water.

'Bravo, Evgeny Stepanovich!' they all shouted and clapped.

'My, he's a quiet one!'

'To think he never told us!'

'We'd never have known!'

Basalaev said, 'We prefer to keep quiet about it. Some beat their breasts and cry, "We spilt buckets of blood!" But those of us who fought out in front, rifle in hand, have no need to crow about it . . .'

Evgeny Stepanovich humbly waved aside the praise. 'We must not overestimate my role. Sergei Fedotovich here has described this battle as though I were the only one . . .'

'Come now, don't be so modest!'

'Fancy only finding out all these years later!'

'It's a good thing we've a living witness here!'

'But I must say, in all honesty, that Sergei Fedotovich has minimized his own role in the battle. He also . . . But let's not go into details.'

'Oh let's! Why not?' urged Elena Vasilevna. 'Details are fascinating. We want details!' And she started clapping her large hands, intended by nature for work but now pampered, soft and perfumed. The ladies followed her example, and the Colonel would have been forced to squeeze out yet more had Evgeny Stepanovich not stepped in to cut short further eulogies.

'It's hard to believe. In everyday life he's so sensitive and easily hurt,' said Elena Vasilevna, her voice full of emotion. 'There was a dead birch-tree here in the garden, and we had to have it chopped down. I called in the workers, and when it fell to the ground, he went to the other end of the garden – he simply couldn't bear it. "Did you hear it groan?" he said. "It groaned like a living being . . ." And do you know, he had tears in his eyes! Even I, a woman, didn't suffer like that . . .'

At this point Basalaev stuck one leg under the table and laid his arm along the stove seat on which he was sitting with his back to the wall. After fidgeting a bit more he rose heavily to his feet. 'I shall not make a long speech – forty, forty-five minutes should suffice, if you will permit me.'

They did, of course, and beneath the encouraging murmurs

Evgeny Stepanovich whispered to his wife, 'Better give Basa-laev's chauffeur something to eat.'

'But there are so many of them out there smoking!'

'Call the man to one side, then. Tell Evangelisha. For God's sake make sure she gives him something! A hungry chauffeur shows disrespect for the boss. Basalaev may ask questions.'

'... I was recently at the theatre with my wife, Antonina Nikandrovna, sitting right here beside me – she'll bear me out. We had a box. And who do you suppose the play was by? Why, Usvatov, of course! Our very own Evgeny Stepanovich! To accomplish that, and in his spare time too, is no easy task, I would suggest. I hope our writer friend here won't be offended ... ,' The writer was not in the least offended, and nodded approvingly. 'Why do we so underestimate our own talents? Why must we die before we discover the genius within us? Die young, and you're a genius! Think of Shake-speare. "To be or not to be?" he asked. To this question we must reply unequivocally, "To be!" '

'To be! To be!' The guests roared and applauded, and Basa-laev, glass in hand, embraced Evgeny Stepanovich.

'A long life! A long and creative life!'

Evgeny Stepanovich was deeply moved; although he knew Basalaev was lying through his teeth, he also managed some-how to believe him, and even shed a few tears.

At this point the brother-in-law dashed on to the veranda bent double, clutching a sheet of cellophane to himself and shielding the next lot of kebabs with his body. He emitted such a fierce heat that the inside of the cellophane was white and streaming with sweat, and water dripped from its surface. Only then did they notice above the hubbub of voices that it was pouring with rain. By this time no one could eat another thing, and they were all heartily sick of kebabs.

After the oppressive heat of the morning, huge drops of rain and hailstones pelted down, beating against the windows and jumping along the tin guttering. With the windows closed, the veranda grew stuffy. There was a flash of lightning, almost invisible in the rain, then lightning flashed directly above the veranda, making the ladies shriek.

Cooled by the rain, the veranda windows sweated with the warmth of the house and the steaming bodies of the overfed guests. High above the roof and the rain the hum of an aeroplane broke through the noise of the party, retreating and growing louder again. It was drowned by a sudden roaring outside, and on wiping a pane of glass Evgeny Stepanovich saw a truck enter the gates and proceed to shed its load. The back rose in the air, tipping down a pile of crumbly black asphalt which steamed in the rain as two little figures in orange waistcoats hopped and danced around with spades in their hands.

When the rain had subsided, the veranda windows were flung open and a sense of lightness and abundance wafted in from the garden. The guests livened up, wiping their necks and faces with their handkerchiefs, while Evgeny Stepanovich slipped out to cast a proprietorial eye over the work. The soaked students were dragging a loaded wheelbarrow and spreading the sticky asphalt with their spades, and he saw again a young woman he had noticed before. Then she had been sitting on the grass dangling her feet in the ditch, and her rolled-up track-suit trousers had revealed strong shapely legs, burnished in the sun. She had been drinking a carton of milk, and her lips were covered in cream as she threw back her head and gulped it down with a gusto which he himself had long since lost. He had envied that young life, and was fascinated by her.

Sensing his glance, she had stared at him briefly as though at some alien, prehistoric being, then had drunk again from the triangular carton before passing it to the boy next to her. Why should she stare at him like that? He could still make people happy; he had things to show for his life which she, poor girl, could never dream of.

When he went out for the second time, she was the first person who caught his eye. She was standing at a slight angle,

19

her sunburnt legs crossed and her arm resting on a long-handled shovel, and the graceful curve of her lovely young body pleased his eye and delighted his senses, inflamed as they were with a few glasses of wine and vodka. What was she doing at the Highways Institute? She should be at the Film Institute, the Drama School, the Institute of Diplomacy! Ah, what a great future she could have had!

'Didn't you manage to keep out of the rain?' he said, bustling up to her. 'You're all wet, you should have told me . . .' To the boys he called out, 'See that dent over there? Chuck on five spades of asphalt, then roll it flat.'

He was so close to her that he could smell the sweat from her wet clothes, her youthful body. The blood rushed to his head and he saw himself before her as a young boy, not an old man of sixty with dyed hair and an ill-fitting lower denture, which caused him endless problems in eating.

At that moment he noticed a woman he did not know rushing down the road. Her face wet with tears or rain, she gave off a powerful sense of danger as she hurried from car to car. She must be somebody's tenant; in summer the smaller families in the village often let our their dachas to outsiders, though Evgeny Stepanovich himself had always been against this. The woman ran up to the drivers, talking to them and entreating them, while a passer-by who had been out picking mushrooms, wearing rubber boots and an old straw hat black with sweat, stood bucket in hand and basket behind his back, shouting angrily, 'Look at all these bloody cars blocking the road!'

The man pointed his stick toward the yard, but Evgeny Stepanovich had already scuttled back to his veranda.

FOUR

When he got back, Elena was slicing a water melon. Huge, red, sweet and refreshing, it was just what the guests needed after so much food. Melons were not on sale in Moscow yet, but a number of these massive fruits had been flown in from the south – purely out of gratitude – and modest, silent, dark-skinned people had filed in with them, then withdrawn again.

While Evangelisha washed the mounds of plates piled up in the steamy kitchen, Elena's huge knife sliced away in circular movements. She cut obliquely, leaving a sharp cone of sweet-ness at the centre. Picking up this sugary heart with her knife as though it was too small to give to any of the guests, she transferred it to her own plate in the most natural way imagin-able, then started on the next melon, laying the slices on clean plates from the kitchen and passing them round.

After his encounter with the young woman outside Evgeny Stepanovich felt as if he were seeing Elena for the first time. How fat she was, how large and heavy her face was. And why did she have to plaster herself with all that make-up? He saw the big blobs of dried mascara on her eyelashes, and the elaborate arrangement of dyed black hair which swelled her head to twice its normal size . . .

Raising her lashes, she threw him a piercing look from under her puffy lids. Then with a slow smile she handed him a slice of water melon on a plate, and beneath her gaze his adulterous imagination wilted.

As the guests enjoyed the melon and the chance to rest from all the rich food and talk, the singer-composer, tapping his toe and strumming his guitar, crashed out a despairing chord and started howling '*à la* Vysotsky'. The veins stood out on his neck in the same was as Vysotsky's, and he had a similarly hoarse voice.

Sitting at the far end of the noisy table like two turtle-doves were Evgeny Stepanovich's daughter, Irina, and the young diplomat she had brought home with her. Evgeny Stepanovich glanced at them shrewdly from time to time. Matters were clearly shaping up nicely; it was one of those conversations where looks speak louder than words. The young man was no genius, but he was well built, he looked reliable, he wore a good suit, and everything, from the tips of his Italian shoes to the knot of his tie, was foreign made. Poking out of the breast pocket of his jacket was the blackened bowl of a pipe. Was it Talleyrand who had advised young diplomats setting out on their careers to wear grey, keep in the background and never take the initiative? This one would certainly take no initiatives, he would leave all that to Irina. Their daughter had her head screwed on. She and her mother had done right in bringing the young man home to meet their friends.

When the plans for the party had been in the early stages – the first draft, as it were – Evgeny Stepanovich had had the bold notion of asking a few gypsies to come with their guitars to liven things up. He knew people who invited comedians to their dachas to amuse their guests. Not the ones seen on stage and TV, but entertainers who performed numbers which had somehow slipped past the censors, allowing their small audience to enjoy the *frisson* of self-mockery and the thrill of the forbidden. Evgeny Stepanovich had finally decided to play safe, however, and had confined himself to the chess-player, the cosmonaut, the writer and this singer.

'Heat the bath . . .' the man croaked mournfully.

'Heat the bath *up!*' quietly interposed the writer. At first the others merely looked puzzled, but the writer's face was so anguished that they soon realized that he must have some personal connection with Vysotsky, and knew how it was meant to be sung. In fact the man had once heard Vysotsky sing his famous 'Bath-house' song in person, and he remembered that when Vysotsky came to the line 'Heat the bath . . .' a certain actor had joined in: 'Heat the bath *up* . . .' 'Heat the bath . . .' 'Heat the bath *up* . . .' And so on, three times.

'Heat the bath till it's steaming white . . .' the singer's hoarse voice continued undeterred.

After all the food and drink and talk of work and promotions people felt sick at the sight of the kebabs congealing on the table, and it was very pleasant to savour other people's emotions and wallow in their pain. The musician was really letting himself go now, and singing from the heart:

> 'We cursed at Sta-alin, our voices a-breakin',
> Even though our hea-arts were achin' . . .'

And without knowing why, Evgeny Stepanovich felt goose-pimples creep over his face.

There were more toasts, to him and to Elena. 'To our dear sweet Elena Vasilevna!' bawled Basalaev. The uneaten meat was cleared from the table, cakes were served, and Elena Vasilevna sliced into yet another huge water melon with the same circular movements.

Suddenly in the place where she was sitting, under her very feet, he had a clear vision of her mother, lying frozen to death on the boards of the veranda . . .

'Tea, anyone?' Elena smiled to the guests, as the men restlessly stretched out their legs and lit cigarettes. Glancing at him, she directed his eyes out to the garden, where their daughter and her diplomat were strolling arm in arm along the path. The young man puffed at his pipe, resting his other hand on her hip, which swayed as she walked. Yes, she certainly had everything going for her, no worries on that score.

At that moment Evangelisha bore in a gleaming samovar, which she banged down on the table, and a pleasant aroma of pine cones and smoking charcoal filled the veranda. It was an old-fashioned copper samovar decorated with medals; Evgeny Stepanovich had taken a fancy to it a few years back

23

in Tambov or some such place, and had immediately been presented with it.

It was still raining as the guests drove off, and it was raining as their cars overtook the students on the road, shuffling bare-foot through the warm puddles in their orange waistcoats, trousers rolled up to their knees, plimsolls in their hands or on sticks over their shoulders.

The Colonel had somehow been forgotten at the end. He stood there unable to draw attention to himself amid the bustle of shouts and farewell kisses as the guests climbed into their cars. During the afternoon he had mentioned his army museum to a number of influential people, but although they had expressed sympathy for the idea, they had quickly backed away from any commitment, saying it unfortunately had nothing to do with them. He could not bear to mention his own purpose in coming, and he now trudged back to the station, covering his bald head with a wet newspaper.

As Evgeny Stepanovich closed the gates after the last guest, he and his wife stood alone in the empty yard with an immense sense of relief that the whole thing was over.

'Thank God for that! I hope they enjoyed themselves!'

'Of course they did! The Eremeevs' do wasn't a patch on ours. I bet they didn't have half as many guests. My face is exhausted from smiling!'

'You were wonderful. D'you really think they had a good time?' He wanted praise, and she gave it to him. And he praised her.

'You can't imagine how tired I am!'

'And Basalav? Do you think he enjoyed himself?'

'Your Basalaev enjoyed himself fine.' Elena Vasilevna smiled mysteriously. When she had served him his third or fourth cup of tea from the samovar, the great Basalaev, red faced and stuffed with food, had surreptitiously grabbed the back of her knee, and she had not moved, understanding only too well how one plump body reaches out for another. From long habit with waitresses or vague memories of youth his hand continued to move up her leg as he proclaimed loudly, 'International problems are all very fine, but we've got our own problems – we should sort out things here at home first!'

'So long as he had a good time,' said Evgeny Stepanovich, as though responding to his own thoughts. He peered out through the gate. In the dull light of the street-lamps two umbrellas steamed weightlessly through the soft mist of the rain above the wet asphalt, and two women's voices approached and grew louder. He waited in the yard for them to retreat, then went outside. Several spades and rakes lay in the ditch, along with the abandoned remains of the congealed asphalt.

'Will people ever learn to work properly in this country! They mess things up, they leave their tools lying around . . .' He glanced up and down the road to make sure nobody was about. Then he quickly threw the spades and rakes – six in all – over the fence into his own garden, saying, 'It's appalling how people treat public property. All these years and we still haven't been able to teach them anything . . .'

The spades were nothing special, but the rakes were excellent, and the shovel – the one the girl had leaned on – was superb, light and with a good strong handle.

After waiting once more for the women with the umbrellas to pass on their way back, he and Elena seized the wheelbarrow in which the students had carried the asphalt and, jostling each other through the wicket-gate, they wheeled it into the yard behind a clump of bushes where it would not be seen. It took Evgeny Stepanovich a long time to clean his hands, first rubbing them against the bark of a tree, which made them as black as soot, then bending down to rub them on the wet grass and wiping them with a rag.

The greasy corners of the barbecue steamed wetly in the rain as they went back to the veranda to clear the tables. 'Goodness, I'm tired!' exclaimed Elena Vasilevna. As she gave out her orders, Evgeny Stepanovich went upstairs and scrubbed his hands with soap, then flung open the shutters in the bedroom. The rain and hail had been followed by a fine drizzle, which seemed set to continue all night. The earth drank eagerly, tempered by the heat, and the air was fresh. He was about to comb his hair before the window but remembered just in time and rubbed it with a rough towel from the cupboard. Long ago when he was a child, people used to rush out into the rain and dance in the puddles, and the village girls would soak their plaits to make them grown thicker. Nowadays when it rained, you could end up with no hair. It had turned chilly, so Evgeny Stepanovich put on a dry flannel shirt. Yes, the human race had made a proper mess of it. Though the fact was that however sensibly we looked after ourselves, we all ended up in the ground, and we ate what was in the ground. Take those strawberry-beds being watered by the rain. It was a fact of life.

Down below the brother-in-law stepped out from the veranda with his shirt unbuttoned to the navel. Standing near the water-butt, he lit a cigarette and stuck his enormous hairy belly into the rain. What did he care? He drank, he ate, he cooled his stomach in the rain. What did life mean to him? Did he ever consider the question? Most people were like him: they just ate, drank and watched television.

'Come here, doggy . . . !' Evgeny Stepanovich heard the man murmur affectionately. 'Get down, rascal, look at your wet paws, all cold on my stomach! Growling too. Doesn't like it, eh . . .? Oh I'll get an earful tomorrow! They don't invite the wife, they don't let you through the door, but when they need someone to do their kebabs, it's different. Don't give him a drink, she says. It's not right. It's just spite. But if someone invites me, I don't like to refuse. That's how I am . . .'

'Is he staying the night?' Evgeny Stepanovich asked irritably when Elena came upstairs to join him, breathing heavily from the two flights of wooden stairs which creaked under her weight.

'I said he couldn't. But he was well away even before people

26

had left and I don't need trouble from Lina. Let him sleep it off and leave in the morning. I don't know – we're sisters, but we're so different . . .'

They stood side by side.

'What a crowd, eh? Haven't you a clever wife? How about a little kiss!'

He kissed and embraced her, and as they stood together by the window, he felt something resembling desire.

'You didn't drink too much? Good!' She laughed meaningfully. 'I was keeping count. You're not twenty-five any more!'

The pine branches outside the window quivered in the rain, making the downpour seem even heavier. Rainwater from the gutter fell into the water-butt, which reflected the light of the swaying street-lamp. Further off puddles gleamed on the sticky asphalt.

'You know what? I'm hungry!' said Elena. 'I always feel hungry after entertaining guests.'

'I wouldn't mind a snack myself . . .'

She laid places for them at a corner of a table on the veranda. They did not turn on the lights, and after the bustle of the party it was very cosy to eat and drink tea by the glow of the street-lamp. Yet he still had a lingering sense of unease. It had happened several times in his life that the day after drinking a lot he had had some premonition of disaster which would make him want to hang himself. But why? A lot of guests had come and blocked the road with their cars. What had poisoned the joy of the occasion? And suddenly the answer came to him: there was no longer any certainty, it had been lost. He had everything, everything! He had been elected to the presidium for the second time, yet there was no joy in it. Even that was gone. He felt irritation seething inside him and seeping into his soul like heartburn.

After a while, when the rain had eased, they took their umbrellas and went for a bedtime stroll. Standing in the shadow of the street-lamp, he spoke to her quietly. 'You know,

I'm beginning to understand why those lorry-drivers stuck pictures of him on their windscreens.'

'Don't say that, please! And at night too. What on earth would become of us if he were alive today?'

'Us? Nothing? If they didn't touch you then, you've nothing to fear now. Because then we had law and stability!'

'But remember what he did to my family! I'm still terrified they might find out from your papers.'

'They can't – there's nothing there.'

'That's what I'm afraid of.'

They both looked around, then walked on for a while in silence.

'There's no certainty any more,' continued Evgeny Stepanovich, 'no stability. The riff-raff have taken over. "You've had your turn, lads, now it's ours." This one's not so bad, he means well. But do people understand that? We're used to the big stick. I used to criticize him too – the euphoria of the 20th Congress, and all that. But at least we knew where we stood. What have we got now? Everything's so – ephemeral.'

'He was on television again yesterday.'

'When they gave him his medals, he had to hold on to the table – he can't even stand up! What a government, what a country!'

'And why does he always say long words he can't pronounce? Couldn't someone help him?'

'No one dares.'

'Is is true he has a foreign pacemaker?'

'It's not just him. Almost all of them have one.' Evgeny Stepanovich sighed deeply. 'They're not actually foreign, they're ours, but they're put together over there. Our people apparently can't do it.'

'Well, God grant him health, that's all I can say!' said Elena fervently.

He sighed again. 'What we need is resolution! A firm hand!' And then it was as if his most sacred thought suddenly burst from his lips. 'Our people must learn to love without judging.'

FIVE

In sober moments – in times of failure or emotional stress – Evgeny Stepanovich would look back over his life. He had achieved a lot, of course, but the more successful he had become and the more limitless the possibilities stretching before him, the less happy it had made him. He had read once that the sun shines equally on man, beast and tree, yet it cast a different shadow. And someone's shadow always lay over him.

When he was about eleven, in the fifth or sixth class at school, he sat next to a dull-witted boy named Fomin, whom they called Foma. Foma had had to stay down a year, and while everyone else in the class had moved up, he had remained at the same desk. In the weekly maths tests Foma always copied from Usvatov, but he couldn't even copy properly, and never got more than a three. It was easy to beat him in an argument; you just had to speak quickly, while he would plod along, struggling to keep up with your ideas. After a day or two he would finally have sorted it all out.

'You know you were saying . . .?' he would begin.

'Me? I never said anything . . . !'

'You did! We were standing right here, under the stairs . . .'

'You're lying, Foma. What stairs . . .?'

And he would drive Foma to distraction, for Foma needed desperately to prove he was right.

Foma did have one miraculous gift, however. Sometimes in the middle of a lesson he would fall into a day-dream, and his hand would open his notebook and start sketching with a pencil. He would screw up his trembling eyelids like a blind man, some vision would flash across the darkness, then he

29

would glance down, the pencil would quickly start filling in shadows on the blank sheet of paper and from the shadows would emerge the familiar face of their teacher, writing on the blackboard with a crumbling chalk and peering distractedly over his spectacles. In that familiar face Foma would show something none of the others had noticed before, for he seemed to have an eerie ability to capture a person's most sacred essence.

Before Foma joined the class, Usvatov had been the best at drawing, and all his father's friends had marvelled at his talent. Once he had copied a portrait of Nekrasov, with his beard and his bald head, on to squared paper. The eyes were particularly lifelike, with an almost natural-looking wetness. He had neatly rubbed out the squares, and taken the picture in to school to show off to Foma. Foma had looked at it, then moved away looking cold and unfriendly. He's jealous, gloated Usvatov.

Shortly after that they had been taken to the country to sketch the woods in autumn, and for the first time in his life Usvatov had experienced what must be meant by inspiration. As he drew, he happily imagined the others clustering around him, and the teacher saying in amazement, 'There! Look at that! That's the way to do it!'

But it was Foma they clustered around. Usvatov forced himself to look too. Foma was not drawing any details, just sketching in lines and patches of light and shadow, yet everything had been brought miraculously to life: the trees, the distant horizon, the sky, the whole of that golden day breathing farewell to the summer.

Usvatov paled. What's so special about it, he wanted to say, but it was the teacher, himself an artist *manqué*, who spoke. 'There, that's what I've been trying to teach you.' His voice trembled and his hand shook. 'But it's not something you can teach. I can't. I don't have the gift . . .' And he walked away, blinking rapidly.

The next day there was a maths test, and Usvatov hid his

work from Foma with the blotting-paper. He realized that the rest of the class would see, so he pretended he was only teasing: he knew Foma was thrashed at home whenever he got a two.

'Does your dad really beat you?' he had once asked him.

'You bet he does, the bastard!' said Foma sullenly.

Later, during the break, Usvatov went back to the classroom. There was no one there, and the register lay open on the teacher's desk. The maths teacher generally put a mark against the names of those he intended to question during the lesson, and little Lyapin, who sat in the front row, would inform the ones who were to be asked. Looking in the register was Lyapin's chief job, and the others all tried to curry favour with him. Sometimes he would deliberately scare someone by telling him it was going to be his turn. The pupil would sit through the lesson shaking with fear, and at the end Lyapin would say, as though granting absolution, 'Thank your lucky stars he didn't get round to you!'

Foma had had threes for algebra all term, and Usvatov could not restrain himself. The register was open, the room was empty, the pen and inkwell were on the table . . . His hand reached out, and he put a thick mark against Foma's name. Then he ran. In the corridor he realized to his horror that the nib was wet with ink; he imagined the teacher coming in, and demanding who had been using his pen. When the break was over, Usvatov joined the crowd of children and entered the classroom with an odd, reeling gait. He stared at the table – the pen was in its place, the nib was dry. Foma was called to the board, given a well-deserved two for his efforts and beaten when he got home.

What made me do it, Usvatov wondered afterwards. It probably hurt me more than it hurt him.

It had not taken Usvatov long to grasp the truth of what his father was always telling him: there would never be enough to go round, it was impossible for everyone to get equal shares. If one person had a lot, the next person would get less. He had lost out. He had to stand in Foma's shadow. Where was the justice in that? Why should Foma get it, not him, when he frankly needed it so much more?

Foma never really made anything of his life. Before the war, in 1939 or 1940, his father was thrown into jail. Like their drawing teacher, the man was a failed artist and had taken to the bottle, but his huge portrait of Stalin continued to adorn the buildings of the District Party Committee while he was sitting in jail. Everyone in the class knew who had painted that portrait, and Comrade Stalin, three storeys high in his army greatcoat, would greet demonstrations when they marched under it during the May Day and Revolution Day processions.

In 1941 Foma disappeared without trace; rumour had it that he had been captured by the Germans and had escaped across Germany, but had been taken prisoner again in Poland. After the war he served time in various Soviet labour camps – for betraying his country. He returned to Voronezh in the mid-fifties and began drinking heavily. During a visit home Evgeny Stepanovich met him and bought him a drink in a café. They sat together at a small table in the open air, surrounded by the din of everyday life. A completely new generation of boys was milling around, sitting on the wall like martins on a lightning conductor, tearing about on motor cycles and chasing girls. Looking into Foma's bleary, drunken eyes and his unshaven, wrinkled face, Evgeny Stepanovich became even more convinced that there had never really been anything remarkable about him, and that real talent will always force its way out, like a blade of grass pushing through asphalt.

'What have you been up to?' he asked. 'Didn't you used to be some kind of artist?'

Foma mumbled something of which Usvatov made out the words 'Get me another vodka . . . And a mug of beer.'

A bit later he muttered, 'Get me another – a big one!'

They were an unlikely pair: Evgeny Stepanovich, neat and

short haired, with his tie and cheap new suit, carefully watching where he put his elbows to avoid beer stains, was already beginning to take the first confident steps in his career and seemed to have a bright future; Foma, destitute and dishevelled, smelled like a cheap bar and looked like one too.

'Didn't you ever get married?' asked Usvatov and, not getting an answer, he added, 'Are your mother and granny still alive?' He had a sudden vivid memory of a grey-haired old lady, almost transparent in the light, who had given them boiled fish to eat and some delicious sweets like noodles baked in honey, which crumbled and melted in the mouth. She had gazed fondly at him, stroking his head with her cold hand, and thanked him for helping her grandson with his maths.

'They hanged my mother,' said Foma.

'Who did?'

'The Germans.'

'What for?'

'Don't you know what people are killed for? For not being scum. For being human – that's what for. Right in front of Granny's eyes . . .' A drunken tear dropped into his beer mug, and as he wiped his cheek with a dirty palm, Evgeny Stepanovich noticed that the third finger of his right hand was missing. 'Mum was hanged by the Germans, Father was killed by our lot in the camps . . .'

His toothless mouth grinned nastily, and Evgeny Stepanovich began to feel oppressed by the meeting. Foma drank his beer messily, spilling it down his sleeve, so that he had to get out a handkerchief and wipe it off. When they said goodbye, Evgeny Stepanovich handed him a ten-rouble note, and this nonentity accepted it without gratitude, as though it were his due, smiling an unpleasant, knowing smile.

After the party Evgeny Stepanovich's anxieties pursued him into sleep. The rain rustled all night in the pine-trees, and he dozed fitfully, shivering under the quilt in the chill of the open window. Towards morning an east wind sprang up and something began to scrape against the guttering. He had a terrifying dream that he was running away from something and had crawled head first into the space beneath the veranda, dirty, dusty and full of cobwebs. He awoke gasping and sweating, and sat up on the edge of the bed, his heart pounding. It was ridiculous – there was a brick plinth beneath the veranda, and the ventilation holes were covered with net to stop mice getting through. It must mean something, though, dreams always mean something. Or had he just eaten too much meat the night before?

He did a few light exercises, squatting down and waving his arms around and observing to his chagrin how flabby his breasts were. There was nothing he could do about it: he wasn't twenty-five any more, but sixty. Yet it was galling none the less. He felt a bit brighter after a shower and a brisk rub. Clean, freshly shaved and smelling of his special French-Soviet aftershave, he sat down to breakfast in the track suit he wore for his morning jog. He was aware of the familiar discomfort in his stomach from all the food and drink he had consumed the day before and not fully digested, and he had little appetite for breakfast. He had also been disturbed, while rubbing and massaging himself under the shower and raising his arms to the taps, to discover under his armpit a lump the size of a largish pea, or even bigger. It could not have got there overnight – so why had he not noticed it before?

He kept putting his hand under his arm to feel it as he listlessly smeared the whites of a couple of soft-boiled eggs with mustard and ate them with several slices of hot crisp toast, straight from the toaster and dripping with butter. Then he picked out some large juicy radishes, dark pink on the outside and white inside, and covered each one with butter and salt. He was beginning to get his appetite back now, but since he would be eating again at noon with a delegation of Hungarians, it would not be wise to overload his stomach. He drank a mug of strong tea with cream – there would be little cups of coffee with the Hungarians. It was real Lipton's tea, fragrant and steaming, which a friend had brought back for him from London.

The car was already waiting outside and the chauffeur was walking round it, wiping its gleaming body, and the moment Evgeny Stepanovich stepped through the gates in his light summer suit, white shirt, starched collar and bright tie, the motor started up.

Sometimes he would leave for work without seeing Elena. She would make his breakfast and lay his place at the table, then go back to bed for an extra hour's sleep, after which she would get up, do her hair, drink a cup of strong black coffee, smoke a cigarette and start on her telephone calls. As he was leaving that morning, however, she put her head out of the first-floor window and yelled out all the various errands he was to do for her in town. Listening to her attentively, he examined the asphalt and noticed some irritating dents. He must get them to throw on some more of that sand behind the gates to make it look less conspicuously new: they would not want everyone knowing it had just been laid. Forgetting half of what she had said – she would ring his secretary several times anyway, and his secretary would remind him what had to be done – Evgeny Stepanovich threw his briefcase on to the back seat and had just got in beside the chauffeur when Elena's brother-in-law dashed out clutching a parcel wrapped in greasy newspaper.

'You didn't need to hurry,' said Evgeny Stepanovich, moving his briefcase to make room at the back. 'I've got to be at work early, you don't have to be there till midday . . .'

Breathing heavily through his nose, the brother-in-law got in, slammed the door shut, tapped the chauffeur on the shoulder in his usual loutish manner and said, 'OK, drive on!' He was unshaved, and looked as though he had slept under a bush all night.

'I'll drop you off at the nearest underground,' said Evgeny

Stepanovich without raising his voice or turning his head on the headrest. 'We're not going your way.'

He intensely disliked having to drive across town with the fellow, particularly as he had the habit of rolling down the window and looking out, or shouting 'Stop the car!' when they passed some food-stall. No wonder they say a stupid relative is worse than a clever enemy.

At the crossroads their path was blocked by a large black Volga – an old one, not the latest model, like Evgeny Stepanovich's. Its chauffeur signalled, and signalled again, and finally a general proceeded imperiously through a side gate. Recognizing Evgeny Stepanovich, he greeted him and then continued to his car.

Roads loomed up on either side filled with pedestrians on their way to the station. Some paused on the kerb with a look of obscure hope on their faces, but Evgeny Stepanovich did not see them. He was already working, looking through the official papers spread out in the folder on his knees. His greying temples caught the light of the morning sun; the rest of his hair was as black as it had been thirty years ago, with just a few reddish tinges. Close up, however, when he inclined his head, it could be seen that the skin on the little bald patch on his crown was also slightly red. Evgeny Stepanovich had been dyeing his hair for some time now (using a special American brand with which one of his friends managed to keep him regularly supplied), but he always left his temples grey, for this gave him a solid, imposing appearance in photographs.

Fresh, smooth and clean after his morning shower, Evgeny Stepanovich's face behind the lowered car window was a familiar sight to the crowds queuing at the bus-stops, besieging the buses and spilling out of their doors. His expression and bearing were identical to those of all the other officials of his rank driving at this hour of the morning from their dachas to their places of work.

SIX

Before the usual business awaiting him that morning Evgeny Stepanovich would have to face a stream of congratulations. That was how he put it: a stream of congratulations. It was only by veiling himself in a tone of light irony that he felt he could carry it off. Good form demanded that he accept all the things he was striving for so passionately as though they were just a general contribution to the larger collective which he merely happened to represent. This was how important figures conducted themselves when accepting their awards on television – and this sort of thing was being shown almost daily now. Someone would read out a congratulatory speech from a slip of paper, and the recipient would listen with a pained, modest, pious expression, then produce from his pocket a prepared speech sprinkled with prophetic wisdom, gratitude to the organizers for their kind words and the various stock phrases which formed part of this familiar ritual, as though the award meant absolutely nothing to him.

Evgeny Stepanovich sometimes imagined himself in that position – speaking on television, with the whole nation watching and listening – and at such thoughts he would have to get up and pace about to calm himself. For a highly placed public servant like him, close to all the secrets of official life, there was a great deal to be learned from these events. He could always detect the driving force, invisible to the uninitiated, by observing who came out with whom and in which order, then drawing the right conclusions. If Brezhnev did not appear at a reception or in the newspapers for a while, anxious rumours would fly, and the foreign 'voices', audible through the jamming, would whip these up by calculating exactly how long it was since he had last been seen in public and conjecturing endlessly about the reasons. 'Well, God give him health, that's all I can say!' Elena would exclaim at these times, and when he returned to people's screens, they would peer at him to see how he looked and listen to hear if he was articulating his words properly, and they would feel temporarily reassured.

In the car Evgeny Stepanovich opened the fresh newspaper which was bought and delivered to him at the dacha by his chauffeur every morning. He knew there would be no official announcement of his award – that happened only with the top medals and to people of much higher rank. Yet he could not resist turning to the second column. Nothing. Still anonymous. He felt slightly cheated. Naturally he would not wear it. Fewer and fewer people wore their medals these days. This woman Djuna who was treating Brezhnev was said to have advised him not to wear his, claiming they gave out some sort of radioactive rays. At that, everyone had immediately dropped down a rung on the ladder, and had modestly forsworn all excess. Yes, things were in a bad way! Charlatans, healers and soothsayers have always appeared at certain periods of history. Just before Stalin died, when things seemed pretty stable, miracles again started to occur, along with a mass of weird phenomena which defied rational explanation. There was some rascal called Bashyan, and a few others – Evgeny Stepanovich could not remember their names. Before that, of course, before the Revolution, there had been Rasputin. It was no coincidence that Rasputin had turned up when he did, just before the end. A strong government has no need of soothsayers.

These ideas about certain periods of history were not in fact his. Elena had heard about Djuna's miracles and had become fascinated by her. 'There was this man with a shaking head, and after three session with her it stopped completely,' she told Evgeny Stepanovich. 'He even got married recently to some young girl . . .' It was not clear what Elena needed treat-

38

ment for: her head did not shake, thank God. But as the rumours of miracle cures multiplied, Evgeny Stepanovich started searching for evidence to disprove them. It was said that the artist N. had presented Djuna with a painting; sometimes his right hand couldn't even hold a paintbrush, but after seeing her it worked perfectly. Evgeny Stepanovich had invited the man to his office for tea and biscuits, and they had had a long discussion about his work.

'How come you haven't had your own show yet?' Evgeny Stepanovich asked him. It then emerged that the man had not given Djuna a painting at all, and talk of the show petered out, though for some time afterwards he continued to ring Evgeny Stepanovich and pester him about it.

After this Evgeny Stepanovich had been told in strict confidence about a certain well-known film director who had had some sort of extrasensory treatment for impotence, and had found it most helpful. Evgeny Stepanovich had called this man in for tea and biscuits too, showering him with kindness. When he eventually led the conversation round to the subject of extrasensory healing techniques, the old cynic started talking about the charlatans who appear at particular moments of history, just before the end. All this he said at the top of his voice, right there in Usvatov's office. So you want to make trouble, do you, Usvatov said to himself, his face turning to stone, whereupon the director sneered and winked offensively at the telephones, as if to say OK, I get it, I'll keep my mouth shut!

At the underground station Evgeny Stepanovich dropped off Elena's brother-in-law, still clutching his parcel – he could not imagine what was in it – and suddenly there was a great deal of room in the car. Among the buses, trolley buses, Moskviches and Zhigulis more and more solid black Volgas appeared, and as they passed, Evgeny Stepanovich recognized more and more number-plates and heads in back windows. He was coming into his own world now, a world in which the dozy, dishevelled brother-in-law with his greasy parcel had no place. We all have lurking in the background some squalid relative of whom we are not particularly proud.

As the traffic stopped at the lights, Evgeny Stepanovich signed a number of documents from the open file on his knees, and when he looked up, he shuddered. There before him, behind the back window of the trolley bus in front, was his old classmate Leonid Oksman – Lenya – leaning on the handrail. Evgeny Stepanovich hurriedly immersed himself in his papers, but the moment the traffic started to move he looked up again. As the trolley bus pulled away, patches of sunlight slid over its convex rear window, swallowing up the sky, the clouds and the tops of the trees, so that it was imposs-ible to see whether Lenya was moving away or he was just imagining it. But at least he need no longer panic.

When he stepped from the car into the Committee build-ings, he was met by a battery of smiles like camera flashlights, and the glass doors were flung open. Acquaintances and strangers hurried up to greet him; he thanked them, nodded and smiled back, and someone held the lift for him, putting his hand under the shining eye of the photo-electric cell to cut the beam. Just as the doors were closing, a man carrying a document-case stuck out his leg, kicked them apart and pushed his way in. He wants a favour, Evgeny Stepanovich surmised. The man was obviously pursuing him into the lift for an intimate chat. That gold-stamped document-case doubtless contained the plans for some project, and clearly indicated his role in some special celebratory event or other.

As the lift was going up, Evgeny Stepanovich chatted affably to the ladies, coldly keeping the petitioner at bay with a glance which told the man in no uncertain terms that any attempt to take him by storm, as he had done the lift, would be both futile and unseemly.

'Evgeny Stepanovich!' a high voice squeaked behind him when they were getting out. 'You don't know me, of course, but Vasily Porfirevich suggested . . .'

Evgeny Stepanovich strode ahead, stern and unapproachable. The fact that they had gone up four floors in the lift together conferred no advantages or claims to friendship. On reaching his office he said to his secretary, 'There's some damn nuisance out there trying to see me. Don't let him in, I'm busy!'

Galina Timofeevna had started out as a secretary some thirty years before, when by all accounts she had been a pretty red-haired girl, enjoying a great deal of success and admiration. Now her bearing was statuesque and her grey hair was rinsed with blue, but the same brightly painted fingernails flashed and swooped over the keys as she touch-typed Evgeny Stepanovich's letters. She could anticipate his every word, and she could be relied upon to let no one in without an appointment.

Long ago, when Evgeny Stepanovich had first stepped over the threshold of this office, he had been amazed by its vastness and splendour. In those days everything had delighted him: the high-backed revolving chair which rolled around on castors, the vast red-wood desk, the other, smaller desk and two chairs at right angles to it, to which he would move if he wished to lower himself democratically to the same level as his visitors, the long conference table lined with chairs, the battery of telephones and the separate rest-room, with its fridge and sofa. Even the tear-off table calendar was special, with its bluish pink leaves of watered silk. There were various pennants and mugs, as well as glass cabinets filled with the usual gifts from official delegations, and several brass-cornered morocco files, with his surname and initials stamped on them in gold. Previously he had only ever seen these files at important meetings; now they lay under his hand, and the leather was soft to the touch. 'It's vital for a man to love his work,' Evgeny Stepanovich would say with feeling. 'Let's face it, it's the most important thing in this day and age.'

As the years went by, and he aspired ever higher, Evgeny Stepanovich's office began to seem increasingly old and shabby, and gave him less and less pleasure. He was especially irritated by the air-conditioning box which had been fitted to the window, a piece of gimcrack rubbish which embarrassed him in front of his foreign guests. Recently Evgeny Stepanovich had been picturing himself in another, better office, and he felt he had been passed over. Today, however, he sank into his armchair and Galina Timofeevna brought him his pile of greetings telegrams, on top of which lay the red-stamped government ones.

'Later, later! I have work to do!' he cried. But the moment she had gone he began avidly to read them. How often he had checked the congratulatory messages brought in for him to sign. Here were the very same messages, couched in exactly the same words, yet when he read them, he was touched. He was surprised by their warmth; those hackneyed words seemed to be genuine. He laid them out in order, according to the signatories' rank and status, then he paced around the office behind the backs of the empty chairs lining the table. It was said that Stalin liked to creep up behind people's chairs as they sat, not daring to raise their heads; one can well imagine what they must have felt as they heard the footsteps of fate behind their back.

Galina Timofeevna came in with her notebook and read out his agenda for the day. She also had some unpleasant news. One of his classmates had died, and the funeral was today. Some people had come to the office, asking him to make sure he was told. 'Ku-li-kov,' Galina Timofeevna read slowly from her notebook, as though pronouncing some strange-sounding foreign name, then glanced questioningly up at him. She always had trouble remembering the names of people who were unknown and unimportant, as though she found it hard to believe they really existed.

'I told them you were inundated with work, and at twelve you have the Hungarians. But they insisted you got the message.'

'Yes, yes, yes,' barked Evgeny Stepanovich, frowning. 'We

must send a telegram ... Sincere condolences ...' He hesitated. 'Have you got their address?'

The man whose seat Evgeny Stepanovich had inherited – or rather the man's wife – had strictly forbidden anyone to tell him about the funeral of anyone of his age, especially his classmates. Everybody at the Committee knew this, and legend had it that during some celebration or other the man had signed a greetings card in thick felt-tip pen to someone who had been dead for years, wishing him happiness, professional success and a long and healthy life. 'How could you leave him out!' the man had reproached Galina Timofeevna. 'It doesn't do to forget. A card costs nothing, and it'll mean so much to him. Remember, people always appreciate a bit of attention.' Galina Timofeevna had heard him out in silence, and the unsent postcard was stored deep in the bowels of the Committee.

'What time is the funeral?' asked Evgeny Stepanovich quickly.

'Eleven.'

'I see. Where?'

Galina Timofeevna told him the address: October 25th Street, formerly Nikolskaya Street, on the corner, as you're coming from the Hotel Metropol. The driver knew where it was, she had told him just in case. The ceremony was to be at the offices of the *Forest and Steppe* magazine, in the conference room on the first floor.

Evgeny Stepanovich glanced at his watch: he could just make it. He gave orders for the car to be outside at 10.45 sharp, then saw four people in quick succession, signed several urgent documents, sorted out one long-standing problem and sent off a number of partly solved problems to various departments, whence in due course they would return to him, loaded with amendments. Everything else could wait. Then, brimming with satisfaction at his own success in beating the clock, he signalled to Galina Timofeevna to call in his co-author.

'Lead him through!' he said.

In the late thirties the Soviet cinema industry was headed by a man who had previously controlled a regional department of the NKVD, and it was reported that whenever some film director came to see him, he would say, 'Lead him through!' This was his chief claim to fame, since he did not last long and soon shared the fate of those who had been led through to see him. But at good moments such as these Evgeny Stepanovich would permit himself this little joke.

His co-author was waiting outside in the reception room, as though preparing a speech. He was a young man from the provinces – something of a country bumpkin, frankly, without a Moscow residence permit or any clear goals in life. Evgeny Stepanovich could give him a passport to life by getting him his residence permit, but this was a high price to pay. He had pulled his previous co-author up from the gutter and given him his passport to life. That fellow too had been young and full of promise, and everything had been working out so well for him. Yet he had repaid Evgeny Stepanovich's kindness with stark ingratitude. Together they had written a hugely topical play. The play had opened, and during the final curtain-call the young man, hungry for fame, had run on to the stage to kiss the actresses' hands. Evgeny Stepanovich had remained seated in his box, and only when everyone, the director included, had lined up on stage did he emerge from the shadows and genially restrain the applause.

The performance was followed by a big banquet. 'Don't skimp,' he had warned the country boy, who had little experience in these matters. 'Tell me afterwards what it all comes to.'

It all came to a considerable sum, as one might imagine, since a large banqueting room had been hired at the Praga restaurant. By the time Evgeny Stepanovich arrived everybody was sitting down, and they applauded him as he made his way to the microphone on the main table. All evening people congratulated him and toasted his health and the groaning table, while his co-author bustled around frantically,

44

conferring with the head waiter and running into the kitchen. At the point when people started tipping cigarette ash into their plates of food and the evening began to degenerate into the sort of drunken binge that is usual on such occasions, Evgeny Stepanovich rose to his feet and made for the door.

His co-author caught up with him at the lift. 'Evgeny Stepanovich, some actors in there have ordered more vodka and six extra bottles of champagne,' he panted, pressing him against the wall. 'Have you any spare cash on you?' His voice was wretched, and he looked sweaty and harassed.

'Come, come, my boy, that's not the way we do things.' Evgeny Stepanovich produced two ten-rouble notes from his pocket and handed them over. 'There, that's all I have on me. You should have sorted this all out before.' The lift arrived, with the elderly attendant sitting inside. 'You should have thought,' Evgeny Stepanovich went on. 'You'll have to get yourself out of this.' He stepped into the walnut-lined cabin, the doors closed and the lift descended.

He owed the fellow no favours. He had paid him excellent wages, wangled him a Moscow residence permit and got him a one-room flat. You can't put a price on things like that. But, as they say, do someone a favour and he'll spit in your face. It transpired that all the time they had been working together the scoundrel had dashed off a little play of his own which he was trying to get staged. Not only that: Evgeny Stepanovich had proposed an idea for a new play, which he had shamelessly dodged. Never mind, he was paying for it now.

'Lead him through!' Evgeny Stepanovich repeated playfully as his new co-author appeared at the door.

On these occasions he would unplug all the telephones apart from one, which was never disconnected, and from that moment on anyone trying to get into his office would be told by Galina Timofeevna, 'Evgeny Stepanovich is in a meeting just now. I can't say for how long ... Try later.' Generally coffee and sandwiches would be brought in, since the man was always hungry, but today there was no time for coffee.

'I'm afraid we have only twenty minutes,' Usvatov warned. 'At 10.45 I have to leave for a funeral. It's just come up. An old fellow student. We were at university together. Clever chap, never made it somehow ... By the way, British military psychologists reckon fifty per cent talent and one hundred per cent character is better in the long run than the other way round.' Evgeny Stepanovich narrowed his eyes enigmatically and rubbed the soft tip of his nose with his fingers. 'Well now, that's given you something to think about. This tragic death presents us with a rather interesting story, in fact – I must tell you about it some time. It might even be the subject of our next play. I can already visualize the broad outline. We just have to fill in the details ... Great love interest too!'

'Perhaps we'd better not read today if we're in a hurry?' the young man said hopefully, and stopped pulling the messy scribbled sheets of used paper out of his file. Evgeny Stepanovich had given instructions for him to be issued with as much top-quality Finnish paper as he needed, yet although he took it, he continued to write on crumpled scraps and the backs of envelopes, insisting that this was the only way he could write. Evgeny Stepanovich, who loved neatness above everything, simply could not comprehend this.

'No, no, it makes no difference, let's get on with it.'

His co-author sat down at the little desk and started to read while Evgeny Stepanovich sprawled above him in his soft revolving chair, listening comfortably and every so often paying particular attention to something.

A few years ago a special meeting had been held for party activists at the Committee, at which Grishin himself had spoken. He had expressed his concern that certain works were beginning to develop a 'subtext' (or 'sobtext', as he had pronounced it). 'They're afraid to come out with it openly, but in the sobtext . . .' He had eloquently stuck his thumb under his ribcage. After Grishin, two distinguished writers had elaborated on the harmful effects of the 'subtext'. This was a signal. On his return from the meeting Evgeny Stepanovich took appropriate measures and called together a small group of people to whom he explained that henceforth special attention was to be paid to the subtext. Now he did not merely listen when works were read out to him, he adjusted his sense of hearing.

'Well,' he said when the twenty minutes were up, 'that's not bad. It's shaping up quite nicely.' He always couched his praise as vaguely as possible. His experience on the Committee had taught him never to be hasty with his judgements and to avoid being specific. 'I like your range of colours. Pity you still haven't given full expression to my ideas about the way people's souls are being crippled by what I call possession-worship. Materialism. Before long we'll be awash with material goods – the threat's already advancing from the West. It's desperately important for us not to lose touch with our moral values, forget our roots, turn into a consumer society. Incidentally, we must have more popular sayings in our play. They enrich our language. "Poverty sings, poverty dances." Lovely image, that. Must get it in somewhere. Now you just leave me this scene, and I'll try to do something with it.'

At 10.45 prompt he got into the car. He had definitely made the right decision in going. He was hugely busy, of course, and under enormous pressure from all sides, with requests and responsibilities clinging to him like burs to a dog. Yes, burs to a dog. He wasn't afraid to debase himself with this image, and he often used it. Ultimately no one would have criticized him if his other commitments had prevented him from paying his last respects. But a voice had told him to go.

He entered the room. A number of complete strangers recognized him, inclined their heads respectfully and stepped aside, whispering as he passed. Then his arm was squeezed by a stout woman with grey hair and a flat, round face. 'Thank you, Zhenya dear,' she said. 'Forgive us for not congratulating you . . .'

'Us?' The light was not good, and at first he had no idea who she was. Then through her tears and the years and the

47

lines on her grey face she smiled, and he recognized her. It was Marta. Once, long ago, she had given him dancing lessons. There had been a brief craze for dancing, and the students would gather in the assembly hall after classes and someone would sit down at the piano. Although after the war girls had outnumbered boys two or even three to one, Marta had had many admirers. Yet he was the one she danced with. He had even been a little in love with her, and then she suddenly ran off to marry a man much older than she was, who seemed to have very little going for him. Meeting them once on the street together, he had realized, not so much from the way they were dressed as from the anxiety on their faces, that all was not well with them. Too bad, he had thought with a certain malicious satisfaction, she had brought it on herself.

'I was the one who insisted you were told. I knew you'd want to come.'

He raised his arm, as though to say how could I possibly not? the other mourners made way for him as he stepped forward to the front, followed by Marta's whisper. Two tables had been moved together, and on them lay the body of Kulikov in his coffin, looking like an old Russian peasant. So this was what the rosy-cheeked Kulikov had come to. He had been the youngest boy in their year at university. Evgeny Stepanovich remembered them all clubbing together for a party at the Balchug restaurant to celebrate their final exams, and Kulikov jumping on his chair and flinging his glass in the air, spilling champagne over himself, and crying, 'To love! To the stars in the heavens . . .!'

This peasant lying in his coffin, surrounded by people, looked just like his grandfather, with his straight, lifeless, grizzled beard, the dark hollows around his cheekbones and temples, the stern brows above the eye-sockets and the fluff of sparse grey hair. All inessentials had vanished, death had returned him to his essence. This thought pleased Evgeny Stepanovich: he must remember to use it some time.

When people made way for him at the coffin, the man reading the funeral speech recognized him and faltered, but Evgeny Stepanovich made a little gesture to indicate that he should go on. It was a gesture he had to make all too frequently when appearing in public, and he could see that it had diverted several people's attention from the dead man.

It must be thirty years since he had last seen Kulikov. What kind of life could have turned that cheerful, naïve boy into this stern, withered old man? It terrified Evgeny Stepanovich to think about it.

In a pause between the speeches a woman who had slipped in late laid some flowers at the dead man's feet. Evgeny Stepanovich felt a pang of shame that he had not sent his chauffeur off for a few carnations. He had simply got out of the habit. If there had to be a funeral wreath, it was generally someone else who laid it; such things were always organized in advance by people whose job it was. His job was merely to give orders. It was simply not expected of him; his presence was what mattered.

He stood with a suitably sorrowful but resolute expression, clouded by thoughts and memories. Out of the corner of his eye he saw the latecomer push her way through the crowd and embrace an old woman standing at the head of the coffin. The old woman kissed her, and as they both wiped away the tears, he suddenly recognized this old woman as Irina. So that was why he had sensed her anxious, malevolent glance. But God, what havoc age wreaks upon people!

As soon as the ceremony was over and the mourners started carrying out the ribboned wreaths, Evgeny Stepanovich took his leave. 'So sorry . . . I've a delegation of Hungarians at twelve . . . everything organized . . . no chance of getting out of it . . .' People thanked him and shook his hand, and some cheerful fellow, whom he had never seen in his life, popped up, shoved out his sweaty palm and announced genially, 'Luchenkov's the name!' Numbskull! Who gives a damn what his name is, thought Evgeny Stepanovich irritably. Sticking out his hand without a by your leave!

When he stepped outside, Evgeny Stepanovich gulped down the fresh air as though emerging from the underground into the light. His life might have been as grey as that funeral, those people. He imagined carrying his briefcase up those dreary, worn stone stairs every day to a world as crowded as a shared kitchen, full of the same petty, narrow-minded interests . . . Then leaving work every evening to be met by a horde of gypsies at the cloakroom, milling around selling black-market goods and telling fortunes.

As he slipped into the car, his face maintained a solemnity fitting to the occasion. In front of him some women were being guided into the funeral bus, and again he saw Irina, her grey head covered in a black gauze scarf. Two women on either side of her propped her up by the arms as she walked towards the open door of the bus and raised her foot to the step. But she could not manage it, and had to be helped up. From the car he saw every detail of the shabby yellow winter shoe with its thick sole. He saw the protruding bunions, the puffy legs strapped with elastic bandages – thrombosis, probably, a widening of the veins – and he saw her grab the handrail, pulling herself up as they pushed her in.

Yet how beautiful she had been in her youth, how light-footed! He remembered her firm sunburnt young body in its peasant shirt darting through the cherry-trees. She and Kulikov had just married, and for some reason she was hugely amused by his name. 'Kulikov!' she would call out, laughing. Usvatov had proposed that he and Kulikov write a book, and the three of them had scraped together the money to rent a hut in the Ukraine for the summer. Irina cooked for them, and they all took it in turns to cycle to the shop for bread and milk, since their landlady was very poor and had no cow or goat, only a hen. The minute the old woman heard the happy clucking sound she would go out to the yard for the new-laid egg; clutching it still warm in her dry hands, she would present it to Irina, whom she adored.

At midday the women would call the two men out to eat.

They would emerge from their morning's work and sit down at the table they had knocked up in the yard, while Irina darted between the table and the makeshift outdoor kitchen, her bare arms and sunburnt shoulders hovering above them, and her cornflower-blue skirt revealing strong tanned legs. Usvatov's gaze would grow heavy, and he would try not to look at her, yet she was constantly before his eyes, and he was aware of her every movement. In the stuffy summer nights when Irina and Kulikov were asleep in the hut and the light was out he lay awake in his hayloft, unable to sleep. And then the impossible happened. How beautiful she was, how passionate she had been . . .

Kulikov had cycled back at dinner-time with the milk and bread, and they ate ice-cold beetroot salad straight from the cellar, with frozen lumps of sour cream on top. Irina first sat at the table with them, then busied herself at the stove under the awning, frying up perch in a pan, and he saw her smiling a special secret smile, just for him.

Nothing ever came of their book. And although Irina did not let him into her bed again, Kulikov furiously sensed something. People said that things did not work out for them, and that they were endlessly separating and getting back together again. But it had all happened a long time ago, and he was certainly not to blame. Looking now at old women like Marta and Irina – or indeed most of the other women there – it was hard to imagine them ever being young, or making anything of their lives.

The bus in front finally moved off, and after waiting a little longer the car whisked him across Moscow. The back of his head ached. A lot had happened in one morning, with one person after another returning from oblivion, like some sort of conspiracy . . .

He lowered the window an inch, made himself comfortable on the passenger side of the back seat – the safest spot in case of a crash – and closed his eyes. He was too old for funerals, it was time to call a halt.

He took the lift up to his floor and entered the toilet, all mirrors, bright lights and tiles, its odours masked by a sickly air freshener. After washing his hands he examined his face critically in the huge mirror, pulling up first one eyelid then the other with his wet finger. The mucous membrane was slightly inflamed – it must be too much reading – but his colour was not bad and his eyes were bright, with none of the dull resignation of old age.

Later, after a brief official exchange of greetings, the entire delegation of hungry Hungarians noisily assembled around the long table, together with their translators, advisers and Soviet assistants – there were always twice as many Soviet comrades as guests at the table – all eagerly tucking in to the food and drink. With a pleasurable sense of the fullness of life, Evgeny Stepanovich downed a glass of chilled vodka and nibbled some hot smoked sturgeon, which made the saliva flood into his mouth and his cheekbones ache. Then he poured himself a second glass, popped a delicious, mouth-watering little pie into his mouth and felt everything become delightfully hazy, as a deep peace entered his soul. Through this haze he had a momentary vision of the cold, echoing marble of the empty hall at the Archangels Crematorium outside Moscow. He imagined the silence and the barely audible strains of the funeral music, the coffin sliding along the gleaming metal rollers, the shutters coming together and closing as it was lowered, and then the end . . .

The guests advanced on Evgeny Stepanovich to touch glasses, and, holding his tall goblet in his hand, he started to tell them how he had just laid to rest a splendid man and dear friend from his university days. Waves of sympathy rolled over him from all sides. Deeply touched, he felt his heart go out to these people, and as he spread mustard on a slice of marinated ox-tongue and put it in his mouth, his gentle eyes were wet.

SEVEN

Evgeny Stepanovich – Zhenya, as he was then – was fifteen when his father's work had taken them to Moscow. Later he realized that this had been their salvation.

They had packed in a hurry. Things were given to relatives or thrown away, the tickets were bought, and then, the very day before they were due to leave, he had come down with scarlet fever. He had caught it from his classmate Kostya, whose flat he used to visit. On that last occasion the door was opened by a stranger in civilian clothes. The man gave him a searching glance and let him in, ordering him to sit down and not allowing him to leave, so that the entire search of the flat and the arrest of Kostya's father took place in his presence. At two in the morning his mother arrived, half dead with worry, having searched the town for him and called all their friends and finally here to find that the phone had been cut off. She too was let in and made to sit on a chair. A line of friends and neighbours sat along the wall, not daring to speak to one another. One neighbour had rung the doorbell, wanting to borrow an iron. 'I only wanted an iron . . .' she kept saying, as though denying any other connection with the family and disowning all the rest. Shortly after that her husband had arrived. He had just had a bath, and had poked his nose round the door in a neighbourly way. Now he sat there shivering in his towel and string vest, his slippered feet steaming and his head covered with a knotted handkerchief.

They took down everyone's names, reducing them all to a state of panic and uncertainty, and at five in the morning Kostya's father was finally led off. From the door he looked back, as though about to say something, then he helplessly threw his hands in the air.

'Why did you have to go? Whatever made you do it?' Zhenya's father shouted at him afterwards. Zhenya had never seen him like this, with his face all blue and swollen like a hanged man. 'Why did *you* have to go too, you stupid woman? And you, boy, stand up when your father's speaking to you, worm!'

Through his own fear and alarm Zhenya could see how mortally terrified his father was, and that this man, surrounded at home by so much respect, was in fact pitifully weak. It was one of those childhood revelations which remain for ever. Later he understood his father's terror in the face of a higher authority and he did not condemn him; on the few occasions when he too came face to face with this terrible authority he himself forgot all shame, and much else besides.

His father left for Moscow on his own, while his mother stayed behind to look after him. He was dreadfully ill, delirious, weeping and gasping for air. Once in a raging fever he saw some huge men in boots which smelled of tar stamping around the flat moving furniture. Then suddenly he saw them taking away Kostya's father again, only this time it was not Kostya's father but his own, and he turned back his blue swollen face at the door. When the fever dropped, he realized that he was lying in an empty room. All the furniture had been moved, and his mother's large wardrobe of Finnish birch had been wrapped in hessian. This smell of fresh hessian was the first thing he noticed as he recovered. Removal men arrived in clean rubber aprons and clumped around, taking away their things, and Zhenya, still very weak after his illness, was driven with his mother to the station in a jolting horse-drawn cab.

His father met them in Moscow. Heads and faces flashed past as the train drew into the station, but his mother at once picked him out in the crowd. 'Look, there's Papa! No, not there – there!' In his white high-collared summer jacket and

54

white linen cap his father seemed different somehow, imposing and rather military. He was followed into the carriage by an athletic-looking youth who beamed happily at them, his mighty chest bulging out of a laced-up sports shirt. While his father pecked his mother on the cheek and inquired about the journey, the young man seized the bags in his strong arms, whose rippling muscles turned Zhenya green with envy, and ran up and down handing their luggage out to the porter, so that when they alighted they had nothing to carry.

They drove through Moscow beneath the hot white July sky and the trolley-bus wires. Zhenya recalled Foma telling him at school that he had read in the Bible that the time would come when these wires would tangle up the earth, and iron birds would land, and the world would end . . . But to Zhenya Moscow seemed like a party, its pavements crowded with people, its streets filled with cars and trolley buses and policemen in white gloves and tunics directing the traffic.

At the hotel the doors were flung open by a bearded commissionaire resembling some pre-revolutionary figure, and they stepped into the marbled magnificence of the lobby as though entering a palace. People were strolling across the marble floors and lounging in armchairs, and a bulky foreigner held an open newspaper before him, one booted foot thrown over his knee. As they walked through, they were assailed with waves of cigar and tobacco smoke, and a scent like Mama's powder-compact wafted from the perfume kiosks, their multicoloured bottles gleaming beneath the electric lights.

Father led the way, his heels tapping confidently in the size thirty-eight boots they used to buy secretly for him at the children's shoe-shop. Zhenya and his mother followed, and the chauffeur brought up the rear with the suitcases, one under each arm, the other two clutched in his trembling hands. People greeted his father respectfully, and when they reached their floor, the woman behind the desk immediately handed them the keys to their room; a chambermaid in a white apron with a huge bow at the back appeared to be expecting them, and went into ecstasies over Zhenya.

Zhenya had known since childhood that his father could not bear pain, and that his pain always hurt much more than others'. He would go into a decline if he had a temperature. Once when he was ill Zhenya's mother had washed him in the bath like a baby and he had thrown a tantrum. Now, however, as they crossed the marble floors and carpeted landings, he seemed an extraordinary man, much taller than in reality. When they reached their room, their suitcases, which had been following them up, were already waiting for them.

On his first night in Moscow's Hotel Moskva Zhenya hardly slept. The breathing of the great city, the hooting of the cars outside the window, the beam of the headlamps wheeling across the ceiling, the silky cream-coloured curtain at the brightly lit window, the circling light and shadows – everything was new and exciting. The moment he dropped off traffic policemen in white uniforms would wave their batons and, shuddering from the noise of the car horns, he would jump up and bump his forehead on the wall, for everything in the room was in the wrong place and he could not remember where he was, or what he was doing there.

It was late when he finally awoke, and he again felt as though he were at a party. Music was playing outside, the sun blazed on the high moulded ceilings, and his mother, her blue dressing-gown bathed in sunlight, carried dresses on hangers from the suitcases to the cupboards.

They went to a café on the other side of Gorky Street and breakfasted on whipped cream and sausages, which he loved more than anything else, while outside a loudspeaker thundered out a popular song:

'Over the land spring breezes play,
Life grows happier every day . . .'

56

Then they returned to the hotel, to find that their room had already been cleaned, aired and tidied.

Over the next few weeks Mama would sometimes wake him in the middle of the night and he would sit up in bed with a plate on his knee and juice dripping down his face, holding in his sticky fingers a huge pear or a bunch of Lady's Finger grapes which his father had brought back from work. He would also bring fresh rolls filled with sweet, succulent ham, or sandwiches or wonderful freshly smoked sturgeon; Zhenya's lips and hands would smell of smoked fish for hours afterwards, and he would sniff them under the bedclothes.

Late one night, through a haze of sleep, he heard his father coming in drunk, and excitedly relating at the top of his voice how he had just seen Comrade Stalin, and how Comrade Stalin, right in front of everyone else, had said, 'Usvatov, Usvatov . . . Tell me, Usvatov, when will you fart off?'

'I was shocked rigid! Comrade Stalin was looking at everybody and waiting, then suddenly – you'll never believe this – he laughed and poked his finger at me, and just said, "Ah, Usvatov!" '

Zhenya crept out in his bare feet to listen, and his father, his eyes shining with alcohol, repeated it all over again for his benefit, painfully jabbing him in the stomach, to show how Comrade Stalin had poked his finger at him, and said, 'Ah, Usvatov!' For a long time that poke served as his father's safe-conduct pass.

But Zhenya was beginning to notice that his mother seemed increasingly fearful of the polite chambermaid in the snow-white apron and of the receptionist who took their keys when they went out and stared after them as they passed, and for some reason she invariably told these women where they had been or where they were going.

They continued to live in the hotel while they waited for a flat to come up. In the mornings the maid would come in and clean their room, and on his way to and from school he would go through the lobby filled with the scent of perfume and foreign tobacco and lined with rows of foreign suitcases covered in stickers. He loved walking past all this to the commissionaire, who soon knew him by sight and would fling open the massive doors for him. Everything should have been splendid, but something was going on between his parents. He would hear them whispering long after midnight, or he would wake up to find their light still on. During the day his mother was quiet and withdrawn, and when he asked her something, she did not hear. His father too seemed to be avoiding him. Once when Zhenya looked questioningly into his eyes, he started as though caught unawares, and for no reason at all thrust a rouble into his hands, saying, 'There, buy yourself an ice-cream.'

Eventually a flat became available. Since his father was at work, the chauffeur helped them to move. They had a long drive across Moscow, then down some side-streets and along a cobbled road lined with old wooden houses and fences, where a little girl in a red cotton dress was washing her bare legs under a stream of water from a standpipe. In this wasteland, facing on to the railway tracks, stood a grey five-storeyed building which shook with the roar of passing trains and was grimy with the coal dust from the engines. The chauffeur carried in their things and apologetically took his leave of them, and Zhenya and his mother were on their own. A bare window, a bed, a narrow oak sideboard topped with a glass cabinet and, against the wall, the hessian-wrapped wardrobe. Somewhere in this shared flat a child was crying, and Zhenya, not understanding anything, went out to look. The door opposite theirs was open, and he saw a little boy standing on a table howling; his shirt was tucked up and he was aiming a stream of pee into an enamel teapot. A distraught-looking woman ran down the corridor, the door into the room slammed and there were more tears and howls.

Dumbfounded, he asked his mother, 'Is this where we're living now?'

His mother stood starkly silhouetted against the window.

'But where's my room?'

She turned round and he could barely make out her face against the light.

'I didn't know how to tell you, but you're a big boy now . . . Your father has a new family . . .'

Stunned by the thought that this crying child and terrible frantic woman might be his father's new family, he embraced his mother, or rather clutched her in terror. She misunderstood his gesture, and saw him for the first time as her protector.

'There, son, never mind . . .' she murmured, gratefully stroking his head with a trembling hand, and he felt her sweating forehead against his chin, for he was now a good head taller than she was.

So began their wretched life together in this flat which they shared with two other families. The bathroom, filled with strangers' underwear, the stench of children's urine and the sinks full of laundry, made him feel sick. The kitchen contained three tables and three electric hotplates, on one of which he would fry potatoes or heat up soup when he returned from school. Too hungry to wait, he would run into the living-room to get bread from the sideboard – ah, how wonderful the inside of that sideboard was, the very wood smelled of black bread! After cutting himself a thick slice he would spread it with margarine, dip it into some sugar and creep back to the kitchen to catch the little boy at his thieving again. Having been lured by the smell, the child would snatch a potato from the pan, or move a stool to the table to scoop some of the thick goodness from the bottom of a pan of pea-soup. Zhenya eventually worked out what to do. One day when everyone else was out he got a wet towel and chased the little boy down the corridor, whipping him on his bare behind. The child could not complain, for he was a deaf mute and could only howl and moan in pain.

Seeing Evgeny Stepanovich now, stepping into his gleaming limousine every morning, perusing his official documents on the way to work, seating himself behind the massive desk in his office, chairing important conferences and charming audiences with his wit and elegance, it was hard to believe that he had once chased a sobbing deaf-mute boy down the corridor with a twisted towel, beating him again and again and laughing with pleasure. Once the boy had filled his pants in terror, and Zhenya had had to overcome his revulsion and wipe him clean, hanging him over the bathtub to wash it all off. His methods had their effect, however, and before long the little boy was afraid even of his smile, and would freeze with fear at the sight of him.

Not far away, polished brass door-handles shone, spotless chambermaids shook specks of dust from rugs and carpets and bearded commissionaires threw open massive doors. There, in the same city but in another world, lived his father. Zhenya ached for that life and dreamed of it at night. Here his mother would bring back a thin paste-like blancmange from the factory where she worked for a pittance as a clerk, and he would eat it on bread.

For some reason he kept remembering the people his mother used to feed secretly in their kitchen before the family broke up. It had been in the terrible winter of 1932, when hordes of hungry peasants left the villages and poured into the town. Zhenya's father, who used to return late from work even then, would dine alone in the large room at the long table laid with a starched white cloth. He always ate the same thing: a cold sliced chop on white bread and butter, washed down with a glass of warm skimmed milk, and another glass of strong sweet tea to aid his brain (which his wife insisted that he overexerted). As he ate, chewing methodically (the doctor had advised him to chew every mouthful thoroughly to break down acidity), he would tell them how carts drove around the town towards dawn picking up frozen bodies from the streets and taking them to be buried in a ravine outside the town. Afraid to warm themselves in the stations, where the police would harass them and send them packing, these people huddled in doorways or at gateposts, and were found frozen to death in the morning.

As the horse-drawn bread-van pulled up Zhenya would see crowds of hungry people running towards the smell of bread and clouds of steam. Terrible scenes of violence followed as women and children in cloth shoes were beaten back like sheep, while the horse, deep in its nosebag, munched away at its oats.

Like all families of important government officials, the Usvatovs were registered with a special food store inaccessible to the general public, and his mother would carry back bags of food to distribute among various members of the family. There were also a number of people whom she would regularly feed in their kitchen. She never told her husband about this, and she begged Zhenya not to upset him needlessly by doing so, for he worked so hard. But his mother's wheedling tones made Zhenya suspect that something was wrong, and it bothered him that he did not know what it was.

Of all those who came to their kitchen that winter, the one who came most was a boy of his age. When his mother first brought the boy in and unwrapped the rags on his legs, he seemed quite plump, but she explained that he was merely swollen from malnutrition. He used to come at exactly the same hour every day, waiting outside if he was early, and Zhenya's mother would feed him and give him something to take away. Zhenya was not allowed in the kitchen at these times, but he was curious about this boy who ate their food, and even imagined himself making friends with him. One day he went in, holding a slice of bread and goose dripping in his hand. He was a well-nourished child and, since their flat was well heated, he had shorts on. For the first time he saw his mother blushing for him, her own son, in front of this strange boy. The boy nervously stopped eating and Zhenya was chased out of the kitchen, but not before noticing that he was wearing one of his jackets. It was an old jacket, to be sure, but he had been fond of it. Then his father's galoshes disappeared, and before he could stop himself, he had blurted out in front of his father, 'Perhaps that boy who comes here to eat took them.' His father then demanded to know everything, and a terrible row ensued. The country was encircled by the enemy, he shouted, the government was forced, yes, forced, to use these methods to carry through its industrialization programme, people had to harden their hearts or we would be crushed, wiped off the face of the earth . . .!

His mother generally listened to him admiringly. When they had guests, she would glance round enraptured, as if to say did you hear that? Isn't he clever? And when he returned late from work and dined alone at the big table, she would have had her hair done and smartened herself up for him as though she were going to the theatre, hanging on his every word as he spoke slowly in the pauses between chewing and drinking. This time, however, she shyly objected. 'But why should we take the bread from people's mouths? Why should children die of hunger? Why should they pay for it with their lives?'

'Fine!' shouted his father. 'I won't eat this chop, then! You can feed it to them!' And, jumping up from the table, he flung aside his unfinished supper and upset the glass of milk on to the starched cloth. Waking up in the night, Zhenya heard his mother heating up his father's milk and bringing him his food in bed; his father was cross and bad-tempered but eventually ate it up.

The boy in Zhenya's jacket had never appeared in their kitchen again. Yet in their squalid Moscow room Zhenya was unable to get the image of him out of his mind. At school he was ashamed of his wretched life, his poverty and his smelly flat. Some of the children in his class lived in the workers' hostel, but some lived in the large apartment building on the Mozhaisk road, and these were the ones Zhenya was determined to cultivate. Once Boris Pimenov invited him home after school. Talking loudly and swinging their satchels, they walked past the lift-attendant, took the lift up to Boris's flat and rang the bell. A loud pedigree bark came from behind the soft, upholstered door, and as they went in a huge dappled Great Dane flung its paws on Zhenya's chest, covering him with repulsive slobber. Boris ruffled the dog's ears and chuckled. 'Silly thing – he's still a pup. D'you know how old he is? Just seven months! He'll end up this big . . .' Zhenya attempted a casual laugh and stretched out his hand to stroke the revoltingly naked animal, but deep down he felt mortified.

The dog followed them through the large rooms, its claws clicking on the floor. The polished parquet gleamed, and a lampshade hung above a large dining-table, covered with a fringed and tasseled velvet tablecloth, and a glass-fronted cabinet containing coloured crystal goblets. Boris had his own room, as Zhenya himself had once had, with exercise rings hanging from the ceiling, a Swedish wall and nickel-plated dumb-bells lying on the carpet. The boys worked out on the rings and boxed with the punchball before being called to the dining-room. Dinner was served by an elderly peasant-like woman in a white headscarf with blue spots, and Boris's mother, a large, imposing woman, sat opposite, plying Zhenya with questions about himself. He ate without lifting his eyes from his plate, both embarrassed and fascinated by the deep cleavage in her cherry-coloured satin dressing-gown.

That evening he picked a quarrel with his mother. 'I'm fed up! I've had enough!' he shouted at her, loudly enough for the neighbours to hear.

Trying to explain their poverty to him, she said, 'Your father only left us because Uncle Gera and Auntie Marusya were arrested.' Gera and Marusya were her brother and sister, and it was the first time she had ever said this.

'Don't tell lies about Father!' he yelled. 'That's not why he left!'

She fell silent, realized that he had not said half of what was on his mind, and suddenly she saw herself as he saw her: withered, flat-chested and grey.

EIGHT

A major event was coming up: a huge delegation was leaving for Uzbekistan, to be led by Evgeny Stepanovich Usvatov. During telephone conversations he would casually remark, 'I'll be away for ten days or so, leading a large delegation . . .' Or, 'I'm afraid something's cropped up – I have to take a group of delegates . . .' If an unwelcome caller kept pestering for an appointment, he would say, 'Let me see . . . I'll just look in my diary . . . Next Thursday? No, Thursday's no good . . . How about Friday . . .? Excellent! Friday it is! We can have a good long talk about work.' But since the delegation was to depart on Wednesday, 'the good long talk' would be postponed indefinitely. Evgeny Stepanovich never liked to turn people away.

The moment the trip was announced the machinery swung into action. The names of the delegates were shuffled, altered, sifted through and revised, until the day finally came for them to be printed out on thick Finnish paper, fastened with an especially large paper-clip, marked with a pink label and placed on Evgeny Stepanovich's desk in a brass-cornered morocco-leather file, with E. S. Usvatov stamped on it in gold. People of his rank were not officially entitled to this type of file, but he would not hear of this, and his assistants had been most helpful. Two types of file were available: the more sought after was the red morocco one, the colour of top-level testimonials, but Evgeny Stepanovich had modestly opted for the brown: he had no wish to be greedy.

The officials listed on Committee documents had always been the President and various deputies but no First Deputy. Evgeny Stepanovich had refused to put his signature to these papers, correcting them by hand and sending them back to be retyped, until everyone, even the typists, had got it into their heads that he was the First Deputy. People had whispered about this in the corridors, of course, and the whispers had got back to the President. But the old rhinoceros, as Evgeny Stepanovich called him, had not made an issue of it, and before long a sign had appeared on Evgeny Stepanovich's door saying First Deputy President.

'Right ho!' he said now, picking up the list of delegates and sticking a cigarette in the corner of his mouth. He did not light it, for he had stopped smoking ten years ago, but when concentrating on something he would occasionally put a cigarette in his mouth to allow his subordinates to appreciate the enormous effort of willpower required to abandon the habit. 'Right ho!' he said again, getting down to business.

Standing to the right of the table, patiently awaiting instructions, was the head of the Central Directorate, Vasily Egorovich Panchikhin, a clever sallow-faced man with small squashed ears and neat hair which had gone grey in the service of duty. Drumming his fingers on the table, Evgeny Stepanovich peered once through the list and raised a puzzled glance to his old ally. Panchikhin spread his hands in perplexity. he enjoyed Evgeny Stepanovich's special confidence, and this made him deferential in public. Although somewhat less formal in private, he understood perfectly where the invisible boundaries were drawn.

'We were aiming for eighty maximum,' Panchikhin said. 'Eighty-two and we're in trouble. If they haul us in, we'll be like partisans in the firing-line.'

Evgeny Stepanovich frowned, drumming more loudly on the table. His fingers were fat and red; as a boy at school his sweaty hands had caused him great embarrassment with the girls. After the war he told everyone that his hands had got frostbite at the front, and then they had commanded respect.

'They mightn't give us a proper welcome,' he said. 'How many were in that delegation to Azerbaijan last spring?'

'A hundred and fourteen.'

'There, you see! Our Uzbek comrades won't give us a proper welcome, and they'll be quite right.'

The delegation the previous spring had been headed by Komrakov. Assuming that Evgeny Stepanovich did not automatically inherit the rhinoceros's seat, he and Komrakov were now neck and neck for the same job. In Azerbaijan Komrakov's people had been received by the Leader himself, who had taken them for boat trips on the Caspian and up in an aeroplane, from which they had scattered salt and fired rifles to disperse the clouds and make sure the delegation had fine weather for the duration of the visit. Usvatov, on the other hand, had been allowed just eighty people. He put on his glasses again, took up his felt-tip pen and began to study the list in earnest. He had already heard on the grapevine that the Leader was not intending to welcome them; they would just have to give him some encouragement by bringing in some more important people.

Evgeny Stepanovich crossed out a number of names, one with a particularly thick line. Panchikhin, who was still standing to the right of the table, immediately assumed responsibility for this mistake, and from then on was always out whenever the man called.

'That's a bit better,' Evgeny Stepanovich said, scanning the list a second time. He reached out for his cigarette-lighter and turned it around in his fingers, but again mastered himself by a sheer effort of will. 'But why haven't we got—?' He named a distinguished elderly writer. 'Why is he not on our list?'

Panchikhin modestly lowered his head. The others were simply not important enough; what would one so distinguished want with a delegation like this? But Evgeny Stepanovich, his eyes shining, refused to be deterred.

'He's an awkward customer,' muttered Panchikhin, looking away, for they understood each other all too well. 'He never goes anywhere without his wife.'

'Well, ask his wife too!' Evgeny Stepanovich needed the old

man, and would spare no expense to get him. 'Ask his children, his daughters-in-law, his grandchildren, his great-grandchildren! God dammit, we'll take his dog too if need be!'

'He's afraid of flying,' mumbled Panchikhin, terrified of being made to look foolish. 'He's difficult.'

'Gifted people always are,' Evgeny Stepanovich said, nodding judiciously. 'Yes indeed, talent is a heavy burden . . .' He seemed to be speaking personally here, forgetting for a while where he was. There was a pause. Panchikhin waited respectfully. 'So, where were we? Ah yes, talent . . .' Evgeny Stepanovich returned from his thoughts. 'Talent is the property of the people, we must remember that. Now, you and I have work to do. What's the name of that new novel of his?'

'*Joys and Griefs*.'

'Aren't you confusing it with a different one? There's another thing with "Joys" in it – I can't remember who by.'

'That was Fedin's *First Joys*. Igor Matveevich's is *Joys and Griefs*.'

'Better check – we don't want to cock it up.'

Once, at the very start of his career, Evgeny Stepanovich's great desire to please had led him to make a cock-up which had taught him a lesson he would never forget. Wishing to impress a certain important composer, he had employed the time-honoured method of flattery. Anyone who says flattery has no effect on him is lying; if it has no effect, it is just not being done right. When praising a certain cantata to the skies, Evgeny Stepanovich had stupidly failed to check first, and the cantata had proved to be by the composer's arch rival, whom he had loathed and envied all his life. 'It's not mine! Not mine!' the man had screamed tearfully, and Evgeny Stepanovich had been so distraught that he had waved his arms at him, crying, 'It *is* yours! It *must* be!' Time passed, the composer departed this world and Evgeny Stepanovich finally felt able to tell the story at intimate dinner-parties. He mentioned no names, of course, but people guessed who it was anyway, which merely enhanced his standing.

Panchikhin gave orders for the Committee to be scoured for someone actually reading *Joys and Griefs*. A man was eventually found with the book and questioned, and it was soon lying on Evgeny Stepanovich's desk with a few choice bits underlined. Before putting him through on the telephone, Galina Timofeevna placed in front of him a piece of paper on which she had neatly written the first name and patronymic of the author himself, as well as that of his wife, for nothing was decided without her. It was she who answered the phone, giving Evgeny Stepanovich the chance to shower her with compliments.

The writer's wife had the voice of a child, the face of an angel and nerves of steel. As so often happens with young women who marry older men, she had aged catastrophically quickly, and needed to disguise this with ever more finery. So, when telling her about Samarkand and Bukhara ('What, you haven't been to Bukhara? Believe me, Anna Vasilevna, you've missed one of the seven wonders of the world!'), Evgeny Stepanovich casually mentioned that Bukhara cured the best karakul in the world – black, brown, golden, white, pink, blue, any colour you wanted. The karakul had the desired effect, and the grand old man was called to the phone. Evgeny Stepanovich's earnest inquiries as to whether he had interrupted the creative process were followed by an impressive silence during which various plosive sounds issued from the receiver. Then Evgeny Stepanovich said with passionate feeling, 'You know, I took your novel *Joys and Griefs* from the shelf yesterday . . . God knows how many times I've read it, but I needed something for the soul – something to take me away from work . . . And, you know, I completely lost myself in it! I was up till three in the morning!' Aware that he was in good form, he waved to Panchikhin to sit down and enjoy a free lesson. 'Yes, three in the morning! Couldn't tear myself away! You can read any book once, but real books you read again and again. What a wealth of colour and experience!' Squinting at the book, he read the note scribbled on the flyleaf. 'Our treasure-house of talent!'

The writer was concerned to know which edition he had.

'I can't tell you exactly the year, my copy's at home,' said Evgeny Stepanovich, quickly going to the title-page with all the relevant information. 'It's blue – an Art and Fiction edition . . .'

This was apparently not the right one – he should have the latest, green one, which contained a number of additions and improvements.

'I can't imagine *how* you could improve it . . . You know, I felt there was something of Bunin there . . .' There was a tense and ominous silence at the other end of the line, and Evgeny Stepanovich realized he had said the wrong thing. 'Only in the immediacy of the images, of course, and the smells . . . ! It's the way you set the whole thing up! I was immersed in a world of smells! But the main thing is the insight. That's something Bunin never had. What a global, comprehensive concept . . .'

From then on, everything went swimmingly: Samarkand, Bukhara . . . Anna Vasilevna needed a holiday . . . Forget Switzerland, forget abroad . . . Publishers in Uzbekistan wanted to bring out his novel too. They had actually rung to invite him over in person . . .

Although the writer did not give his final answer at once, it was understood that he would go. What a shame it was, the old man said, that when most people read a book these days, they so rarely had the simple spontaneous warmth to get on the phone and tell the writer what was in their heart, but saved it all up for the obituaries. One should always say these kind words while the writer was alive, he said. Put off other things, but never a kind word . . .

'I'm speechless!' Panachikhin enthused as Evgeny Stepanovich put the phone down.

'I told you so! The thicker you lay it on, the more effective it is. Writers and artists are a special case. You can never praise them too much, only too little.'

By the end of the day the directors of four Moscow and Leningrad theatres had agreed to come, as well as three well-known film directors and a host of popular actors and actresses, and when each of them asked who else was coming, Evgeny Stepanovich would casually mention the names of those who had already accepted. The list was once more sifted and shuffled, printed on high-quality paper and finally placed on his desk. The delegation now consisted of one hundred and twenty-one people, seven more than Komrakov's party – and what people those seven were! Leading them all was Evgeny Stepanovich. The laws of the theatre rule that the tsar must never be played by himself, only by his understudies.

After his victory Evgeny Stepanovich wished to show his thanks to Panchikhin; it was Panchikhin who had once taught him everything he knew, and now he could give him a few tips in return. They had worked well together over the years, largely because Panchikhin had long since abandoned any ambition of his own. As time passed and all passions were spent, Panchikhin emerged as master of his own little domain, happy to have his views and comments sought. He was irreplaceable in another way too: with him around, Evgeny Stepanovich could afford to be generous in allowing projects through, knowing that Panchikhin could later throw them out. Panchikhin did have one secret passion, however: his collection of match-boxes. He had thousands of them, and Evgeny Stepanovich would return from his various trips and foreign assignments with entire sets for Panchikhin to add to his collection.

He now ordered tea to be brought to his office. He sometimes wondered whether the old man would think people were being kind to him simply because he was on the verge of retirement. Yes, the old chap would soon be packing up his matchboxes – who knows, he might even write a learned treatise on them. Evgeny Stepanovich had set up a highly complex manoeuvre whose ultimate goal was to establish his future son-in-law in Panchikhin's job. Clever Irina had got things going nicely, and her young man was first to be posted to the Soviet embassy in Thailand (too soon for anywhere better, but not bad for a start) before slipping into Panchikhin's seat. People involved in elaborate housing swaps rarely know one another, but there is invariably one person who ends up getting far more than those for whom the whole thing was ostensibly set up. Thus, as Panchikhin conscientiously helped Evgeny Stepanovich to organize the delegation on the eve of his retirement, he little suspected that this would be his swansong.

The tea arrived with three kinds of biscuit, including Panchikhin's favourite, a pretzel shaped like a figure of eight and sprinkled with coarse salt.

'We could use some beer with these, eh, Vasily Egorovich? What do you think?' chuckled Evgeny Stepanovich.

'You really must let me treat you to some of my home-cured fish one of these days, Evgeny Stepanovich. We've a little stream near our dacha . . .'

No, he suspected nothing. As Evgeny Stepanovich sipped strong tea from the saucer, he observed him with curiosity. It was interesting the way even the most observant people can be blind to what is happening to them. One could do anything with people, since they never believed the worst until it was too late.

Panchikhin's venerable silvery hair was ever so slightly out of place at the end of the working day, and his porous nose was flushed from the hot tea and the pleasant talk.

'Do you remember, Evgeny Stepanovich, how our then minister of culture of the RSFSR once rushed over to the dacha of a certain very important figure? The man was a genius on the mouth-organ, incidentally. "Why don't you pop over some time?" the man had said. "I'm having a little celebration . . ." And you know what he did . . .?' Panchikhin gave a little laugh. 'Here he was, an experienced man, and off he rushed

71

with a present. An expensive present too – he'd really pushed the boat out. Well, the guards stopped him at the barrier. "You do that," he said. "I was invited, here's my present . . ." They checked on the phone and told him to leave his present there, so he had to walk back. He told me there was an endless stream of limousines passing him on the road . . .'

'He must have been frantic!' exclaimed Evgeny Stepanovich.

'On the contrary!' Panchikhin sat up very straight, all trace of tolerance gone, his voice hard and his gaze inexorable. 'No, Evgeny Stepanovich, he wasn't frantic, he was glad. He told us this story for our edification. "How could I have forgotten my place, old fool that I was!" Yes, that's what he said, and he struck his forehead with his fist. If all the cogs of the state machine worked as smoothly as they do in our office, the state would be unshakeable!' And at these words Evgeny Stepanovich felt all his old longing for stability and order stir within him. 'I tell you, Evgeny Stepanovich, the entire structure rests upon us – we built it up, and we maintain it!' Panchikhin spoke with dignity, and even a touch of menace. 'We are like the hoops on a barrel – knock away the hoops and the rivets disintegrate. *He* understood that.' Panchikhin pointed to the ceiling.

The old fellow's right, thought Evgeny Stepanovich, his heart pounding. Ah, he could still be useful to me. I know everything has its price, but it's a shame, a shame . . . !

Evgeny Stepanovich himself would not be here for much longer either, of course. He had gone as far as he possibly could in his present position, and the award had been the final acknowledgement of this. But now he felt like a tree whose buds had swollen painfully and had nowhere to go. How he would have thrived in a new post! He would have brought new energy to it, and some of that enthusiasm with which he had started out all those years ago. He had made so many good suggestions then – half of them totally unworkable, of course – and he had impressed everyone as being a shrewd and energetic administrator. Now it was time to move on, leaving his successors to start afresh. The new people couldn't be answerable for the past, they too must have time to show their worth.

One thing he now knew for sure, however: if this trip made its mark and attracted favourable attention, that would be a step in the right direction.

NINE

Evgeny Stepanovich spent a great deal of time before his departure dashing around the Committee building. By picking up something someone said in one department and dropping an amended version of it in another he was able to enhance the importance of his mission and to suggest that great things might be expected of it. He was seen scurrying along the corridors of power, and while people on one floor might have had their doubts, those on the next floor up would be saying, 'Usvatov will pull it off, all right!' And this too he would repeat, overcoming modesty in the interests of the business in hand.

Sweet was the moment when he was driven to a certain building. The car door was opened and after giving the driver his instructions he stepped out on to the asphalt. With a remote, official expression he strode briskly past a man in plain clothes loitering on the kerb, past identical-looking pedestrians, and up to the main entrance, where after a routine check he was allowed in. And how sweet it was to emerge through the doors of the building, to see his car swing out from the line of gleaming nickel radiators, to climb inside, slam the door and drive off deep in thought.

The initial result of all this promotional work was that another nine people were added to the list of delegates: four eminent men of culture were to be flown in from Kiev, three from the three Baltic republics and one from Moldavia, and an ancient Georgian actress from Tbilisi would fly to Moscow to join the other delegates before flying back south with them to Tashkent.

The evening before leaving Evgeny Stepanovich took a

shower, put on his pyjamas and unhurriedly started to fill his case. He always packed for himself, ticking things off against a list. He and Elena felt especially close to each other in the hours before a journey, and the flat always seemed especially cosy and precious.

He gently patted down his starched shirts, then put in his sponge bag and shaving gear, along with a Philips safety razor in case he needed to shave on the plane. Just as Elena entered the room bearing a list of her measurements and all the things he was to get her in Uzbekistan ('You must have *some* time off!'), the phone rang; apparently a Tupolev 104 from Leningrad had crashed while landing at Vnukovo airport. Evgeny Stepanovich hung up and decided to say nothing to her about the crash. Fired by a thousand desires, she showed him an old silver ornament with green stones which she had got in Armenia but was sure could be found in Uzbekistan. He listened patiently. On another occasion he might have snapped, 'Stop babbling! Can't you see I'm packing? I might forget something!' But now he felt full of warmth, and was pleased not to have told her about the crash. Let her find out when he got back.

He waited for the inevitable call from the distinguished old man he had been so determined to recruit, who would obviously now be unable to fly. Of course when the phone rang, it was not the old man himself but his wife, whose life's mission it was to protect this national property.

'I'm sorry Igor Matveevich can't . . .' she said. 'His work, you know . . .'

'Oh, what a shame!' Evgeny Stepanovich no longer needed the old fool anyway. He had served his purpose as the bait to lure the others, raising the delegation to the level where the Leader would now definitely be receiving them – and that was official. 'To be utterly frank, dear lady, I was thinking primarily of you. Samarkand! Bukhara! The karakul . . .! Science feeds from the ever generous hand of the state – why should not the arts partake of that warmth? And its foremost practitioners, as one might say . . .'

It had all worked out beautifully. It was just as well that tedious couple weren't coming; he wouldn't have to flatter them endlessly and put up with their silly whims. Evgeny Stepanovich glanced again at his list to check that everything was packed and realized that he had almost forgotten his travel slippers. They had a special leather case, and had accompanied him halfway round the world; nothing had ever gone wrong, so they must bring him luck.

At seven the next morning Evgeny Stepanovich's car whisked him to Domodedovo airport. Sprawling on the passenger side of the back seat, he gazed absent-mindedly out of the window. Houses flashed by and vanished, and then he was in the countryside. The breeze wafting in through the lowered window was still fresh and unpolluted by fumes. Life was not so bad, if one was philosophical about it and undistracted by trivia. The problem was, nothing could ever be repeated. It is said that in an eternity of time and space everything is reconstituted from its particles – if you can wait that long . . . He had not paid much attention to this idea when he had first heard it, but if there were ladies present, he might announce, as though peering through mists of prophecy, 'I have a sense that I have been here before . . .' Women were a powerful force: nobody weighed one up so shrewdly as the wives of important men.

He saw his delegation at the far end of the echoing, deserted airport building, huddling round their bags like shivering chickens and looking out for him. He waved cheerfully and marched towards them with a carefree, purposeful step, his fawn raincoat slung over his arm, his shoulders thrown back, his hat at a jaunty angle and his driver hurrying along behind with his bag.

The airport was totally empty after the accident at Vnukovo; people had presumably just remembered the existence of the railways and cashed in their air-tickets. All the more warmly, therefore, did he greet his delegates. He kissed the hand of the ancient Georgian actress; as he lifted it to his lips, a heavy bracelet fell from her wrist and the large green stones of her rings clunked against each other on her withered fingers. They were exactly the same stones as Elena had requested, and they were as cold as the shiny, emaciated skin of the woman's hand. He felt a momentary revulsion as he brushed the dark protruding veins with his lips. When he raised his head, her black eyes were fixed upon his in a tragic, questioning gaze.

'It will be all right,' Evgeny Stepanovich assured her quietly. 'It's always safest to fly straight after an accident – they check everything ten times over. In a month's time I wouldn't be so certain, but now you may rest completely assured.'

These grand old men and women baffled him. There was no life left in this old crone, the blood ran cold in her black veins, yet people packed the theatres to pick over her decaying bones and suddenly, as if by magic, an eagle would step on to the stage and the hushed audience would hold its breath. Drops of rain started to fall from the scudding clouds – a good sign – and as they stood outside on the damp tarmac, the ladies opened up brightly coloured umbrellas and a long-legged, short-skirted stewardess came down the gangway towards them like a heavenly apparition. Then all at once Evgeny Stepanovich heard a familiar voice in his ear: 'You're killing yourselves . . . !' There, standing beside a composer from Leningrad, like some dishevelled visitant from another planet, was his utterly earthly wife, her throat swollen and her voice roughened by copious brandy and the cigarette that perpetually dangled from her bright lips. Evgeny Stepanovich threw her a tender, encouraging smile, then was distracted by one of the humorous writers tapping his teeth to the tune of Chopin's Funeral March:

'Tupolev One-O-Four is the quick-est way to fly,
Tupolev One-O-Four is the quick-est way to die.

77

A plane crash in your pri-ime
Saves a lot of ti-ime . . .'

Evgeny Stepnovich shook his head angrily and turned away. No one could call him a nationalist, let alone anti-Semitic, but insensitivity ran in these people's blood. They were incapable of seeing themselves as others saw them. They were born that way. This was why so many of them were comedians. Could they think of nothing better than to laugh at life? Why were there three humorists in the delegation anyway? Two would have been quite enough.

The huge Ilyushin 86 had seats for over three hundred passengers but no first-class accommodation, so Evgeny Stepanovich democratically joined the others in the main body of the plane, where he heard the crew announce, 'Managing this flight will be . . . Your captain is . . .' The little word 'manage' was certainly no accident – more appropriate, surely, to a dangerous circus trick. Very Freudian, very Freudian indeed. He had not actually read Freud, but he always contrived to make some reference to him when subconscious matters were being discussed. He never developed these ideas, of course: discretion is always the wiser course.

Over three hundred lives were strapped into their seats and the huge, lumbering contraption cruised towards the runway. The engines revved up with a roar, and through the porthole the earth tilted away as they took off. Now everything was falling headlong beneath them. Cars, roads, houses and clumps of trees all grew smaller and smaller, veiled in a shimmering haze which cleared as they reached the cold heights – minus fifty-five degrees outside. Under the wing of the plane the huge maw of the engines glared with an unbearable brightness. There was an ominous jolt. Down below a small white plane wandered towards them through the shadowy cumulus clouds. High above the earth the engines swayed and the wings shook. In the cabin people stretched in their seats reading newspapers, and a woman cosily took out her

78

knitting. But the question was, what if one of those engines came off and hurtled to the earth? What would all our dos and don'ts mean then, dear comrades?

The stewardesses changed into grey aprons and rolled the drinks trolley up the aisle, serving drinks in little plastic oriental bowls. One walked backwards while the other advanced, asking, 'Squash? Fizzy water . . .?' Their grey aprons, white shirts, red chiffon neck-scarves and bright make-up were most attractive. Perhaps the stewardesses in that other aeroplane, five or six years ago, had put on aprons and rolled out the bar. No, they would have had no time. The plane had just gained height after taking off from the seaside resort of Adler, and had plunged straight into the Black Sea. The passengers, tanned and relaxed, were returning from their summer holidays, peering through the portholes for a final glimpse of the sea. Some, reluctant to leave, had probably run down to the beach for an early morning swim, throwing coins in the water as a pledge that they would return, bundling their wet trunks and bathing-suits into their bags . . . For many weeks afterwards *Evening Moscow* had carried announcements of the deaths, framed in funereal black, along with their degrees, titles and awards. Most were couples. Of course news of the crash was never announced officially since mourning is not permitted, but the rumours spread none the less and everyone knew.

Evgeny Stepanovich somehow could not get this tragedy out of his mind. It was like a denouement, the resolution of some crisis – maybe even a kind of liberation. What if the hermetic seal had not broken on impact with the sea and the plane instead of being smashed to pieces, had plunged into the black depths, and – ghastly thought! – they had all sat strapped into their seats, until there was no air left to breath . . . Sat there, waiting . . . God knows what had actually happened. But the point was whether in that moment all the things to which we attach such importance – all our precious dos and don'ts – had had any meaning for them. And if not, what in God's name was the point of dragging this burden around for the whole of our lives like a tortoise with its shell? If none of it meant anything at the moment of death, why should it eat away our souls during our lifetime?

It had indeed been Lenya whom he had seen at the traffic-lights as he drove into town that morning after the party. Evgeny Stepanovich had hastily immersed himself in his papers again, but what had he been so afraid of? The two men had moved so far apart, they inhabited such different worlds. What did he have to fear? Yet he was haunted by premon-itions of disaster, and he felt a growing dislike for the man. It was Dostoevsky who said we can never forgive those we have harmed – or words to that effect.

Yet what harm had he done Lenya? Lenya, Kulikov and he had all been friends at university. Kulikov was just a boy then, who hadn't even done his military service, and they tended to patronize him. Hard to believe that Evgeny Stepanovich's last sight of Kulikov was as an old Russian peasant lying dead in his coffin. Evgeny Stepanovich had recently had a terrifying dream about him, in which he was standing dressed in a white shirt, his feet bare and his toes stiff, and his calloused, emaciated fingers were beckoning Evgeny Stepanovich. But Evgeny Stepanovich did not move – he remembered this quite clearly when he awoke. Kulikov had called to him, silently, wordlessly, and he had not gone. That dream must have been trying to tell him something. We know so little about the human psyche and what it is trying to tell us.

It is hard to accept there are times when the individual is powerless, a mere product of its times, and it is not we but history which determines our actions. Who had condemned that little boy who had come to their kitchen? Who had con-demned the people whose frozen bodies were scooped up into carts in the morning and driven to the ravine outside the town? One could comprehend all these things on a mass scale, when set against the political transformations of the epoch. But why that little boy? What had he done wrong? And what of all the other countless, nameless victims in a long line of nameless victims? What too of those blessed by nature and capable of great things? Must all that too be smashed to the ground? No, Evgeny Stepanovich did not want to be the manure on the rose-bed of history, even if it did produce beautiful flowers.

The engines throbbed evenly, everything was reassuringly familiar, the seats and armrests were in position, and again he heard, 'Your attention, please!' Removing his spectacles from the bridge of his nose and swinging them in his hand, Evgeny Stepanovich listened to the stewardess announce which towns the flight path lay over, and that the plane was travelling on course.

In Tashkent the whole ritual of cars, flowers, smiles and welcoming speeches would have been laid on. He would step out of the plane first to clicking cameras, embraces, hand-shakes and triple kisses, while the ordinary passengers, pushed to the back to allow the delegation out, would observe the joyful welcome from afar, marvelling at the importance of their fellow travellers. Evgeny Stepanovich shoved his folded newspaper into the net pocket of the seat in front, eased his head against the white paper headrest and closed his eyes.

So many psychological mysteries elude our understanding. What had made him cling to Lenya then? What had made him follow him around all that day? Was it some premonition which had made him reluctant to leave him alone? Lenya would have seen it differently, of course; he must have thought his friend had been told to tail him.

They had walked down Pyatnitskaya Street and along the embankment, then drunk a beer somewhere under an awning. Chilled by the cold beer and the breeze from the Moscow river, they strolled up to the Sparrow Hills.

Even more chilling, though, were Lenya's words: 'The swine! Now they're saying the Jews didn't fight. According to them, only two per cent of the infantry were Jews. Shiryaev said that to me!'

'You shouldn't have anything to do with Shiryaev . . .'

'So what am I supposed to reply?' Lenya continued. 'He said he hurt his neck lugging ninety-six-kilogram sacks of sugar in the rear. "Come off it!" I said. "Don't tell me you were at the front – you did your back in at a sugar factory!" '

'He'll never forgive you for that, don't you understand?'

'The hell with him! Who cares!'

And Evgeny Stepanovich's heart bled for Lenya, sensing already that he was doomed.

'Two per cent . . .' said Lenya. 'So where did I lose my arm, if not in the infantry? What's amazing is that there were as *many* of us as that, considering Jews are only two per cent of the whole population. And who are the ones who throughout history have always been chucked into the infantry? Why, the people with the least education. Mainly the peasants, of course. And who gave land to the Jews before the Revolution, when they were forbidden to own it?'

Terrified that someone might hear him, Evgeny Stepanovich glanced around and smiled hastily at a passer-by who turned back to stare at them.

'What an idiot I was. I was sent off to study, and this major at the enlistment centre, some little rearguard pig, narrowed his eyes at me and said, "How come you lot are always skiving off to study, while ordinary Russians are fighting at the front . . .?" I nearly gave that bastard a lesson he wouldn't forget. Everything's *their* fault. The masses are such idiots. Why can't they realize that *they* are the yeast – without *them* the dough can't rise.'

Lenya paid for the beer. Evgeny Stepanovich offered to, but Lenya said with a crooked grin, 'Don't bother, I don't expect I'll be needing it much longer.'

Did he know already? They walked on, and Lenya continued, 'Didn't fight in the war? So why did Jews get a third of all the Hero of the Soviet Union medals? Nearly half of 'em posthumous as well. I suppose they wormed their way into that too!'

And then he said. 'We fought the fascists at the front, but the fascists were waiting for us at home.'

At these words Evgeny Stepanovich's blood ran cold and his head froze under its cap. Running behind a bush, he threw up the beer from his stomach, then looked around. Nobody was there. Nothing but the wind to carry the words away. It was then that he finally knew Lenya was doomed. He had known these things for a long time, of course: his mother had been told by Lidka, the building's accountant whose amorous fortunes she used to tell with cards, that the house committee had been ordered to make a list of all the Jews living there. Yet he could not abandon Lenya. He felt a macabre terror, mingled with a strange, morbid curiosity.

'Did we really come back from the front for this?' Lenya said. 'Is this how we thought life would be after the war? At the front I learned what I was worth. Bodies lying outside trenches, some killed in the last attack, some the day before, black in the heat . . . What's a human life worth, people said. But it opened up our souls. Then they got frightened of the people. And now they're harking back to 1937 again. And who are our most trusted students, in charge of everything? Why, Mukhin, Shiryaev and Zyatkov, of course! The swine! Mukhin spent the whole of the war inside the Kremlin.'

'But they were all sent to the front,' said Evgeny Stepanovich wretchedly.

'Well, well, you don't say!'

'Mukhin told me. They sent them off . . . to kill a German . . .'

Lenya laughed angrily. 'Yes, did you see those people with their assignments to the front . . .? Taken out on the lead, and told to kill one German each? Go on, they said, kill a fascist swine . . .'

Evgeny Stepanovich found himself shivering again. Lenya noticed. 'What's the matter? Are you cold?'

'No – it's nothing . . .'

It was late that evening when he returned to the hostel. He

was unable then or later to remember fully what happened. The three of them – Mukhin, Shiryaev and Zyatkov – appeared to be waiting for him, sitting on the two beds in the room shared by Shiryaev and Zyatkov. It was a small base-ment-like room with a barred window. When the students went home for the winter holidays, Zyatkov would melt down all the fat he had been unable to eat that term and put it in a jar which he would place inside the bars; all the students in the hostel could see it, but they couldn't remove it, even if they broke the glass. Almost everyone was hungry then, for ration-cards had not yet been abolished and the girls would use fish-oil from the chemist to fry up fritters made from anything they could lay their hands on. But the jar of melted-down fat and crackling awaited Zyatkov in the cool space behind the bars: his father was director of the local machine and tractor station, so he always got as much as he could eat.

Now they all sat on the two beds, facing one another as though in a railway carriage. With them was a soldier from Mukhin's village and army detachment who had come to see his old friend. For some reason they did not seem surprised to see Usvatov at this late hour. He was Lenya's friend, of course. But still they weren't surprised. They had evidently decided in advance what they wanted from him, and when he realized this, he felt utterly humiliated.

He tried to defend Lenya, saying, 'He fought at the front, in the infantry . . . He's a war invalid . . .' But even as he spoke he knew that the very mention of Lenya's experiences at the front and the loss of his arm would merely compound his fate and spoil the picture already fixed in their minds.

'Huh! You won't travel far in the carriage of the past,' said Shiryaev with his genial grin. This grin of his was very strange: the crueller the words, the sunnier his grin. He him-self had not fought at all, and by injuring his neck in a sugar factory in the Far East he had managed to avoid the war with Japan.

When he grinned his good-natured grin, the soldier grinned

84

too, but his was a cold and knowing grin, and he always said 'we', as if speaking for some higher authority. He was dressed in cotton civvies, and his legs were set squarely before him in polished cow-hide boots which smelled of leather and wax. Some power forced Evgeny Stepanovich to confess to these three men and to the tall cow-hide boots planted on the floor, as though fear were wringing the words out of him.

'It seems quite straightforward to me,' Shiryaev finally said with his grin. 'There's a clear dialectical consistency in all this.' (Shiryaev was able to find dialectical consistency in anything.)

Something warned Usvatov not to tell them everything, and he did not mention Lenya's phrase about the fascists waiting for them at home. On the floor above, virtually over their heads as they sat talking with their heads and knees together, Lenya was probably going to bed or reading, and this thought tormented Zhenya for a long time to come.

Lenya was picked up not that night or the next but a week later. He had walked his girlfriend home, returned to the hostel and put himself to bed. He was just falling asleep when they shook him awake, demanding, 'Have you any weapons?'

'Yes, a machine-gun under the bed!' he joked, still half asleep.

They actually searched under the bed before taking him away. As he was going, Shiryaev went up to Lenya and kissed him in front of all the students, and afterwards people whispered about how brave he had been to kiss Lenya in full view of everyone.

Evgeny Stepanovich suffered terribly. For three years he and Lenya had sat next to each other. Now Lenya's place was suddenly empty, and that empty seat taught him more than anything else had done about the person who had occupied it. At nights he would cry in his sleep, and during the day he would sit through his lectures frozen with fear, waiting for his turn to be called out for questioning, and feverishly remembering everything. He remembered how Lenya had once visited the local court. A woman in a blue overall stood behind the barrier, pale as a saint, and the judge and two chairmen of the court stood before their tall chairs as the sentence was read out: eight years for stealing a bottle of Carmen eau-de-Cologne from the factory. The woman's children were in court too, and as they led her away, she cried out, 'My babies! My babies!'

Walking back past the underground station, they had seen a young war cripple standing in the bitter cold, selling cheap cigarettes individually from the packet. He was their own age, drunk and trembling, and in his blue stumps of arms he held an open packet of Belomors. Lenya had whispered there was a new law known as the 'three ears of wheat law', which meant that even a child of twelve could be shot for gleaning ears of wheat from the collective farm and taking them home. The law had apparently been signed by Kalinin . . .

What if Lenya were forced to confess, and then *he* was taken off? Why hadn't he said anything? He recalled a story that had been going around Moscow about a group of boys who all stood up together in court when their sentence was read out and shouted in unison, 'Thank you, Comrade Stalin, for our happy childhood!' He and Lenya had discussed this too. What would happen now? His mind went numb. Should he go to them straight away and tell them everything? But then they would say, 'Why didn't you come before?' And what if Lenya did confess to something . . .?

Once when the students went outside for a smoke during break someone had pointedly told a story about a prisoner who, when asked by his cell-mates why he was there, had replied, 'For not being active enough!' Three of his friends had had a drink and a chat, but he had been too lazy to tell on the others then and there, and had decided to let it wait until morning. By morning he had already been taken in – there were plenty of others more active than he was . . . At this Evgeny Stepanovich blushed painfully, and everyone noticed.

Before long he was indeed taken off. But some sixth sense

prompted him to tell them nothing they didn't already know from the other two witnesses required in such cases.

When the reselection of the student party committee came up, Zyatkov put forward Usvatov's name, declaring, 'This comrade has proved his worth!' He was supported by Shiraev and Mukhin. The whole thing had obviously been fixed from above.

Yet he had genuinely loved Lenya. Nobody would ever know how his soul wept, and how there were times when he hated himself so deeply that he longed to die . . .

As the plane touched down, Evgeny Stepanovich peered through the porthole. It was all pretty much as he had expected: the black limousines dazzling in the sun's glare parked on the tarmac, the sunburnt men in skullcaps and striped gowns, the men in severe suits and hats, the slender girls with long plaits and bright silk gowns bearing flowers, and the long native trumpets whose name he did not know. Everyone was waiting, everything was ready.

The air-hostesses had been warned in advance to hold back the other passengers. As Evgeny Stepanovich emerged in his pale suit from the dark depths of the cabin through the open door, a gust of dry Asiatic wind grabbed at a lock of his dyed hair and exposed his bald patch. Holding his hair down with one hand and gripping his hat and briefcase with the other, he stepped down the gangway. Drums and tambourines struck up below, the long trumpets tilted their throats to the sky with a roar, three boys in skullcaps standing on tall stilts concealed in vast stripy trousers broke into a wild dance and the girls advanced with their flowers. There were smiles, embraces and triple kisses. Cameras clicked as film crews hovered around, squatting on the ground and adjusting their lenses. The ordinary passengers, finally allowed out of the plane with their bags, walked past and watched with interest as the delegates climbed into the cars parked beside the gangway, the drums beat, the boys on stilts danced for their lives and the girls in bright gowns whirled weightlessly in the air, their slender arms floating and their plaits circling their waists.

TEN

The two-room luxury suite, the flowers, fruit and wine, the fridge stocked with brandy – Evgeny Stepanovich looked inside to check – all spoke of the high esteem in which the delegation was held. Removing his jacket and loosening his tie, he threw off his slippers, walked in his stockinged feet across the soft carpet and stretched out in the armchair. The air-conditioning hummed quietly, cooling his feet. He should really have a wash and brush-up, since in half an hour's time he was meeting the delegates in the lobby to brief them on the programme. But he lay back in the chair, resting his elbows on its velvet arms.

All things were relative, of course. He remembered the time twenty or thirty years before – could it really be that long? – when he had joined his first delegation. 1956 had been a bumper harvest year, at the very height of the Virgin Lands programme, and as part of the propaganda campaign numerous brigades had been sent off to help with the harvest. There had been four of them altogether: an agronomist from the ministry, a journalist from some farming newspaper and an instructor from the Central Committee, their leader. He was a young man, but he had already defended his doctoral thesis at the university and generally secured his rear against all odds. Since it was during the struggle against the 'personality cult', they had nicknamed him Cult.

There was a sixty-kilometre car journey in the Orenburg heat through a vast black dust-bowl, then through walls of red dust. Yet it was good to be rolling along. On the way they stopped beside an icy stream and had a swim, and it was midnight when they arrived at the state farm, feeling their way through the dark with the headlamps. By then he was too tired to think. The buzzing voices mingled with the buzzing flies on the ceiling, his lids closed, he started, stared around him and plunged again into sleep.

Early next morning he sat on the jetty with the farm director, dangling his feet in the water. The smell of a meaty tomato stew wafted from the outdoor summer kitchen, and some odd psychological quirk made Evgeny Stepanovich long to be invited to breakfast with them. Cult had presumably already ingratiated himself with the District Party Secretary, and was bound to be asked, but they could not all go. The way he saw it, the agronomist didn't need to and the journalist wouldn't care, since his newspaper was extremely obscure, and those two would be just as happy eating with the driver. But he desperately wanted to be asked – he was even prepared to bring his own sausage. He had brought with him two large, fine smoked Moscow sausages, and when he sliced them into thin diagonal discs, it would smell so delicious that people's mouths would water. Yes, he was prepared to give away the lot.

The director, a burly steppe-dweller, scooped up his naked little grandson into his broad hand and warmed him next to his body. Then, narrowing his eyes against the low sun – or perhaps merely from a lifetime spent in the sun and wind of the steppe – he told Evgeny Stepanovich of the people who had lived here two thousand years ago; he had found some herbs and wild grasses which proved it, and the canal over there was man-made ... Evgney Stepanovich nodded and looked interested, all the while consumed with anxiety as to whether he would be invited or not.

Sighing, the old man raised the child up by his arms, making his little ribs stick out, then lowered him over the jetty, dipped him in the water, rinsed him like a fish and slapped him back on the path, saying, 'Run about and dry off!' Then he lowered himself in his wide swimming-trunks into the water, and Evgeny Stepanovich diligently swam after him, still desperately hoping to be invited.

Now, of course, Evgeny Stepanovich would spit on that director from the eighth-floor luxury suite where he was reclining with his elbows on the soft armrests of his chair. Then, however, he had felt that nothing could possibly be sweeter than to dine at his table.

That trip had merely been a tick in somebody's book, he had realized that from the start. The whole country was helping the farms with the harvest that year. Their papers for the visit were stamped 'Harvest assignment', and the trucks, grain pouring through every crevice, had 'Harvest' crudely stencilled in gloss paint on the sides. The harvest was indeed spectacular: where rain had fallen just once, the farm chairman would be awarded the Order of Lenin; twice, and he would be a Hero of Socialist Labour. Millions of tons of grain were gathered. Lorries scattered trails of grain across the steppe to the elevators, and people scooped it up in buckets from the ruts in the road. The state-farm driver ferrying them around had made a bucket from an old inner-tube and he used it to collect grain to feed to his geese at home.

Of course, there were not enough elevators for a harvest of this size, so the grain had no time to dry out, and the extra trains arrived too late. The fast-growing wheat picked from the Virgin Lands was reaped indiscriminately, stripping the perennial ground cover from the steppe and producing duststorms which blotted out the sun. The four of them drove around, exhorting and threatening and adding to the general chaos. Meanwhile the grain scorched in its trenches, and he realized that if you were to put in your hand, it would be hot and wet when you took it out again. Part of that spectacular harvest was doomed to disappear under the snow, and he heard later than the bottom fifteen to twenty centimetres of the trenches were ploughed under in the spring, so the whole glutinous mass ended up as fertilizer. Nevertheless, their reports back to Moscow were upbeat – 'militant', as one said at the time. They described the number of wall-newspapers, and what was in them, and accounts of the various progressive experiments . . . Evgeny Stepanovich even had a short article printed in *Komsomol Pravda*, which got him noticed for the first time.

True, there had been a sticky moment in Orenburg on the way home, but the episode went no further than the four of them and never got back to Moscow. They had stopped by a little wood to pick mushrooms. It was a lovely spot. Clumps of orange-caps spread out before them like in a fairy tale, tall, large and bright. The agronomist said he didn't mind getting his old coat dirty and ran back to fetch it, and they fell upon the mushrooms like drunkards. Yet the further they went into the wood, the more mushrooms they saw rippling before their eyes. 'We don't touch those on the steppe,' said the driver. 'Some of 'em are poisonous, you could make yourself ill . . .' The raincoat was by now piled high with mushrooms, and they realized that some of the ones they had thrown in were as mangled and wormeaten as old foot-rags. Tipping the mushrooms out, they threw half of them away, keeping only the firm young ones with thick bases and orange caps.

After that they shot a duck and her ducklings in the reeds by the lake. The driver happened to have a double-barrelled shotgun in the boot, but Cult volunteered to do the actual shooting. He crept up on the duck and took his time aiming while the duck and her brood paddled across the little patch of water. A shot rang out, then a second, and the ducklings scattered over the pond flapping their webbed feet and their tiny naked wings, for they had not yet learned to fly.

Naturally it was the driver who stripped naked, covered himself modestly with his hand and waded into the water to retrieve them. The bank was marshy. Somewhere in the reeds a surviving duckling quacked, probably in pain. Having fished out as many as he could, the driver carried them back by their yellow feet, their little heads dangling. The mother was still alive and twitching.

They drove to a restaurant, where Cult went to the manager and introduced himself, and the driver and the agronomist then carried the ducks and the mushrooms into the kitchen at the back. A tacit hierarchy had quickly established itself in their little delegation: first came Cult, of course, followed by Evgeny Stepanovich, then the agronomist and the journalist. The agronomist always eagerly volunteered his services whenever anyone was needed to help the driver or with domestic matters. He had joined the ministry late in life to draw up documents, and was in fact the sharpest of them all; he knew exactly what was what.

While their food was being cooked for them in the kitchen, two tables were moved together under a palm-tree in the dining-room and covered with a large cloth. At first the driver discreetly declined to join them, but since it was his gun they had used, and he had been the one to go into the water, he washed his hands, plastered down his hair with water and took his place at the table, as pleased as the father-in-law at a wedding.

The waitresses fussed and fluttered around them rather too much, and the other diners were not slow to notice. Soon people were banging their knives on their glasses and crying 'Waitress!' Evgeny Stepanovich heard someone sneer, 'Here come the bloody bosses!' And when people looked up from their plain restaurant fare to see the duck being carried out on its dish, along with two large black frying-pans piled with dark mushrooms and sour cream, the atmosphere became electric. The four of them were so hungry, and everything tasted so good, especially after they had washed down the salad with the first glass of chilled vodka, that at first they paid no attention.

'Nothing's too good for the bosses!' said a loud voice at the next table.

'Come on, Petro!' another voice reasoned. 'Cut it out and drink up. S'all right for you, stuffing your face while the bosses are sitting there worrying about you!'

'Irka!' someone else yelled out to the waitress. 'How much longer do I have to wait? Why aren't you serving me?'

'Stop bellyaching!' said the waitress calmly without turning round, and went straight to the delegates' table to ask whether they wished her to serve the mushrooms or preferred to help themselves.

'We'll help ourselves,' said Cult hastily. And to the others he said in a muffled voice so no one else would hear, 'Take no notice.'

He refused to let them pour a second glass of vodka, even though there was still half a bottle left and they had planned to order another to finish up the hors-d'œuvres. As the muttering grew louder at the next table, they sat there with their heads down, pretending it had nothing to do with them. The ducklings, plucked and roasted, were as tiny as sparrows, their soft little bones poking out in mute reproach. The meat stuck in their throats, and they ate in silence. Suddenly the young man at the next table, egged on by the other diners, came up and stood over them, his legs wide apart, saying, 'Can't eat what we eat, huh?'

The agronomist attempted some placatory remark, but this merely made matters worse, and the driver, looking uncomprehendingly at each of them in turn, shouted, 'Shall I smash his face in?'

'You keep out of it!' hissed Cult, his faced white, and, bowing their heads over their plates, they went on eating, ignoring the young man above them who was becoming more aggressive by the minute.

'Are you real blokes or what?' cried the other diners.

They felt utterly mortified; they were not 'blokes' at all, of course, but important officials on an important mission, and the last thing they needed was for reports of a drunken restaurant brawl to follow them back to Moscow. Try as they might to prove what had really happened, an official report would be impossible to disprove, and Moscow would hardly be interested in sorting out the details. Cult said people in the provinces were always setting up this sort of thing to discredit men of importance; he knew all about it.

'This is what happens when you loosen the reins and give the people their heads . . .' he muttered, his lips pale and trembling. 'We must call the police.'

But the young man was already being tackled by the waitresses, fearless princesses in white caps and aprons, waving napkins at him and shouting, until eventually a policeman waddled in to dispense justice.

They felt even more humiliated the next morning when they were called to the police station. On their arrival yesterday's hero was led out of his cell, crumpled and sleepless and humbly begging their forgiveness, his lowered eyes flashing hatred at them. The police chief tried to smooth things over, urging them not to ruin the boy's life just because he had had a drop too much to drink, and the agronomist started to relent, saying it could happen to anyone. But then it came out that the fellow was a former army officer who had recently been discharged for insubordination. Not just an ordinary officer either, but a political worker. He was by now completely unsuited to civilian life, and should not really be drinking at all. Cult was incensed: fancy a man like this organizing political pep talks for the troops! What the sober man keeps in his head, the drunkard says out loud. No, this was more than mere hooliganism, this was a political crime.

He turned to the agronomist: 'You've got the best handwriting. Sit there and take this down.'

A deposition was drawn up, filled with cast-iron formulas, and all four put their names to it.

For the first time in his life Evgeny Stepanovich had a sense of what it meant to be alone in the world, with no defence against those who must always be referred to in terms of the highest praise, like huge babies.

ELEVEN

At the entrance to the theatre that evening stood a vast Zil limousine, flanked by black Volgas. The empty square was blocked off by turnstiles, behind which groups of police stood on guard, accompanied by a police car with flashing head-lamps. Curious passers-by milled around outside the build-ing, grudgingly stepping aside for the arriving guests. Inside, inconspicuous men in plain clothes lined the passages and stairways leading to the stage, inspecting all who passed with well-trained X-ray eyes.

Beneath the brightly lit stage a multi-ethnic crowd of faces blended together in the dark and silent auditorium – the top people, all hand picked. It seemed a lifetime ago that Evgeny Stepanovich had been invited to his first conference. He had sat in a corner at the back, unable to see or hear, but thrilled to be one of the trusted, one of the chosen. Anyone who has experienced it will know the feeling.

Not long before that, in 1951 or 1952 – shortly before Stalin's death, when things were already very tense – he remembered travelling on a correspondent's pass on the bottom berth in a compartment of an ordinary train along with three others. He was working for some obscure little magazine at the time; the others were a factory engineer, with whom he later shared a hotel room, a middle-aged female party zealot and an elderly lieutenant in the special internal forces. The lieutenant soon explained – or somehow it emerged – exactly what this meant, and about the camps he had been in charge of. Perhaps it was because the lieutenant was still surrounded by the aura of these invisible camps that the rest were suddenly seized with an inexplicable urge to give proof of their loyalty, ecstatically vying with each other to please him with their orthodoxy. The woman tried especially hard, virtually tearing out her righteous heart and offering it to him in her hand, but Evgeny Stepanovich was not slow to come forward either. Oh, the joys of self-negation! Meanwhile the lieutenant, an old hand in these matters, sat there with his two little stars on his epaulette, accepting their protestations in approving silence and giving nothing away. It excited Evgeny Stepanovich to know that they were all trusted. Yet something repulsive stirred in his soul, and with the other side of his brain – he was frequently struck by the peculiarities of the human psyche, and concluded that this must be a feature of the creative personality – he realized how pathetic they must appear to the lieutenant. He must know things about them which they did not even know about themselves, and God help them if they did, or betrayed so much as a hint of it. Only when faced with the bottomless abyss can we appreciate what we have escaped. Each of them in that compartment had gone to the edge of that abyss, and it could have collapsed beneath any one of them.

But all of this was now buried in his old life, as in a deep, dark well, and he had long abandoned public compartments for special two-seated saloons, where one found a very different class of person and far better amenities.

That evening, as he followed the Leader with dignity on to the stage, the entire audience rose to its feet and clapped. After those on the platform had taken their places at the table behind the podium, they applauded back, as the ritual required, the Leader quietened the audience with a motion of his hand and everyone resumed their seats. All this would be shown on television – the people rising to their feet and Evgeny Stepanovich and the Leader sitting side by side. Their photographs would be in the newspapers too . . .

Evgeny Stepanovich had still not recovered from the elation as he walked to the podium, took from his breast pocket a piece of paper with a prepared text and read out a short speech opening this evening held in honour of leading cultural figures from the fraternal republics. The Leader nodded approvingly and touched his arm as he sat down. Now the Leader's small dark hands with their shining nails lay quietly before him on the table, and his narrowed eyes seemed to be smiling in his swarthy face. It was the face of a man accustomed to people standing and applauding whenever he appeared, and it radiated a peculiar glow and lustre. It excited Evgeny Stepanovich to imagine the power concentrated in those small hands lying on the table.

Yet he was also acutely conscious of the cameras trained upon him, and under their gleaming eyes his face assumed the appropriate expression of gravity, animation, concern and, above all, benevolence. He was working as he sat there. He was representing himself. The few represent the many, and since he was one of the few, he now revelled in the attention of the cameras.

These good people sitting sedately in the auditorium had not gathered to see him: he was merely a small part of the vast Machine. But he knew exactly how that Machine operated. Push a button, the wheels turned and it sprang into action, and none of those entertaining him now or later would have dreamed that the indirect result of all this would be his promotion one step up the invisible official ladder. Thrilled by the sheer impudence of this idea, he was suddenly filled with a consciousness of his own power, and could barely suppress the glint in his eye.

It all went well, indeed excellently, and was marred only by a young poet (who should never have been invited in the first place) reading some dubious verses claiming it would be better if some of our achievements had never happened, since so many heroes had had to pay with their lives for others' stupidity. The Leader, however, generously deigned not notice.

In the interval afterwards a select group of people were ushered into a special room backstage. Thick carpets muffled all sounds, and tables were piled high with fruit, sweets and grapes such as were never seen in Moscow. As the Leader quietly greeted the fraternal ambassadors, Evgeny Stepanovich's gaze was again drawn to the small dark hand and the slender fingers plucking grapes from the bowl and popping them in his mouth. That hand aroused many ideas, as did Elena's green stones, which flashed before his eyes, large as grapes, on the withered fingers of the Georgian actress.

The Leader swivelled round in his chair with a sudden glare at the dignified waitresses in their black uniforms, white apron-fronts and bow-ties, and they silently slipped behind the guests' chairs. Raising and lowering bottles wrapped in starched napkins, they poured the wine without spilling a drop, turning the tall cut-glass goblets a gleaming amber colour. Then they froze in anticipation as the Leader raised his glass. 'We have been told that Comrade Usvatov was recently honoured . . .' he declared.

A flush of satisfaction spread over Evgeny Stepanovich's face. Although several times in the course of the evening he had been addressed as Andrei Stepanovich or Evgeny Semyonovich and the Leader's thick accent made his name sound like 'Us-fatov', he felt touched and flattered.

'. . . Unfortunately Comrade Us-fatov did not invite us, but we shall take this happy opportunity to congratulate him and wish him well . . .'

Evgeny Stepanovich was suddenly brought down to earth by the lordly, slightly contemptuous expression in the Leader's lazily narrowed eyes, which told him that he knew exactly what 'Us-fatov' was worth and where he belonged, and that it was certainly not he who would benefit from these paeans of praise. The Leader was a wheel in the Machine too, but a much bigger wheel. Both served one god, and that god gave to each according to his rank and station in life. The Leader was granted limitless possibilities and immeasurable wealth, vastly surpassing the few crumbs 'Us-fatov' could

99

grab for himself, and Evgeny Stepanovich felt he was small fry indeed in comparison.

Outside the theatre the police still stood at their posts on the now almost empty square, the ranks of black limousines waited and a few people clustered curiously round the turnstiles to see who would come out. Finally the meeting drew to a close and the soft pressure of the Leader's small dark hand when they said goodbye remained with Evgeny Stepanovich throughout the trip.

Next morning two police escort cars, three black Volgas and two large buses were waiting outside the hotel for them, and they all took their seats, a select few in the Volgas, the rest in the buses. One police car tore ahead, red and blue lights flashing, while the other followed. Sentry-boxes at the squares and crossroads cleared the roads of traffic, and people clustered at the crossings and waited. 'Turn right!' blared a megaphone from a police car on the road out of town as people stepped aside and trucks, cars and buses hurriedly turned off the road. Evgeny Stepanovich found it a trifle awkward bowling through the streets as if the delegates owned the place, scattering everything and everyone in their path. But this was the way they did things here: when in Rome, and all that. Since it was a long journey, someone had thoughtfully reclined his seat for extra comfort, and now he calmly leaned back. Behind him a Ukrainian composer was sitting with his knees drawn up to his chin, and Evgeny Stepanovich could feel those knees sticking into him.

'Got enough room back there? Sure I'm not squashing you?' he inquired politely, turning round.

'No, no, of course not!' the composer assured him hastily, and Evgeny Stepanovich no longer felt the knees in his back.

Bukhara's very name spreads bright silks before the eyes. Since childhood Evgeny Stepanovich had associated it with dusty Asiatic bazaars and men in quilted coats sitting on the hot ground before mounds of fruit, but by the time the trip was over and they were back in Moscow the endless images were so jumbled that he could not remember if it was here or in Samarkand that they had had their photograph taken beside the monument to Khodja Nasreddin. They were received in Bukhara by the First Secretary of the District Committee, who was even darker than the Leader, almost black in fact, but very pleasant none the less, and surprisingly young for such an important post. (It transpired that he had fathered ten children, which had a somewhat reviving effect on the wilting delegation). When he spoke of the achievements and prospects for the region, a mouthful of gold teeth lent a dull glow to his plump face; it was not white gold either, but pure, dark gold. Teeth flashing, he brought out some karakul – black, gold, white, and some new pink and blue samples from Germany which unfortunately could not yet be made in the Soviet Union – and the long table in his office groaned with oriental fruits and delicacies.

The following day, again escorted by flashing police cars, they were driven off to a collective farm for dinner. First there was a meeting with the women and children cotton-pickers in the middle of the cotton-field. The sun was unbearably hot, and Evgeny Stepanovich cut down on the jokes as he introduced the delegates who had come with him. The policemen in their light-blue sleeveless jackets, their bare arms crossed and their backs dark with sweat, hung about on the main road by the hot cars, chatting with the drivers and smoking. The dark-faced cotton-pickers sat on the dry earth. (Evgeny Stepanovich later learned about the various poisonous substances sprayed on this earth, and when he got back to the hotel, he carefully rinsed the soles and uppers of his shoes under the tap, then polished them.) 'Next we have . . .' He introduced each of the speakers by name, listing their occupation, title and awards. The poets raised their voices against the wind and proclaimed their verses to the vast snow-white field, fluttering with open pods of soft, ripe cotton. Then finally one of the humorists was brought on in a desperate bid to liven up the audience. But even he read his funny story into the void. True, the schoolchildren laughed, and the local boss accompanying the delegation smiled as he fanned his face with his hat, but the women's faces remained as blank as those of deaf mutes. Only over dinner was it explained that none of the women from this village understood a word of Russian. Evgeny Stepanovich, cursing the absurdity of his position, recalled angrily that the humorist was the same man who had made those insensitive jokes at Domodedovo airport. 'Who invited him anyway?' he demanded of his assistant. His assistant bashfully lowered his eyes. It was in fact Evgeny Stepanovich himself, in his own hand, who had written the man's name on the list of delegates.

Dinner was served at the farm sanatorium on the banks of a lake. A very grand affair it was too, and it lasted for several hours. Roast chicken, golden brown and straight from the spit, cold chicken, steaming pilaff, vegetables, oven-hot bread which they tore at with their hands (what did they call it in these parts? – lavash? churek?) and tender young lamb on skewers . . . The farm manager in his skullcap dashed here and there, making sure everything was all right, and never sitting down for a moment, his face glowing and greasy from the heat of the ovens. Toast followed toast, and silent women served and fetched and carried, gathering up the plates and leftovers, carrying them out and replacing them with clean ones. When the fruit arrived, along with little painted teapots and bowls, Evgeny Stepanovich remembered to propose a toast to their host, the manager. They finally managed to track him down, and he ran in with glazed eyes while the guests played host and filled his glass for him. As the man listened to the speech of thanks, it suddenly occurred to Evgeny Stepanovich that perhaps he too understood no Russian. In fact he did, but since he had no idea which delegation they were or why they had come, he merely thanked them in the most general terms possible for the honour of their presence.

Filled with food and drink (Evgeny Stepanovich disapprovingly noticed some of the delegates stuffing their bags with grapes and persimmons from the bowls on the table), they all walked to their cars past the hissing spits, draped no longer with chickens but with some vast creatures resembling turkeys. Two venerable skullcapped old men in striped gowns belted with scarves, wearing overshoes on top of their boots, swung open the wrought-iron gates of the sanatorium, and just as the cultural delegation was leaving, a flashing police car escorted in a convoy of academicians, so that one group was stepping briskly out of their cars as the other was getting into theirs.

They sped back along the country road into an extraordinarily beautiful Asiatic sunset. Flashing past them on the right, women trudged home from the fields with mattocks on their shoulders. As the cars passed, they clustered beside the road, and their faces, their calves and blackened heels were smothered in dust.

That night in his room Evgeny Stepanovich was awakened by voices and footsteps running down the corridor. It turned out that the composer had eaten something that disagreed with him, and an emergency medical team had been called in to pump his stomach. It was not a pleasant sight: the sick-bowl sitting on the floor bearing the contents of the composer's stomach, and the composer himself lying prostrate on his bed, blue in the face and bathed in sweat.

The emergency staff were replaced by doctors from the Party Committee, and in the weak voice of a dying man the composer grumbled from his pillows about his stomach: he had bought some ravioli earlier on in the market, and it had looked so good . . . The ravioli had plopped out into the bowl like frogs – he had evidently swallowed the things whole. A nurse with drugs and syringes was left to watch him, and Evgeny Stepanovich retired to his rooms. His accommodation left quite a bit to be desired: some repulsive black insects as big as his finger – scorpions? locusts? tarantulas? – were warming themselves on the white ceiling around the chandelier as though about to drop on his head, and when he finally

103

managed to turn the light off, he was kept awake by the quiet voices of a group of delegates roused by the bustle whom he had passed sitting in their pyjamas in the corridor. 'Go to bed, go to bed!' he had advised them genially. 'We have been assured that the dying man will live!'

They did not go to bed, though, and stayed there talking in a mixture of Ukrainian and Russian. 'That fish was completely off . . . Did you see the driver? They each got a bottle – you have to give 'em one . . . When our secretary goes off to some farm in the country, they say, "Feed these people". Who is he? Nobody! He's as backward as the bloody natives . . .'

As they chatted on amiably, Evgeny Stepanovich, suffused in sweat, stuffed a pillow over his head. It's all right for some – they've got someone to blame, he thought as he fell asleep. Who have we got?

Next morning the delegation was joined by an ambulance as well as the usual police escort. At the border with Bukhara province there was a solemn farewell ceremony, at which Evgeny Stepanovich downed a small glass of brandy and kissed the loaf of bread and the blushing cheek of the girl with the wondrous plaits who offered it to him on a towel-covered dish. After driving for just a kilometre they were greeted by an even more magnificent ceremony at the border with Samarkand province. Once again everyone clambered out of their cars, once again he kissed the bread, and after a second tot of brandy he happily kissed each of the girls in turn. There were speeches of welcome, and he spoke too.

After the brandy and the oppressive heat he was soaked in sweat and gasping for breath as he got into the car. His ears buzzing, his heart thudding and the anxiety mounting, he loosened his tie, and the wet collar of his shirt cooled his neck pleasantly in the breeze.

The whole day passed in a whirl of meetings: first an official reception, with grapes, fruit, sweets and speeches about the achievements of the province, then meetings with factory workers, and more speeches . . . Towards evening they were driven, many hours late, to a fabulously prosperous collective farm, where the manager, a large heavy man in knee boots with overshoes, breeches and a jacket festooned with jingling medals, showed them round the beautiful kindergarten and the sports stadium. The delegates, who had just risen from yet another meal, gasped with admiration, 'You won't see anything like that in town! There's discipline for you! They make people work here!' The manager then took them to a room whose floor was covered with clean mats. He removed his boots at the door, and the others eased tired feet out of hot shoes, sat down at the table and happily stuck their sweaty socks underneath. The smell was quickly smothered by the spicy hors-d'œuvres, but the mere sight of the cold meat before him made Evgeny Stepanovich want to vomit.

'Is it spicy?' he asked the manager. They were sitting not opposite each other, as protocol required, but side by side. The manager said something, but Evgeny Stepanovich could not hear him through the ringing in his ears.

'What is it?' he demanded more loudly. This time the manager did not hear him, just smiled apologetically. Then his face grew stern, and he stood up, glass in hand. The toast went on for a long time, and Evgeny Stepanovich, wearing his usual expression for such occasions, was not so much listening as bracing himself to stand up and say something. The guests clinked glasses and half rose from their seats, while he took a sip of his brandy. A wave of nausea rose to his throat. He tried to eat something, but the salad seemed stale. I might get food poisoning, he thought. God knows how long it's been out in the heat . . . Reaching out for another glass, he poured himself some pomegranate juice, and the manager politely pretended not to notice. He must get the better of himself, stand up and speak, yet he knew he could not. What if I collapse on the floor, he thought in sudden panic, and with a commanding gesture he yielded the honour to the well-known Moscow poet sitting opposite him, whose silvery mane belied his still youthful manner and Komsomol ardour. 'The poet delivered a passionate speech . . .' they always said of him on the radio. The man nodded eagerly, and spoke in a loud, resonant voice, his glass in his left hand and waving his right hand above his head, as though reciting his own verses.

Just as the hors-d'œuvres were finished and the main course was about to be served, the manager announced that a young couple from the farm – a machine operator and a vet – had invited the delegation to their wedding. 'Five hours they've been waiting,' he said bashfully. 'Not that they mind, of course . . .'

'What a wonderful present!' beamed the poet.

'Five hours, though!'

'Why didn't anyone tell us?'

'To the wedding, the wedding!'

'Oh, how embarrassing!'

The chattering crowd put on their shoes. Outside, the silver-haired poet threw his arm round the manager's shoulders in a fraternal gesture, and they walked to the cars out of step, the medals on the manager's jacket jingling louder than ever. Feeling increasingly ill, Evgeny Stepanovich decided to have his blood pressure taken. As he stepped up into the ambulance, he staggered back, the blood rushed to his head and he regained his balance only by grabbing hold of the rail.

There was a light breeze blowing through the ambulance, and it seemed cooler in here. The composer lay on a blanket reading a newspaper which already contained their photographs. He had quite recovered but was taking it easy and not eating too much to be on the safe side.

'How are you?' asked Evgeny Stepanovich, dully hearing the sound of his own voice. The doctor pumped up the bulb of the sphygmomanometer, the cuff swelled painfully against his bare arm and he gasped with shock at the position of the needle. The doctor impassively pumped up the machine again, and the figure this time was still higher.

He was chilled to the bone, and a band of steel gripped the back of his swollen head. The doctor made him lie on his back, at which the blood rushed even more painfully to his head, as though all the fluid in his body were swilling about inside him. He sat up. The doctor had long, narrow eyes, and her uniform was a dazzling white against her dark skin; she held out some tablets and a glass of water. As he nibbled the tablets off her cool palm, he suddenly felt so old and so sorry for himself that he longed for the young woman's hand to stroke his cheek.

They had been driving round the sports stadium all this time, and now they came to a stop. Through a wide-open door opposite he could see bright lights, crowds of well-dressed people and the bride and groom sitting side by side in national costume, not touching the food. All this he saw with one eye as though through a fog: the other eye refused to open, and he felt as though the entire left side of his head was being split in two.

People were looking for him. 'Evgeny Stepanovich!' they called. 'Where's Evgeny Stepanovich!'

He wanted to tell them to call the silver-haired poet, but the poet himself poked his head into the ambulance.

'Do the honours again, will you?' said Evgeny Stepanovich. 'Congratulate the young people. I must rest . . .' His voice was low, and the words buzzed in his eardrums and banged against his temples.

After a while the doctor took his blood pressure again, this time so that he could not see the dial.

'Any lower, Doctor? Did the medicine work?' He tried to sound nonchalant, but his voice was weak and his smile frightened and pathetic. The doctor did not reply, merely saying that he would have to have an injection, and no, it could not be in his arm. While the drums beat and the people shouted outside, he humiliatingly dropped his trousers and lay with his face to the wall as the doctor stuck the needle into his plump buttock, saying, 'Relax the muscle now, relax!' He only remembered all this later. At least the composer tactfully stepped outside without being asked. Soon he was given a second injection – a sedative, in the arm this time – after which his head went muzzy and the blood stopped pounding in his temples. He lay there with his eyes shut, unable to concentrate, his thoughts all over the place. We ought to have been at the wedding ... But did we really ...? At least people are working ... Fabulous farm ... Five hours, though ...

He suddenly had a strong urge to throw up and as his mouth filled with watery saliva, he was struck with horror: God forbid he should have a sick-bowl, like the composer ...

He rested, and gradually he began to feel better. Opposite, the wedding party continued behind the door. The poet would be standing before the young people reciting his poems, waving his arm over his grey head and spilling wine from his glass. Even the doctor, watching from the darkness of the ambulance, basked in the reflected glow of the festivities. Here I am dying, and there they are enjoying themselves, Evgeny Stepanovich thought, turning his face back to the wall so as not to have to see. He was all alone, no one needed him, no one cared. The doctor was sitting there with a smile on her face. Did he enjoy lying in agony in this stuffy ambulance? Did he enjoy dragging this delegation around Samarkand? How many ideas for plays had he borne in his head, which was now being split in two? Heavens, to think of the things he would never write, because, unlike a lot of homespun geniuses he could mention, he was not free, he had served the Cause and, like Mayakovsky, he had stamped on the throat of his own song, yes, stamped on it, suppressing his talents and sacrificing himself to the Cause, and no one had ever noticed or understood ... Drumbeats echoed in his temples and tears trickled down the bridge of his nose. Brushing them away with his finger, he rubbed his face on the pillow, and the doctor, hearing him stir, bent over him ...

Three days later Evgeny Stepanovich, sunburnt and slightly thinner but once again fit and fully functioning, was reviewing the trip, which was nearly over. His cool air-conditioned hotel suite was filled with flowers; a starched napkin poked out of the fruit-bowl and there was a tiny fruit-knife on the little plate beside it.

The vast delegation had been split into three so that they could cover the entire republic, and on their return they all came to his room to display their gifts. In Bukhara he had been presented with the traditional striped quilted coat, but his, unlike the others', was made of silk, with a matching embroidered skullcap. Later on at the farm, where the manager in his boots and overshoes had swept the others off to the wedding, the absent Evgeny Stepanovich had received an entire tea-set consisting of a huge painted teapot, a dish and native tea-bowls; since he had been ill, it had been packed up and taken away before he saw it. As everyone told their stories, it emerged that each group had been more spectacularly successful than the last. 'You mustn't forget to put all this into your reports,' he reminded the group leaders as he heard them run over what they were going to say.

The group which had visited Karakalpakiya was the smallest and did not contain a single celebrity, yet they had been presented not with quilted gowns but with velvet ones, embroidered in silver thread, and their skullcaps were much better too. Evgeny Stepanovich felt a twinge of irritation: he didn't need such a gown himself, of course, but Elena could certainly have done with one.

Just as the group was removing one of these gowns from its cellophane wrapper to show him, there was a shy knock at the door of his room. 'Yes?' he said sharply, motioning to the others to hide the presents, and a local man peeped round the door and hastily closed it again, having presumably got the wrong room.

Later, getting ready for the farewell meeting, he shaved in the gleaming bathroom, with its pink tiled walls and pink bath. The panic and humiliation of his insignificant illness seemed far, far away, as though it had never happened. He had gone out of his way to show everyone that he was completely recovered, dismissing his concerned hosts' inquiries

109

with a careless wave of the hand: 'Too much sun probably – a touch of radiation exposure . . .'

Massaging his electric razor over his full cheeks and chin, and the bit under the chin where the neck sagged slightly, he examined himself critically in the mirror. No, there was nothing wrong with him now, he had a healthy spark in his eye. First he assumed a tough look, then a generous smile. The only thing that let him down was his hair. He lifted up hand-fuls of it and twisted his head, squinting till his eyeballs ached. Yes, dammit, there was some grey there – the roots were growing out and the ends were exposed. Couldn't be helped. Hair goes on growing after you die, and he was still alive, thank God. He was skilfully combing it in a way that hid the grey when the man who had appeared at the door earlier knocked again. He was as dark as to be almost black, his Russian was halting and he was so nervous that for a while it was impossible to make out what he was saying.

'I'm afraid I haven't much time. People will be coming for me . . .' Evgeny Stepanovich glanced at the thick gold Swiss watch resting lightly on his wrist.

The man hurriedly stammered out his story as though stumbling over the hem of his gown, but the words 'Aral Sea' kept coming up. Gradually it emerged that he was part of a delegation, and was bringing up the rear to put their case. The Aral Sea was drying up, the Aral Sea was dying out. The waters were receding from the shores . . . boats lying stranded on the sand . . . water poisoned with pesticides . . . children falling ill . . . death rates soaring . . . an entire race of people dying out . . .

Evgeny Stepanovich knew of course that there had been certain local problems and warning signals, but the picture the man was trying to paint was radically different from any of this. He simply could not believe – he had no right to believe – that an entire people was facing extinction. And his confi-dence was not inspired by this nervous little man who had crept in to see him, begging him not to tell anybody here but to tell them all about it in Moscow. He might indeed be some sort of spy. Evgeny Stepanovich began to feel he was being dragged into something unpleasant which had absolutely nothing to do with the cultural aims of their trip.

'You must put it all in writing,' he said, resorting to his usual tactic and coldly turning aside. 'I believe you, of course, but actions speak louder than words . . .'

Having checked his appearance in the mirror, Evgeny Stepanovich set off for the meeting. In his dark suit, his tie and white collar, which emphasized his youthful tan, he joined the presidium on the brightly lit stage. It was not the Leader sitting next to him this time, it was the Second in Command, but the Leader had served his purpose in making the whole thing happen. Every so often Evgeny Stepanovich and the Second in Command would chat to each other, as people do on these occasions, knowing that the cameras are on them and the audience is scrutinizing their every gesture.

Several times on the podium and afterwards, when they had democratically stepped down from the stage and were sitting in the front row to applaud the performers, he felt like casually mentioning the little man's story. But when he glanced at the Second in Command's stern profile, something stopped him, and as always in tricky moments he evaded the whole thing with a joke: 'It's always nice when the people come to see you, but even nicer when it's good news.'

Once again the hall was filled up with an illustrious, medal-bearing crowd, and the evening went like a dream, as Evgeny Stepanovich would say. The Leader's views of their trip around his republic were already known to be most favourable. These would be relayed to Moscow, and Evgeny Stepanovich had already decided exactly what he would say to the relevant authorities about the delegation's achievements, and how timely and essential the visit had been in cementing fraternal relations between the peoples.

After the banquet was over, he returned to his room, where he found waiting for him a black velvet gown embroidered in silver for his wife and a little silk box, lined with crimson velvet, containing a dark silver antique ornament set with the green stones she had asked for. It was totally unexpected. He could not for the life of him remember having mentioned it to anyone, yet someone had found out, and he felt touched and pleasantly embarrassed.

Each one of the delegates received a present. Even the young poet who had almost ruined the first evening with his verses was presented with a cardboard box containing four varieties of tea.

TWELVE

They flew back in a different plane, a Tupolev 154. It was smaller and more cramped but had a first-class section with wide, comfortable seats, which immediately put Evgeny Stepanovich at his ease. His coat was lifted off his shoulders by a pretty stewardess with thick blue eye-shadow and patches of rouge on her cheeks, then the curtains separating them from the rest of the passengers were drawn, drinks were served and two starched napkins were brought, one for the table and one for their knees. When the hors-d'œuvres arrived, Evgeny Stepanovich turned round from his front seat to the other first-class delegates and with a smile wished them, on behalf of the rest, a safe journey. Out of the portholes he could see the sun shining behind the clouds, and the fat brandy glass in his hand was shot through with its rays. He took a second glass with the man sitting next to him, and they drank to their acquaintance.

A general in civilian clothes, the man was most sympathetic, and as they drank, everything looked brighter. Stuffing sprats into his mouth, he exclaimed affably, 'I entrust my life to communism, but my health to capitalism!' The way he lisped his 'isms' betrayed him as a member of the upper echelons of the state. Evgeny Stepanovich always remembered Lenya saying, 'They'll never build communism till they learn not to lisp their "isms"!' – a remark which could have cost both speaker and listener their lives.

It was eight years after Lenya's disappearance that they had met again. Evgeny Stepanovich had been walking down the Tverskoy Boulevard during the spring thaw. Big flakes of rainy snow clung to his face, the snow under his feet was melting and the cars swept through wet slush. The tramlines had not yet been removed, the A-tram trundled down the inner-city ring road and Pushkin stood in his old place – or had he already been removed? Evgeny Stepanovich walked on, his head bowed, worrying that his smart new lightweight coat would lose its shape: he had never in his life owned such a garment, and it still hung on him as it had in the shop. Engrossed in these thoughts, he almost bumped into Lenya. At first he had difficulty recognizing him, in his skimpy black naval greatcoat and glasses. Lenya had never worn glasses before, and what on earth was he doing in that appalling coat?

Lenya peered at him through his glasses and the years with the kindly eyes of a saint, apparently making his acquaintances all over again. Wet snowflakes dripped off his lenses. 'I thought about you there,' he said, as though it had all happened yesterday. Evgeny Stepanovich did not ask what he was talking about since – he realized this later – it was important that he should appear utterly mystified. But Lenya noticed nothing, and went on as if they were merely continuing a conversation they had been having for the last eight years. 'I thought about things a lot . . . After they interrogate you, they bring in the witnesses. I was sure it would be you. It all figured. But do you know who it was? It was Kulikov. I'm sorry, please forgive me. I vowed the moment I got out to come and ask you to forgive me. The most terrible thing about those days was the way they made us suspect everyone and believe anything.'

Evgeny Stepanovich was deeply moved. Choked with emotion, he stood there in his expensive coat, gesturing weakly like a man who has been unjustly maligned. Then he embraced Lenya and kissed him gratefully, and drips of snow fell on to his cheeks as Lenya's cold glasses jabbed into his face.

Later there were times when he longed to tell Lenya how he had almost betrayed him, but he had realized that, human nature being what it is, he would merely think no smoke without fire, and word would spread, and soon everyone would believe it . . .

Soothed by the glasses of cognac and the even hum of the engines, his new friend related a few inoffensive anecdotes, and Evgeny Stepanovich matched them with a story about a deputy minister who was challenged to a duel. The seconds had arrived at the appointed spot, and the challenger waited anxiously for his opponent to arrive. Finally his secretary appeared, saying, 'Ivan Prokofevich has asked you to start without him . . .'

Long ago, as Evgeny Stepanovich was taking his first steps up the official ladder, he had been told this story on a train by a deputy minister; the fact that this man's name was Ivan Prokofevich had added extra spice to the tale. It had been no coincidence that they were both travelling in the same compartment: Evgeny Stepanovich had strained every nerve to bring it about. He had even had the foresight to pack a bottle of Armenian cognac in his bag, and when he saw the look of weary disgust on the Deputy Minister's face as the glasses of train tea were brought in, he bravely put his bottle on the table. They were soon chatting away like old friends – at least Ivan Prokofevich was. Evgeny Stepanovich remained polite and deferential throughout.

'I hope to God you don't snore!' the Deputy Minister said brusquely as he got ready for bed, then proceeded to rend the compartment with deafening snores all night. Next morning the man washed, shaved and put on his tie. As they drew into Moscow, he no longer recognized Evgeny Stepanovich, barely nodding to him as he stepped off the train and into the arms of a joyful crowd of subordinates.

But mysterious are the ways of the Lord, and it is not for us to fathom them. Thus in the fullness of time Evgeny Stepanovich inherited the seat of this very same Ivan Prokofevich, and Ivan Prokofevich, now on a decent pension, made an appointment to see Evgeny Stepanovich, since even a pensioner sometimes needs a few favours, if not for himself then for his

115

children or grandchildren. He was received into his old office with surprising alacrity and was made to feel most welcome. He was treated to tea and crackers, as he himself had once treated the select few, and again they chatted away like old friends; but now it was the other way round, with Evgeny Stepanovich calling him 'my dear chap' while he remained polite and deferential throughout. He left, touched and encouraged by Evgeny Stepanovich's promises and assurances, and Evgeny Stepanovich immediately called in his secretary and gave strict instructions that the man – he pointed dramatically to the chair where he had sat – was never to be admitted to his office again . . .

The clouds above which they were flying stretched over a hilly snow-covered field. After peeling a large juicy orange and wiping his fingers on his crumpled napkin, Evgeny Stepanovich pulled apart the segments and put them in his mouth. Way down below, far beneath the clouds, rain poured on to the earth and the day glowered, but in this world the sun was shining; only when glimpsing the soft folds of the earth through the clouds did one realize that in the expanse beneath the wide seats in which they sat chatting, heavy with food, stretched ten kilometres of emptiness.

Evgeny Stepanovich's cheek blazed in the heat, and as he lowered the plastic porthole blind, it was hard to believe that outside the thin wall of the plane the temperature was minus 150. He lay back in his seat and closed his eyes. As often happens, the stimulating effect of the first few glasses of brandy was replaced by a feeling of lassitude, and he was tired of his neighbour, with whom he had talked so pleasantly and even exchanged cards. 'Hah! Having a snooze!' barked the General, as though issuing a command. Evgeny Stepanovich did not reply, and breathed heavily through his nose.

At the airport he was met as usual by his wife, and the driver followed with his bag. 'Anyone phone?' Evgeny Stepanovich immediately asked. There had been no urgent calls, nor any of particular importance.

His daughter greeted him when he got home. She swung her hips like a pedigree cat or a fluffy lynx, and as she embraced him and pressed her bosom against him, she filled the air with her French perfume.

'Hey, you're crushing me!' he said, patting her behind. She's a handsome girl, he thought admiringly. That's her main weapon, and she knows it! And he decided then and there to give his wife the silver ornament with the green stones and Irina the embroidered black gown.

There was a party at the Committee building the next day. By this time everyone knew that the trip had been a success and the reports favourable: Evgeny Stepanovich had presented the whole thing in a glowing light, he had been showered with praise and the Committee had greeted him like a hero. It was just as well the President was away in one of the capitalist countries, for his presence would have marred the unanimous display of enthusiasm. Everyone who entered and left Evgeny Stepanovich's office that day felt somehow part of the celebration, almost as though they had been promoted, and the very air – which normally reeked of fried fish, stewed cabbage and tomato sauce from the first-floor canteen – was now filled with all sorts of vague aspirations.

Having signed various documents, Evgeny Stepanovich called in his co-author, who had been languishing outside in the waiting-room. The young man had added a number of new scenes to their play. After a tray had been brought in with tea and a plate of sandwiches under a napkin, the reading began. Evgeny Stepanovich's Asiatic tan, emphasized by the whiteness of his collar, had been nothing remarkable down south, but everybody noticed it in Moscow, and as he sat listening in his revolving chair, his face stern and attentive, his thoughts drifted around the corridors and offices of the Committee building, reliving the day's pleasant experiences.

'Well, then . . .' he said when his co-author had finished. The young man looked like an anxious rabbit, frightened not for himself but for something dearer than himself, and Evgeny

117

Stepanovich's heart contracted with a twinge of dislike and even envy. 'Well, then . . .' he repeated. 'Not bad, not bad at all . . . We're getting there . . . The characters are coming along. Do you have two copies? Just one? We'll have to make a copy. I want to run my eye over it. It's definitely got something . . .'

At this moment Panchikhin entered with some urgent information for Evgeny Stepanovich, and the two men stepped aside to the little telephone table. Panchikhin delivered a brief report, during which he twice glanced severely through his glasses at the co-author. Then, gesturing to Panchikhin to stay, Evgeny Stepanovich paced along the chairs, addressing the young playwright: 'Boldness is all! We need more boldness! The task of art is to discover causes. And to interpret them too, not merely show the consequences! We must dig deeper. Not one spade deep – one and a half spades! Boldness is what distinguishes the best from the rest!'

As he lectured his little audience thus, he sincerely believed in what he was saying. It was the natural familiarity of a lie which he no longer even noticed. Before long the Committee corridors were buzzing with rumours: something was stirring on high. Writers must be bolder and dig deeper, word had gone out from the top.

Later that day Panchikhin spoke to an author whose play had been lying in the drawer for the last six months since it dealt with unacceptable subjects. 'So are we to dig a mere half-spade?' Panchikhin demanded. 'The task of art is not merely to register consequences. Boldness is all! What we must do now is to reveal causes!' He lazily leafed through the pages. 'My premiss is simple. We sit here watching each person catch one mouse. And if someone catches two, we rap him over the knuckles. You, if you'll pardon my saying so, haven't even *seen* a mouse – nothing there to rap you over the knuckles for!'

'Deeper, we must dig deeper . . .' During the course of innumerable telephone calls these words were carried beyond the walls of the Committee and repeated a thousand times. It was still not clear where the phrase had issued from. What mattered was that it had been issued by various sources and repeated by various people. Thus the rumour had its intended effect: major changes were in the air.

THIRTEEN

Youth is said to be the happiest time of one's life, but Evgeny Stepanovich had not enjoyed his very much. There was so little he could remember without shame, especially after his father left. He felt they had been branded, and he even forbade his mother to visit his school, lest people discover their disgrace from the sight of her unhappy face. He did not invite any of his classmates back to the flat, with its stink of babies' urine, paraffin fumes and steaming soapsuds. People were endlessly spilling paraffin and boiling clothes in the communal kitchen, and he could not free himself of the ineradicable reek of poverty, so that he no longer knew if he really smelled or was just imagining it. Even on cold frosty mornings on his way to school he would first make sure nobody was around then unbutton his coat to air it, shaking it and sometimes taking it off and carrying it under his arm in the hope that people would think he was toughening himself up. Yet he blushed crimson with shame if any of the boys at school stared at him too closely.

Was it possible that he had once lived in a flat with a huge dining-room and a long dining-table with a starched, freshly ironed tablecloth, and that his father had sat at its head, his smallness somehow adding to his stature? Chewing methodically, he would speak slowly, and his mother would absorb his every word as though it were a revelation. When his father was at work during the day, Zhenya would ride his tricycle over the floors of that empty dining-room. Had it really been so large? Every two weeks a man called Uncle Petya would come to polish the paraquet. First he would smear the whole floor with yellow wax from a bucket, then he would go off to the kitchen for a smoke while it dried, and the flat would smell of polish, damp oak and Uncle Petya's coarse tobacco. After his smoke Petya would take off his boots and stuff his foot-rags into the tops; the soles of his feet were as yellow as the wax in the bucket. With his hands loosely behind his back, he would start dancing, one foot weaving about before him with a brush strapped on to it, backwards, forwards and to the side, while the other foot, which bore his weight, inched forward with the toes, then the heel. There were no electric floor-polishers in those days, just Uncle Petya, with a stream of light pouring from behind him over the waxed floors.

It seemed unimaginable now that the hotel had once been part of his life: that the commissionaire resembling an admiral had respectfully opened the doors for him before he entered the marbled lobby, sauntered through the hubbub of foreign voices and casually swung his satchel as he waited for the lift, then walked along the carpeted corridor, where snow-white chambermaids polished, dusted and cleaned . . . That period of his life had its own special light and colour: the crimson of the velvet tasselled curtains, the gleam of burnished bronze. Not long after they left he had walked past those doors, which were now permanently closed to him, and the commissionaire had not even recognized him.

On his way back from school or when he was alone at home he sometimes wondered what he would ask for if he had just one wish. As he cut himself a slice of black bread, dipped it in the sugar-jar and sprinkled a thick layer of sugar on top, he thought that his wish would be for a kilogram of cheap sausage – not even the best sausage, just the cheapest garlic sausage – and he would devour whole mouthfuls of it, not cut it into tiny, economical slivers as his mother did . . . A kilogram of sausage, and a kilogram of soft white bread. Or perhaps hot white French rolls, with the cold meat melting inside . . . Sometimes his mother would heat up soup in the kitchen after returning from work, and find there was no bread left in the sideboard. 'I forgot, don't you understand! I forgot!' he would shout. 'They gave us too much homework! I forgot . . .!'

All his classmates knew that Vera Kizyakova liked him, and he knew it too and it embarrassed him. Vera lived in the workers' barracks. She was a pale girl, with hair combed smooth like a spider's web in the sun, a face of translucent whiteness with transparent veins on her temples. She once came to school in tears because the neighbours had had a fight and deliberately spilt a bowl of cabbage soup over her school books. Three families lived crammed together in one room in their squalid hostel, and they all had to eat at one table, the same table she did her homework on.

One day, when he was already sixteen and in the ninth class at school, he invited Vera back to his place. The day before, he and Borka Pimenov had gone swimming in the Moscow river, and as they clambered up the bank on their way home, they heard voices calling to them from the bushes. They looked around and saw three women sunbathing on the grass, stark naked and dazzlingly white, giggling and calling out to them, with their clothes hung out on the branches. The boys ran away in terror, and reading one another's thoughts afterwards, each was ashamed to look the other in the face. He spent that night in agony and the next day in a trance, and finally he invited Vera back. It was all over very quickly, for they were both scared out of their wits; some youths from next door were rollicking about in the corridor, and one burst in seeking refuge from the others, who were beating him up.

Afterwards he avoided Vera in mortal fear that something might have happened, as they say. She looked out for him and waited for him, but he was careful never to be on his own and always left school with the other boys. Thankfully, nothing did happen, but by the time the whole thing was over he had gone through agony. Later a group of boys met at Borka Pimenov's flat, and as the huge dog lazily padded from room to room, its claws tapping on the polished oak floors, they competed to see who was strongest, doing press-ups, lifting weights and generally showing off. And because he had nothing special to boast about and did not want to be outdone, he told them, without really wanting to, that he had slept with Vera Kizyakova. 'You dirty liar!' the others had said, and demanded to know all the details. After that the boys kept clustering around Vera and squeezing her. He did nothing about it and he hated himself, especially since Vera understood everything. Once he caught her watching him when Borka Pimenov deliberately squeezed her in front of him, and that look of hers said everything.

Then war came. By that time he was in his first year at university, and sported a fluffy little moustache which he would stroke with his fingers, saying as he did so, 'Now look here . . .' What elation there was in those first days of the war! How enthusiastically they had all joined up! At one meeting their old professor had declared with tears in his voice, 'Let them carry me to the front on a stretcher!' and he waved his withered little fist above his head. The old man had promptly donated his car to the war effort until transport was properly mobilized, and from then on his niece used to bring him to lectures on the tram.

The students were handed their weapons straight from boxes on the ground, moving forward in turn to be presented with a rifle and bullets. His was an Austrian First World War rifle with a heavy welded butt, which he realized was supposed to have a bayonet. He was given it by a comrade in an army cap, striped civilian trousers and a military tunic without badges of rank, who slapped him farewell on the shoulder with his free arm. Each of them received a rifle and a farewell slap, on the back or the shoulder. Later, as he lay in his dark dug-out one dull autumn day surrounded by rumours of a German advance, Evgeny Stepanovich remembered this young man and knew it had been ordained from the very start which of them would hand out rifles and say farewell and which would go into battle, rifle in hand.

They had marched down the streets in columns four deep,

rifles clasped to their shoulders. Unfit for singing or drilling, they had shuffled along wearing their everyday clothes, in wide flapping trousers, sandals, boots and gymshoes whitened with toothpaste, while the military commanders proudly stepped forward at the front or by their sides, bawling out commands, and the people of Moscow huddled on the pavements gazing after them in amazement.

Little could he have imagined then how quickly everything would collapse, and how on that cold dark October day when Moscow had been abandoned by its citizens, when the German armies were advancing and the ashes of burning papers wafted over the streets, he would finally look for his father.

When he appeared, his father was terrified, not for him but for himself. Understanding his fear, Evgeny Stepanovich had said, 'Don't worry, I'm not a deserter, I've been at the front . . . We were surrounded and I escaped.'

Hastily closing the inner door of his office, his father said, 'Keep your voice down! We don't want any shouting here!'

The drawers of his desk were wide open, and he was destroying papers. In a desperate bid for his sympathy, his son told him how some of them had scrambled aboard the last truck out, and how those left behind had grabbed on to its sides, were dragged alongside down the sandy road and then were hacked down. Only Senka Konobeev had clung on, his fingers all mangled and bloody, and his face covered not with pain or outrage but with a happy, grateful smile. They would have pushed him off too, but he had got on ahead of the others and had managed to squeeze into the cabin itself. That night as they forded the icy river the smallest of them had trodden in a dip and gone under, crying out in fear. They had pushed his head down, saying, 'Drown quietly!', and he very nearly had. Human life counts for little in such moments; he had seen that for himself.

As his father seemed to be listening, he plucked up his courage and told him that students were being selected for the

Military Medical Academy, and that there was still time to telephone . . . Emaciated, green faced and pathetic, he stood before his father's desk like a petitioner or subordinate. At the front, as rumours of the German advance spread, he had seen one of the students quietly slicing a bar of soap and eating it, soapy saliva foaming out of his mouth. In those last days, before deciding to look for his father, he too had eaten soap, and afterwards he had had blood in his shit.

His father leaned over, banged one drawer then another and opened the doors of his desk. When he straightened up, he was a different person, dry, official, a stranger to all emotion.

'Comrade Stalin sent both of his sons to the front!' he said loudly, not just to him, but to anyone else who might be listening in the walls.

And his son mumbled numbly, 'I'll go . . . I did fight . . . I joined up . . .' Then he beseeched, 'But one person can't do anything there! I'm not even trained. If I went to the Academy . . .'

His father maintained an inexorable silence. And Evgeny Stepanovich understood that if he died, his father would survive: he would have sacrificed his son to his country and done his duty. At that moment he hated his father and the entire order of things which forced people to sacrifice their sons. He would never have believed then that a lifetime later he would envy his father and mourn for that unchanging order.

His mother, with neither power nor contacts, managed to achieve what his father, with all his opportunities, had not. He knew she did not approve, and that however much she loved him she would have accepted it as inevitable if she had lost him at the front. Some new quality had appeared in her, as though submitting to a higher power and sharing the common grief had made her equal with others. Yet she was unable to tell him to go off and fight. So she accompanied him on that shameful journey which he would never talk about, and as the years passed, the episode gradually drove him further and further from her.

Late one night he and his mother turned up at the railway station, and were admitted on to a hospital train. How she contrived to get around the guard he would never know, but they climbed in with their things, and later on as the wheels thudded through the night, bowls of hot beetroot soup with red-stained lumps of meat were brought into their crowded apartment, and he thought he had never in his life tasted anything so delicious. But his inflamed bowels could keep nothing down, and afterwards he suffered from excruciating cramp.

Next morning, when he ventured outside the compartment and walked down the corridor, a round shaved head peered down from a top bunk and shouted, 'Hey there, hero! Why aren't you fighting?'

The man was his age or even younger, and was badly wounded, with his chest bandaged and his arm in plaster. The stubble on his strong chin and dark cheekbones gleamed like gold in the shuddering sunbeams of the rocking train, and his pale eyes bulged from hanging upside down.

'I've been at the front!' Evgeny Stepanovich wanted to say. But realizing how bad this would sound, he prevaricated. 'I'm about to be called up . . .'

'Called up, huh! Skived off, more like! Lousy coward!'

He did not leave his compartment again, but he was puzzled by the bursts of laughter he heard gusting through the carriage; the nurses received a good deal of attention, and people talked more about the soup they had had for dinner than they did about the front. Primitive creatures he thought they must be, incapable of comprehending the disaster hanging over their country. What he did not understand, not having experienced it himself, was that each of them had done what his duty and conscience required; they would all march back to the front, from where not all of them would return, but it was best not to upset each other by talking about it.

126

After the train journey came an interminable boat ride up the river Kama. As the steamer dragged its way upstream loaded with refugees, the dark river lashed the deck and a strong head wind soaked everyone on board. People bundled up against the cold and sat or lay huddled together with their bundles and belongings. In the midst of these people a shaggy thickset old man opened the suitcase on his knee as though he were sitting at his own dinner-table, and enjoyed a leisurely snack. 'We're not scarpering from the front, it's the Yids!' he declared. 'They're the ones who are scarpering off!'

And before the eyes of the hungry passengers he cut himself a thick slice of roast meat, rosy-pink inside, and nibbled a juicy onion, saying as he broke a huge chunk of bread, 'I'll get my stick and I'll thrash those bastards . . .'

He choked and coughed, scattering crumbs, Evgeny Stepanovich would gladly have eaten those crumbs from his mouth, for he was so weak and hungry that the sight of the meat and the smell of the bread and onion made his stomach contract in agony.

'. . . I'll get 'em, I will. "Stay where you're put, bastards!" I'll say. "Don't you dare run! Stop hiding behind our backs and letting us do your dying for you . . . !" '

Under his rabid gaze three Jewish women, mother, daughter and grandmother, froze in terror. Evgeny Stepanovich was not a Jew, of course, and did not remotely resemble one, but he looked so ill and emaciated that he kept his eyes down to be on the safe side. He began to notice there were indeed a disproportionately large number of Jewish families crowded on to the boat. There was a youth of his own age, thin and thoughtful looking, with a straggly beard. His yellow face was buried inside his upturned collar to protect himself from the wind, or maybe to hide his frozen nose, so that only his glasses were visible. He kept glancing at Evgeny Stepanovich as though wanting to make friends with him, but Usvatov kept his distance. He happened to be sitting in the corner furthest away from the Jewish family.

127

Dark clouds loomed over the black waters as the boat ploughed on into the unknown. There was no past, no future; the rumours drifting from the shore grew increasingly ominous. Thanks to the peculiarities of memory the image of that old man thrashing around the deck with a heavy knotted stick in his gnarled, calloused hand was etched in Evgeny Stepanovich's memory. He later put this down to his vivid imagination, since he knew quite well that in fact there had been no stick.

When he and his mother were almost dying of hunger and had nothing left to barter, a woman on the boat gave them some bread. Turning aside so no one would see, the woman had cut bread for herself and her daughter, then, sensing Evgeny Stepanovich's hungry eyes on her back, she had impetuously cut into her last loaf and given him and his mother a slice.

'But we've nothing to give you,' his mother said. 'Not even for this little piece . . .'

And the woman had replied, 'Give someone something later when you have it . . .'

That slice of bread in her hour of need seemed to turn his mother's head completely, and for the rest of her life it was as though she was trying in vain to repay the debt.

They drew into the harbour of a small town, where the local people met them and the evacuees were parcelled out among various homes and families, all united in grief. He and his mother were taken pity on by a young soldier's wife, who saw them standing about aimlessly on the shore. The woman had a large room in the workers' barracks, with a bed, a table, a mirrored dressing-table and a sewing-machine under a knitted cover. An enlarged framed photograph of the tense, gaunt faces of her and her husband hung on the wall. After heating up some water she dragged a trough in front of the warm stove, which was heated from the corridor, and he and his mother each had a bath. He spread his coat on the floor and immediately fell asleep, and for the first time in weeks he slept well. A thousand kilometres from the front he felt he was disappearing into peace and silence, and from then on his stomach miraculously calmed down.

Their hostess was about twenty-five, yet she seemed older because war had given her new independence and she was doing both a man's and a woman's job. She was not large, but she was plump and strong, with a pretty face, or so he thought then. She made him look like a weakling, and had he told her that he had been at the front and escaped from enemy encirclement, she would never have believed him. If she had, of course, she would have asked him why he was not still there, along with everyone else of call-up age, including her husband, from whom she had not heard a word.

When she took off her coat as she came in, her cotton short-sleeved blouse and the sateen skirt covering her strong hips would fan him with the smell of her warm body. When she ran out into the cold, or poked the stove, or soaked clothes in the wooden trough, he would follow her quick, graceful movements as though intoxicated, and he would dream painful dreams about her at night.

Shortly afterwards a regiment arrived in the town to regroup after being defeated and losing all their heavy arms. The commanders would visit the barracks, bringing along rations and bottles of drink. Some even started staying the night, and he would hear the women discussing and comparing them.

One day the woman came to Evgeny Stepanovich and his mother, and demanded sternly; 'How much longer are you two going to be here?' After that they moved out into the cold corridor with its innumerable doors, and there they stayed, huddled round the furnace, for it was almost impossible to find accommodation in a small town crammed with soldiers and refugees.

One evening the woman invited the commanders and her female neighbours to her room, and fried up potatoes in vegetable oil on the paraffin stove. Ah, the smell of those potatoes!

129

He hoped they might invite him in. They had no reason to ask his mother, of course, but he did wish they would ask him.

The party went on until midnight, and when it broke up, he noticed that not everyone left. The next morning a captain stepped out of the front door in his undershirt, and the woman tipped a can of water down his sinewy neck. He snorted in the cold and said something which made her laugh, and that laugh froze Zhenya's blood. The captain was quite a bit shorter than he was, and older too.

After the woman had seen the man off and was leaving for work herself, she brought out the remains of some congealed reheated potatoes for him and his mother, as though putting out scraps for the cat. Hating himself and feeling ashamed, he sat by the furnace on the old padded coat with which he and his mother covered themselves at night, and he hungrily ate those potatoes, given to him out of charity.

He did not know then that soon he would be fighting again. The road to the front was long, through military school and the hungry reserve regiments in which an endless succession of marching detachments would rapidly group before leaving for the front line. He went with one of these detachments, and he was in at the end, marching into Vienna with three stars on his epaulette. During the heady days of victory, when all sorrows were cast aside, he was working at army headquarters and there he was awarded a military medal: not the biggest or the best, to be sure, but a medal on his chest none the less, so he had something to be proud of when he returned home to his studies.

Many years after the war his father sent a telegram asking him to come. His father's loyalty had not ultimately saved him from the fate visited upon even the most loyal servants of the state: his turn had come, and maybe indeed he had something to tell them. He spent seven years in the camps, and was released shortly after the 20th Congress, of which he always spoke with loathing. After that he moved to the little town of Bolshevo, just outside Moscow. Here he either rented or occupied free a small glazed veranda-cum-pigeon loft on the first floor, where various bits of rubbish and old furniture were dumped. He had been barred from his old flat. His second wife, for whose physical charms he had left his first wife and his son, opened the door a fraction and saw the toothless, shaven-headed old man on the landing with a string bag containing a bottle of mineral water and some herrings wrapped in wet newspaper. Recognizing him, he told Zhenya later, she had stepped outside to bar his entry, and through a crack in the door he saw his teenage daughter in the depths of the flat. 'Go away and leave us in peace!' the woman had screamed, locking the door. 'Get out of my life!' There had been someone else in there with her too.

If his mother had still been alive, she would have given him warmth and shelter, for she had never hurt a fly. Over the years she had developed an increasingly strong sense of her obligations to the world and she would gladly have taken on the burden of caring for him to the end of her days.

It was late autumn when Zhenya received his father's telegram and went to Bolshevo to see him. He searched for a long time before eventually finding his cold little room. He was lying fully clothed on an iron cot, covered with a quilt, from which his child-sized shoes poked out. Draughts blew through the windows and the thin glass rattled, yet there was a noticeably unpleasant smell coming from him, and Zhenya realized at once that he had not long to live; his temples were hollow, his eyes were sunk into their sockets and glittered feverishly, and his transparent hand was an anatomy lesson of bones and ligaments.

His father remained lying down while Zhenya sat beside him on an old office chair, whose once comfortable upholstered seat was now badly worn, with all the innards poking out. Even at the end of his life his father was still surrounded by office paraphernalia, the framework for a shelving system, a large ink-stained, two-drawer desk and a battered oval plaque. Zhenya looked at the old man and deeply regretted that he had given way to his feelings and come. He could not leave him here: it was autumn and the weather was bitterly cold. Yet he could not take him in, for he himself had just started a family.

He thought again what a fitting end this was: the Revolution devours its own children, as someone once said. His father had had almost no connection with the Revolution, of course, but he had served its terrible power, and in time it had repaid him. But what a fearsome contrast to the long dining-table on the paraquet floor waxed to a glassy sheen by Uncle Petya's bare feet, and the starched white cloth which seemed to have been laid for eternity, and his father sitting at its head, with people listening with bated breath to everything he said . . . And now this death, unwashed and stinking on another person's bed, surrounded by their rubbish . . .

'You have a new grandson,' Zhenya said loudly. His father lay on his back without replying, and crumbled the edge of the blanket with his pale, feverish fingers.

Then after a while he spoke. 'Well, you've let the genie out of the bottle now! You've moved the cornerstone! That stone kept the whole building up! How are you going to live now, eh?'

'He threw you into jail, and you weep for him!' said Evgeny Stepanovich in amazement.

'Stupid idiots you are to attack him . . . Blood will be washed away with more blood. Lots more blood. Everyone else will be forgotten, but he'll remain! For thousands of years! He knew what he was doing! You lot are afraid of his name!'

As Zhenya was about to leave, his father reached under his pillow and pulled out a wallet, fumbled inside it for a long time, took out some pieces of paper, looked at them as though he wanted to give or tell his son something, then put them back. Finally he buried the wallet under his pillow again and said, 'When I die, make sure they open me up first. I don't want to wake up and find I'm still alive. Promise me that!'

Zhenya gave him his word, but he did not keep it. He

was away on business when his father died. He had already completed his assignment but had problems getting a ticket, and was delayed. He knew that his father would not wake up, of course, and that he had nothing to wake for, since he had had no life even when he was alive.

FOURTEEN

The winter following the trip to Uzbekistan was long and hard, and Evgeny Stepanovich emerged from it as weak as an invalid. It was not clear what, if anything, he had done wrong. Perhaps it was simply that life was full of ups and downs, and when a bad patch came along, everything went to pieces. He had sensed some sort of nasty underhand business at the Committee; the first ominous signs of this came when he was twice passed over for a job which by rights should have been his. These things never happen by chance: there were jealous people out to get him. And it was at that time, when the situation was at its most tense and he had to devote all his attention to it, that his mother-in-law decided to commit suicide. Purely out of spite.

She had always had her funny ways – maybe she was even a little touched. He and Elena had been married three years when she had suddenly put on her glasses and peered into his face, saying. 'Do you mind if I look at you, Zhenya dear?' It turned out that she was so short-sighted that she did not actually know what his face looked like. She had failed to recognize him several times, in fact, and had once passed him on the street, leaving him gaping after her in amazement. Yet she stubbornly refused to wear her glasses, which was why her eyes remained so clear and undimmed, filled with a look of childish delight. Elena, thank God, did not take after her. One of the many family stories about his mother-in-law told of her going to the market for eggs, and trying to buy some of those plaster ones used for putting under laying hens. She had even haggled and demanded to know why they were so expensive.

Evgeny Stepanovich had learned from Elena that at the height of the terror, when they imprisoned first the old woman's brother, a well-known surgeon, and then his wife and son, she had started carrying a portrait of Stalin in her bag as proof of her loyalty, as well as a safety razor with which to slit her veins in case they took her too. So she was thinking of death even then; she had evidently been a bit touched for years.

Her nephew had managed to smuggle a letter out of the camp, and some nameless person had dropped it into a letter-box in Moscow. 'Dear Auntie Manechka,' he wrote, 'please send me some food if you can, even a few rusks, I'm dying of hunger. I enclose a little blade of grass to plant on my grave. It's the only thing that will grow here . . .'

She had taken fright and had burnt his letter, the only thing remaining of him in the world, and, unable to forgive herself for this sin, she spent the rest of her days trying to atone for it.

Initially Evgeny Stepanovich had had nothing against his mother-in-law, even though an outsider in the house always creates problems. They never discussed important matters when she was in the room and stopped talking when she came in, in case she unwittingly blurted something out. But it was when he discovered that his wife had been unfaithful to him that he began to hate the old woman.

Elena had slept – the very word stabbed his heart – with old Kokovikhin, a leading light on the Committee. And what made it doubly painful was that it was this man he had to thank for the first steps in his career. Evgeny Stepanovich learned that it had all happened in Kokovikhin's office, or rather in the little room behind his office. He had even seen the sofa they had used. Kokovikhin had called him in, all unsuspecting, and they had had a friendly talk in which Kokovikhin addressed him with lordly disdain, and through a crack in the door he had seen the magnificent soft leather sofa gleaming in the sun. That evening at dinner, excited by the new possibilities opening up before him, he had stupidly

135

recounted to Elena the conversation which she herself had engineered. At some point he had made some playful reference to the sofa, implying that an old man like Kokovikhin would probably be unable to make much use of it, and not until later did he understand the odd look that flashed across her face.

Afterwards he would lie awake at night, torturing both himself and her by forcing her to tell him all the details. First they would excite him, then he would hate her even more. Kokovikhin had probably wanted him to see the sofa to ensure his complete humiliation. It is the creative man's misfortune, Evgeny Stepanovich thought, to imagine everything in excessive detail. He could even feel the touch of cold leather against bare skin . . . It was only when Kokovikhin was felled by a stroke and crashed overnight from power that Evgeny Stepanovich finally laid the whole thing to rest. Semi-paralysed and mumbling inarticulately, Kokovikhin would have his boots polished and his tie and jacket laid out for him every morning, setting off for 'work' and standing outside the doors of the Committee building. Having forgiven him, Evgeny Stepanovich transferred all his hatred to his mother-in-law. He was not sure if she had known about the affair, but she might well had done; she was Elena's mother, after all.

She was afraid of him. He would see her stretch out her hand to the bread-basket at dinner, and pull it back under his stare. He would not dream of keeping watch on her. Why should he grudge her a piece of bread? One's eyes simply followed a moving object. As she withdrew her white, extraordinarily youthful, almost veinless hand with its clipped nails, he remembered something she had said to her daughter: 'Better eat under the table of your son than at the table of your son-in-law.'

She had once let the boiler go out, freezing the radiator in the corner room. But the most appalling thing was the lie which this episode revealed.

Each family has some secret which must never be mentioned or life becomes unbearable. With Elena and Evgeny Stepanovich, this was their son, Dmitry. It had taken them a long time to choose this pleasantly patriotic name. The moment he was brought to Elena's breast, swaddled as tight as a log, with only his face showing, they were considering his future. Notes were passed back and forth between the maternity hospital and home, and finally they agreed upon Dmitry. Dmitry Evgenevich Usvatov. It sounded good.

Dmitry was a tall young man, a full head taller than Evgeny Stepanovich. He was handsome, good at sports, clever and talented. He had inherited this from his father, of course. But whereas Evgeny Stepanovich had once appeared to have something of a future as an artist, Dmitry's talent was for music. He had perfect pitch, and by the age of seven or eight he was composing songs and picking them out on the piano. He soon moved on from songs, and before long his teachers were predicting a brilliant career for him as a pianist. What Evgeny Stepanovich could have done with half the boy's chances!

One day when Dmitry was out playing with friends he had found a hand-grenade (it was probably the other boys who found it, but they never discovered the exact details). It had exploded, blowing off the index and little fingers of his right hand. Instead of running home, as any normal boy of twelve would have done, Dmitry had gone straight to the hospital with his friends, where his hand was treated and bandaged up, and he had also deliberately given the wrong telephone number so his parents would not be called. That's the kind of boy he was. He was afraid they would be angry with him because he would never play the piano again. The only person he confided in was his grandmother, and the old fool protected him like a hen. This did not dispose Evgeny Stepanovich any more kindly to her, and Elena too, and even Irina started addressing her in a cold and formal tone.

Dmitry possessed one sterling quality, which opens many doors in life: he inspired affection. He didn't even have to try.

People just liked him. Unfortunately, though, most of these people were of no possible use to him.

'Look here,' his father said to him, 'the people you need are legion. Charm them, and they'll tell you all their griefs and woes. Let them get close to you, and they'll do the dirty on you. You don't know human nature. The more you do for people, the unhappier they'll be, yet they'll still praise you. The wise man decides who he needs, then concentrates on them. It's as simple as that.' He went on to illustrate his point. 'Now, you like football. The ball's moving towards the goal-posts. The players shout, "Pass it here, pass it here!" Just as it's going into the goal, it's suddenly passed to someone else. Learn to get rid of those you don't need, pass them off to someone else.'

He told his son how during one of his trips to some autonomous republic the master of ceremonies at the farewell banquet had walked behind the guests' chairs, showing the waiters what each was to have. He went briskly down the line, saying, 'Tea, tea, tea . . . !' Then he stopped respectfully behind a chair and said, 'Koumiss!'

'See? That's what you must go for! You get the koumiss, son, not the tea. Sort your life out!'

It often mortified Evgeny Stepanovich to see what a poor figure Dmitry cut in the circles where he himself reigned supreme. He would observe people casting puzzled looks at Evgeny Stepanovich, as though unable to believe that this boy was his son. Yet he realized that youth would pass, and life would knock sense into Dmitry. Life didn't break people like him. Someone once said that if you're a liberal after the age of thirty, you're an idiot, but if you're not one before the age of twenty-five, you're a scoundrel. Dmitry had his head screwed on and a great future ahead of him. He just had to accept that his father had some pull with the government, where everyone is in some way connected to everyone else. The only people who did not like this age-old order were still trying to get a foot in the door; once they had got themselves in, they understood that things were not so badly organized and that the status quo must at all costs be maintained.

Dmitry had indeed had a great future, but he had thrown it all away on a stupid marriage. A grasping little tart (Elena had researched the girl's background) had dug her claws into their son and deliberately got herself pregnant.

They had already found him a most eligible girl, who was just recovering from an unhappy love affair. Evgeny Stepanovich had sat next to the girl's father on the presidium of an important conference, and as they nibbled smoked fish canapés in the presidium room during the interval, they had got talking, canapés clasped between their fingers, and everything began to fall into place. Shortly afterwards the girl and her parents happened to have seats at the theatre next to Dmitry and his. Old-fashioned? Not a bit. Telephone calls were exchanged, and Dmitry was said to have made a delightful impression. In short the prospects seemed excellent. Evgeny Stepanovich and the girl's father – what an alignment of forces!

It then transpired that Dmitry had barely noticed the girl and refused even to discuss her, proposing instead to present his parents with some relatives by the name of Bender from Moldavia. How would that make his parents feel? How would his father look in the eyes of the other girl's father? It was outrageous, an insult they would never forget!

The day before Dmitry was due to bring his so-called fiancée home to meet them Evgeny Stepanovich decided to talk some sense into him. It would have been better if Irina could have done it, since brother and sister are more likely to see eye to eye, but unfortunately there was little love lost between those two, and she might well have had the opposite effect. So he decided to do it himself.

He at once took the bull by the horns: 'Say what you like – no one could accuse me of anti-Semitism. Quite the contrary. They do have some irritating habits, of course. I'm amazed they don't notice it themselves – they're not stupid. In fact if you count the members of specified nationalities on our Committee, they're easily the largest group . . .'

'*Have* you counted?'

'No, but there are plenty who do, and they've told me. Anyway, if you ask me, it's not what your name is, it's what you do.'

'I know. You've told me that before.'

'And I stick by it. At university I shared a desk for three years with a chap called Lenya Oksman. Only a miracle saved me when he was arrested. He and I were friends during the years when . . .'

'I know, Dad – every anti-Semite has his favourite Jew.' Evgeny Stepanovich put down the newspaper he had been toying with when Dmitry came in. 'I don't blame you, Father, I understand: feelings are stronger than reason. Especially for people of your age.'

Evgeny Stepanovich sat on the sofa, his bare winter-white feet shuffling over the floor for his slippers. The flat was well heated, and the highly polished parquet felt unpleasantly warm and alive. He had considered in detail what he would say to Dmitry, running over all the options in his mind. He could deliver wise advice, based on his own experience, but he had the feeling that this would not work. He could speak sternly. Dmitry was his son, he was concerned for his future, and the couple would probably be moving in with them, after all. But Evgeny Stepanovich decided to adopt another tack: a cosy father-and-son chat. In order to create an opportunity for spontaneity and openness he had put his dressing-gown on; it had been given to him during one of the republics' festivals in Moscow, he couldn't now remember which, there were so many trips and festivals . . . But something in this carefully planned and mentally rehearsed tête-à-tête had gone wrong: the opportunity for openness did not arise, and he felt from the start that he was being resisted.

'I must emphasize that I had no intention of raising this subject . . .'

'Father, they all emphasize that, from government ministers up. Some minister did it just the other day – I don't suppose even you're that big yet.'

He was trying to joke, but his smile was angry. Evgeny Stepanovich felt a pang in his heart. What a fool the boy was, bristling up like a little wolf! Couldn't he see how things were? Did he think he could change the world?

'Your mother and I,' said Evgeny Stepanovich evenly, 'know the girl is of specified nationality . . .'

'For Christ's sake, Father, she's a Jew! Tough, I know, but you'd better accept it – are you ashamed even to say the word?'

'For me personally it's of no significance . . .'

'It burns your ears, you mean.'

'As I said, for me personally it's of no significance . . . *They're* the ones who are ashamed, not me. Ask them straight out, "Excuse me, what is your nationality?" and they become embarrassed and defensive. I don't want my grandson to be embarrassed and defensive. I don't want that! If I ever have a grandson, that is . . .'

Dmitry sat there, his paleness making him even more handsome, with his straight ash-grey hair, his black brows and his white face – his brave, manly face. How could they let him go? That cunning trollop had turned him against them!

'Let us be frank,' he continued. 'I confess your mother and I are not entirely indifferent to the nationality the girl happens to have in her passport. But it's not our life, I must emphasize: it's not our life, it's your life. And as you know, kings don't rule us, but the times we live in. I'm not talking about your career here, but I must ask you again if you've considered your children, should you have any. The children take their mother's name with these people, as you know.' Dmitry jerked his head as if about to speak, then thought better of it. Perhaps all was not lost. 'We're not living in a vacuum, you know. We must look the truth in the eyes,' Evgeny Stepanovich went on in ringing tones. 'Your sister Irina said to me

141

recently, "What if some Negro comes up to me in the street and grabs my breasts? They're breeding like flies these days . . ." Believe me, I have nothing against Negroes as such, but I have to consider my daughter. We've taken brotherly love too far, in my view. Our boundless internationalism would be all very well if they loved us as we love them – and feed them and help them . . .'

'We don't feed them, we steal the bread from their mouths! We have more cultivated land than anywhere else in the world, yet we produce the least and steal the grain from those who can't afford to buy it. That's how low we've sunk . . .'

'They breed like flies . . . But I don't want to go into that now. Yes, yes! They breed in geometrical progression . . . ! I'm beginning to understand why people in America say, "I don't want a Negro marrying my daughter. Someone else's – fine, I'm no racist. But mine? No thanks . . ."'

At this point Elena burst into the room. She had been standing outside the door all this time, and could restrain herself no longer, even though they had agreed in advance that they would keep their temper, for they knew their son only too well.

'Why don't you get to the point?' Elena screamed. 'talk to him, go on, then I'll have my say . . . Don't you understand anything? Hah! That slut got inside his trousers! It's sex, that's all, sex! Her parents want to worm their way to Moscow and into our family. "Our daughter's marrying Usvatov's son . . . !" What kind of name is Bender! Bandits, I call them! My darling boy . . . !' Elena stretched out her arms to Dmitry. 'It's someone else's baby. I've found out everything!'

A few days before their large deluxe colour television set had broken, and since they had been unable to mend it at home, it stood dismantled on the floor as they had left it. When his mother cried, 'My darling boy . . . !' Dmitry slumped on top of it. In the daylight the grey convex screen glimmered between his legs as he sat with his fingers thrust into his hair. Elena and Evgeny Stepanovich exchanged glances: the arrow had hit its mark. A poisoned arrow, true, but it had saved their son none the less. They could not have known then what the consequences would be, or what he was thinking as he plunged his head in his hands. But they chose to put their own interpretation on it.

Evgeny Stepanovich had a Second World War photograph which he would use to illustrate some point when making a speech. It showed a shell-shocked German sitting with his head in his hands by the side of a smashed field-gun, his whole world and everything he held dear in ruins. After what happened to his son, Evgeny Stepanovich could no longer bear to look at that photograph.

Dmitry practically stopped coming home. His meals would be left out in the kitchen, then taken to his bedroom covered in a napkin. Yet he refused to touch them, and he grew so thin that people would take him for thirty rather than twenty. He barely even said hello to them. Every so often Elena would sob hysterically, 'I know something terrible's going to happen!' But Evgeny Stepanovich would reassure her: a bit of character was no bad thing in life – character was destiny, and time wore down the rest. 'But what if he leaves home?' she demanded. Well, that wouldn't be so terrible either, he would reason: at least it would part salvage their reputation with the other girl's family, or rather her father.

Then out of the blue Evgeny Stepanovich had a phone call at work from the rector of the university department where Dmitry and his trollop were students, asking Evgeny Stepanovich, with profuse apologies, if he knew that his son had requested a bed at the student hostel. They were having a lot of problems with space and were even limiting the number of students from out of town, but if Evgeny Stepanovich thought it necessary, they might make an exception . . . Evgeny Stepanovich did not think it necessary. The rector had hoped this was the case, and happily declared his deep respect for Evgeny Stepanovich personally and for his great work.

Evgeny Stepanovich's work took him to Cuba, and when he

returned, he found that Elena had taken matters into her own hands and had pounced on the little bitch outside the lecture hall. She had told the girl exactly what she thought of her, and demanded that she leave her son alone. She also threatened that if Dmitry got to hear about the conversation, it would be the worse for her.

Dmitry did get to hear about it, not from her but from her enraged girlfriends. If Evgeny Stepanovich had been in charge, none of this would have happened, of course. And it was while he was still away that the rector telephoned to announce that Dmitry was transferring to the extramural department.

When he went down for the newspaper one evening, Evgeny Stepanovich opened the postbox and the housekeys fell into his hand. He and Elena rushed to Dmitry's room, and on the hard sofa where he slept they found a note under an ashtray which said, 'The keys to the house are in the postbox.' They rummaged through the cupboard and the drawers of his desk and his bed. Still hanging in the cupboard were the jeans his father had brought back from abroad, which he had always cared for so lovingly. He had taken nothing with him but what he stood up in and a change of underwear, a towel, razor, toothbrush and toothpaste, as well as his books and lecture notes.

Their daughter immediately took their side, but his mother-in-law was another matter. She was really afraid of them now, and crept around the house like a mouse. Once they found her with a blissful smile on her face, admiring a baby's blue flannel blanket with rabbits on it which she had bought on the sly. This was how they learned of the birth of their grandson. 'He's the image of our Dmitry,' she said, shyly trying to make them share her joy. It was a long time after this that they discovered that their son, who had had the whole world at his feet, had gone out and got a job as a loader at the railway station. He and his wife had rented a room in an old woman's cottage miles out of town on the Byelorussian line. Later they were to see this cottage. It had a little vegetable garden and was sunk up to its windows in mud.

They had assumed all along that Dmitry would come back and everything would sort itself out; these things happen in families, they reassured themselves. They had even said as much in the mother-in-law's presence, to make sure she knew where matters stood. That winter, however, in the middle of a freezing blizzard, their darling son had run out for baby food (apparently the woman did not even have enough milk for the poor baby, so Dmitry had to run out to the dairy every morning before work), and was knocked down by a suburban train. Again and again they pictured him, harassed and hurried, dashing over the level crossing in the blinding snow, the flaps of his fur cap turned down in the frost. Afterwards they had found that old cap by the side of the road . . .

Official condolences appeared in the newspapers, there were telephone calls from numerous important people and even from the coroner's court; although none of it meant anything to them at the time, it helped to keep up their strength in those dark days, and those who rang were not forgotten. His subordinates entered his office diffidently, and he tried to guess from their faces what they might say about him when they were out of the door.

He kept going through all his relatives in his mind; father, grandfather, grandmother, even the most distant cousins . . . Which of them had Dmitry got it from? He thought of Elena's father. Could it be that nature took its revenge on the second or third generation? If so, why? What kind of infernal mechanism was that? He had not got it from his immediate family, at any rate. So was it in his genes? If so, whose? Then he would start all over again. The only person who did not occur to him for some reason was his mother-in-law; of all the various relatives who might have influenced his son, he somehow failed to include that strange, dotty old woman.

Quite apart from the unendurable heartbreak of losing a child, he and Elena had to contend with endless vicious rumours and backbiting. It was in those difficult days that he discovered who his true friends were, and the forces he had always felt to be behind him did not give him up to be savaged by the mob. One of the newspapers interviewed him, his various public-spirited activities were twice mentioned on television and his critics fell silent, allowing him once more to hold his head high. There was another matter too in which his friends went out of their way to be helpful. Their old flat, with all its painful memories, where they had to rub shoulders in the lift every day of the week with the neighbours, was exchanged for another one in a quiet central side-street, where several prestigious apartment buildings were going up. This new flat had a large number of modern conveniences (which meant nothing to them, of course). The layout was also much better, and the kitchen, bathroom and corridors were far larger, so that they ended up with a lot more space than they were theoretically entitled to, and even had to buy a certain amount of new furniture to fill it. In short, the place felt right.

It was after they had unpacked everything and arranged their books and dishes on the shelves that they discovered three of Dmitry's old music tapes, and decided to play them. (Dmitry had started recording music when he was still at school, and had had quite a passion for it at the time.) Suddenly there was his voice: 'Testing. One, two, three . . . I think it's recording. Can you hear me . . .?' They remembered that his tape recorder had broken, and he had mended it himself – there was nothing he couldn't do. They listened, deep in memories, as he whistled the Cavaradossi aria – he was always singing that. Tears trickled down Elena's cheeks. What a fine ear he had had! 'Yes, it's working,' they heard his voice again; their son was gone, but they still had his voice. 'The tape's a bit jammed . . .' Then: 'I wish they'd leave Granny alone! I can't walk out, or they'll take it out on her . . . Because Granny's *human*.' They wished he had not said that, it was not what they wanted to hear . . .

They had also been robbed of their baby grandson. They

had seen him just once, when their eyes were dimmed with tears and grief. On All Saints' Day Elena had dressed modestly and slipped off to church to light a candle. She later described feeling something there which she had never felt before, and her soul was at peace.

Evgeny Stepanovich's position and beliefs made it impossible for him to do such a thing, of course, but once on a sightseeing trip in one of the capitalist countries he had visited a church renowned for its stained-glass windows dating from the thirteenth (or was it fourteenth?) century. As he stood beside the lighted candles, people came up and stuck in their own, whispering and crossing themselves. He could have gazed for ever at the throng of living flames cradled in the warm air, and the dripping wax which would eventually make new candles, had not their little guide, burdened by knowledge, anxiously rounded them up to tell them all about the church and its stained glass.

'Ye-es,' Evgeny Stepanovich said to the others as he left the church and put on his hat. He was carrying his raincoat over his arm and was wearing a starched white shirt, a green tie and a brown suit shot through with a lighter colour which glinted in the sun like a cockchafer's wing. 'Ye-es. Generations of craftsmen laboured to create this.'

As the delegates merged with the crowds outside and gulped the fresh air, it was hard to tell them apart (though they themselves would naturally have denied this). Then the entire group, led by Evgeny Stepanovich, headed off for dinner, paid for by some society or other.

FIFTEEN

It turned out that the old woman had secretly kept in touch with Dmitry's widow. Elena used to say, 'I simply don't understand you, Mother! Why are you so mean? Your stockings are all laddered, and here you are darning them all over again. What on earth do you spend your money on?'

'I don't need anything, dear. My life is over, I have no needs.'

Evgeny Stepanovich happened to overhear this conversation, and felt obliged to intervene. 'No needs? Rubbish! A man must have needs. No needs means spiritual death.' She listened respectfully to this, as she did to everything Evgeny Stepanovich had to say, and made no reply.

She had inherited a black rail-worker's greatcoat from her father (he had had a decent job, so it had once been a good coat), and she had found a private dressmaker to turn it into a light coat, which she lined with wadding and used as a winter overcoat. Not one shop in town could be found to do it, and even the consumer services centre turned it down, saying, 'Give it to your poor relations, love.'

'How can you disgrace Evgeny Stepanovich!' said Elena indignantly, seeing her wearing this hideous garment and lifting it off her shoulders. 'We can buy you a nice winter coat if need be, if you insist on hoarding your pension.'

She made excuses, saying that she liked wearing something of her father's, and Elena finally accepted this.

Yet they noticed that any reference to her pension would throw her into a panic, and this began to worry them. Not that they needed her measly thirty roubles, but she did live with them. She smoked – the cheapest cigarettes, naturally. In the past Dmitry had loved smoking with her in the kitchen, and the two glowing tips would flare up alternately in the darkness as they talked together. What on earth could this clever, well-read, precocious boy find to talk about with her? They once eavesdropped outside and heard him say, 'Tell me, Gran, do you believe in God or not?'

'I don't know, Mitya darling. I do believe in him, of course, but I don't understand how he could do such terrible things to children.'

'Clever people say it's to punish the parents. He finds the most painful things to punish their parents with. To make them suffer.'

'No, Mitya, that's just what people say in their wisdom. God's mind doesn't work like that.'

'How do you know how God's mind works?' he said, and they could hear the smile in his voice.

'It just doesn't,' she repeated. 'Aren't children people too? Fancy robbing a little angel of its life, just like that . . . What sin did it ever commit?'

She did not observe the religious holidays or attend church, and if she had ever known any prayers, she had long since forgotten them. But every so often she would go into Mitya's room and whisper to herself (she had no room of her own). At these times Mitya would let no one in, saying, 'She's having a word with the Boss.'

They had eavesdropped on her there too, and heard her telling God about some silly incident one wouldn't even report to the house committee, then asking forgiveness and muttering inaudibly. It was complete mental degeneration, they had tried to tell their son, but he had refused even to listen.

Once a week for some time now she had been asking their permission to go to the cemetery, where she apparently wanted to put a headstone on her father's grave. There was a fence there, but she wanted to put up a stone, 'while I'm still alive.' So that was what she was saving all her money for. And it was perfectly understandable, of course.

One day the caretaker at their dacha suddenly walked out on them, and since it was impossible to find anyone to replace her (before the war such people had been two a penny, but now everyone was desperate for higher education), the old woman was packed off to the country to take care of the house, keep the boiler going and feed the dog. She had acquired this dog when it was just a puppy. They had been promised a pedigree Alsatian guard dog, but one New Year's Eve a stray bitch had had a litter of pups under the porch of the next-door dacha. As the Kremlin chimes peeled the last minutes of the old year on people's television screens and the toasts rang out, flushed villagers smelling of alcohol dragged themselves from their warm homes and noisy tables and poured on to the street. Beneath the porch, which was newly powdered with snow and permeated with the aroma of roast meat, the old bitch lay quietly trying to warm her blind squealing pups against her body.

Elena's mother took out little bowls of warmed-up soup and leftovers; she had seen the bitch running twice a day to the rubbish heap in the yard of the sanatorium where they threw out the scraps, then running straight back and quietly lying down again with her pups, as though anticipating what lay ahead.

Sure enough, after repeated complaints that the strays were frightening the children, grabbing people's legs, ripping their best coats and generally making it impossible to walk down the street, they were rounded up and shot. But the old woman managed to save one of the puppies, and took him home wrapped in a blanket. The moment she let him on to the floor he made a puddle, and she frequently had to wipe up after him as he grew up.

Evgeny Stepanovich and Elena, often with Irina too, used to go to the dacha late on Friday night for some fresh air and skiing. They always remembered to bring a bit of food –

usually some oatmeal and a few bones – for the dog, who was no pedigree but had grown into a huge shaggy creature and needed constant feeding.

Then they discovered by pure chance that the old woman had been secretly slipping off to the cottage on the Byelorussian line to visit their grandson. They had been quite sure that their grandson and the harlot who had robbed them of their son would be taken in by her parents in Moldavia, which was what any normal parents would do. But no, she had apparently remained at the cottage, and the old woman had been visiting her there.

One weekend there had been a fierce frost of over thirty degrees, and they had been in two minds whether to go to the country or not. But everything had its charms. Elena had a Bulgarian sheepskin coat which she kept exclusively for the dacha, and Evgeny Stepanovich had a marvellous battered black sheepskin, warm as an oven, whose fur was of the silky pedigree Romanov breed, once the pride of Russia but now extinct, so that the coat had had to be sent especially from Yaroslavl. How good it was to don a pair of thick felt boots and walk out of the heated house crunching the snow under-foot – how well Pushkin put it: 'Sun, snow, a marvellous day!' Then, freezing cold and bursting with invigorating air, they would go back into the warm to find fiery bortsch waiting for them on the table, along with streaky pink pork fat spiked with garlic and sliced in thin discs just the way Evgeny Stepanovich liked it, and crunchy cabbage, and firm little purple gherkins straight from the brine, and perhaps even a little glass of something too . . . What were they waiting for!

At work he told people he had a speech to write and, feeling like naughty children, they set off not on Friday night as usual but early on Friday morning. They arrived to find the side gate locked and the snow outside unmarked. They rang, knocked and shouted – the side gate was of iron, like the main gates, and they had not thought to bring their spare keys. The

151

only sign of life was the dog, who recognized their scent and tore about barking frantically behind the high fence.

They finally managed to get in by climbing over the neighbour's wall and creeping along in each other's footsteps like thieves, their boots full of snow. The yard was covered in dry snow, marked only by the dog's pawprints. Standing under the windows, they yelled and shouted and banged. It seemed clear by now that no one was there. Elena panicked that her mother might have had an accident and be lying inside, but the driver assured her that if there had been a dead body in there, the dog would be howling instead of racing about happily. He was evidently hungry.

They sat in the car getting warm and eating their provisions (the driver had fortunately thought to bring a thermos of hot tea), then got out again, hopping and stamping their numb feet. They could not see the slightest wisp of smoke from the chimney, which was covered in thick snow. Through the grey tops of the frosted pine-trees a round dark-red sun hung in the sky like a window on to another world, in which everything was melting in fire, about to decline. It was impossible to go home and leave the dacha now.

They were standing in the yard when they heard a key scraping in a lock and the side gate opening. Perspiring and panting in the cold, the steam rising from her body and her woollen shawl covered in frost, the old woman saw them and gave a little start, while the dog went into paroxysms of joy, yelping and jumping around her like a puppy.

They silently let her pass, and silently waited behind her as she struggled to get the key into the lock of the front door. It was as cold inside as it was out, the breath steamed from their mouths, and all the radiators were off. Mercifully the boiler had not burst and there remained a little heat at the heart of the system, but the radiator in the far room, where she had forgotten to close the ventilation window, had frozen.

They shouted at her all right – they were only human. It would have been strange not to, given what she had put them through. She confessed everything. For over a year she had been going not to the cemetery but to see Dmitry's wife and son. The reason she never spent her pension money was that she was saving it all for them. 'It's odd how people change when they're old,' Elena sighed. 'My mother's become unrecognizable.' She had given them everything, all the money she had saved for her father's headstone, and perhaps even some filched from the house. And to think that had it not been for the cold and the fact that there had been almost no transport for the last twenty-four hours, they would have been none the wiser!

'It's nothing to do with the cold!' shouted Elena. 'It's because lies don't pay! That's why you've been found out. Because lies don't pay!'

It was unfortunate that the neighbours heard the whole thing and promptly spread it around the village. They were not usually there during the winter months, but on that day, as though to spite them, they too had apparently decided to enjoy the sun and frost, and they saw and heard everything.

The old woman begged their forgiveness, she promised and wept, but they got into their warm car and drove off. To teach her a lesson, they decided to ignore her for a bit, and they negotiated exclusively with the village warden while organizing the repairs, looking for plumbers and getting the tools (a pipe had burst in the attic too, causing a flood).

A society in which information is not spread through normal channels lives on rumours, and the appalling thing about rumours is that they are always believed. Some old woman in black, complete strangers, told the entire village that Elena's mother was living in the depths of winter in an unheated house, with all her clothes on and nothing but a pair of felt boots on her feet. Whenever people invited her to their homes to get warm, she refused to go, and when they brought her food, she took offence and insisted there was nothing she needed.

True, they deliberately did not visit her for a while, and

then, of course, Evgeny Stepanovich had had problems at the Committee, for troubles never come singly. But they refused to believe she had nothing to eat. Everybody knew that their house was overflowing with good things.

One day she had telephoned Evgeny Stepanovich at work from the office of the village sanatorium. Galina Timofeevna put her through. Her voice was barely audible, for the phones at the sanatorium did not work properly, as he himself knew from the time he had had to make a call there, and the director had respectfully left the room to let him use his own private phone. The public extension was in the bookkeepers' office, which was crammed with five desks, and everyone at these desks would stop what they were doing to listen, which was presumably why the old woman was mumbling.

'Forgive me, Evgeny Stepanovich, I know I've lived too long, but what can I do? I haven't the strength to take my own life.'

This made him furious. How dare she publicly disgrace them like this! It was not even his direct line – he would not have dreamed of giving her his private number – and Galina Timofeevna could easily have overheard.

'I'm in a meeting,' he said frostily.

Psychologists say that those who threaten suicide never do it. That evening he had been about to tell Elena about this ghastly blackmailing call, but something held him back – she was the woman's daughter, after all.

The unspeakable trials they had had to endure! The rumours gradually formed a coherent picture. She had apparently let the dog go, and since it was such an odd-looking dog, people soon noticed it rummaging through the rubbish heaps. They also noticed that the gate was open. The bitter cold had been followed by a warmer spell and a fall of snow, which again showed only the dog's pawprints, and people said he howled terribly at night. Oddly enough, the heating did not go off this time, probably because the weather had been a little warmer and a well-insulated house retains the heat; after the last disaster the chimneys on the roof had been wrapped in several layers of insulation.

They telephoned from the village to say that she was lying on the veranda. They had looked through the frosted windows and had seen her lying there on the floor. It is hard to describe Elena's state as they set off, arrived at the house and saw her there. Normally an unusually self-controlled and level-headed person, on that day Elena was driven to a state of hysterics by those frozen white eyes, which seemed to be staring at her. It made a deep impression on Evgeny Stepanovich's vivid imagination too, and for a long time afterwards he would hear the veranda's frozen floorboards creaking underfoot.

The old woman lay on her side in her railway coat and a clean white funeral shirt. She had evidently thought the whole thing through and knew exactly what she was doing. There was a scratch on her forehead, and a chair had tipped over. She must have fallen from it and banged her forehead as she dropped off to sleep. She had taken all the sleeping pills in the house, and had come out into the freezing cold in her felt boots.

The disgrace was appalling, as one can imagine; they heard only snippets of gossip, but that was enough. As he later tried to work out the exact sequence of events and put them into some kind of perspective, he realized why she had chosen to die in this way.

At their polyclinic at work there was a forty-year-old nurse (always a dangerous age for a woman) who had swallowed a handful of sleeping pills after an unhappy love affair. She had had a bath, brushed her hair, made up the bed with the best sheets and a lacy quilt, put on a clean shirt and climbed into bed. People said how lovely she looked lying there as though fast asleep.

The old woman had curled up like a dog on the floor. Her head was completely grey (he did not remember her being so grey when she was alive), and her parting was yellow. Mitya had loved to kiss her parting. 'My gran . . .' he would whisper, kissing her again and again. 'My gran . . .' Evgeny Stepanovich personally thought she smelled; he had always been exceptionally sensitive to smells, even as a child.

The more he thought about it, the more he felt able to guess the terrible truth of her death. She had made sure the house was warm, since she did not want to cause another accident and did not know when they would discover her. After all, a dead body lying around in the heat . . . Yes, she had obviously thought it all through. What a terrible burden to place upon them. It could only be the work of one out for revenge. During all the time she had lived under their roof as a member of their family she had led her own private life and thought her own secret thoughts. Of course, here too psychiatrists have discovered that those contemplating suicide are not completely responsible for their actions, and their perception of their surroundings is often confused. To spare Elena he did not tell her the conclusions he had come to. But she could not rid her mind of the old woman's words: 'I'll forget how to talk if I stay here much longer . . .'

With no experience of how to handle this kind of disaster, they felt utterly lost and helpless, not knowing where to go or who to turn to. The Committee had a man who dealt with funerals, but the very last thing they wanted was for everyone at work to know about it; things there were bad enough for Evgeny Stepanovich as it was.

The situation gradually sorted itself out; a funeral was arranged and things got back under control. A special windowless khaki minibus with a red cross came to the dacha and the old woman was laid on a stretcher covered with a sheet and bundled out by two orderlies reeking of alcohol. From his first-floor window Evgeny Stepanovich saw them carry her down the snow-covered path between the banks of snow she herself had piled up when clearing it for their arrival. Under the sheet he could see her body lying on its side, the knees drawn up to the chin. The stretcher was pushed through the open doors of the minibus and slid across the icy floor, the two halves of the red cross joined as the doors were slammed shut and the bus drew away. Evgeny Stepanovich went out to close the main gates behind it, and the petrol fumes lingered in the icy air long after he had drawn the bolt.

Then there was the visit to the morgue. They were led down a worn staircase and were shown the body lying in its coffin buried in flowers, the face made up and the eyes closed. Struck by his own detachment, Evgeny Stepanovich detected through the formalin the ineradicable smell of stale meat clinging to these underground walls, like the smell of a salt-sprinkled butcher's chopping-board.

Earlier on they had received a visit from a deputation of old crones demanding that she be brought home so that her friends could bid farewell to her.

'Don't you know suicides can't be brought into the house?' barked Elena, who could be quite sharp when the need arose.

The veranda then, they insisted. She could come as far as the veranda. Or the garden.

'All right, dammit!' Evgeny finally snapped.

It was dark by the time they got her to the local cemetery to be buried. They would never forget that terrible night – the biting cold, the darkness and the steam hovering in the black air. There had been a fierce frost all day, and the only place to escape from it was the car, where Elena huddled trying to keep warm. As though to curse them further, the ground was solid frozen clay, which not even a crowbar and pickaxe could shift. They lit little fires on the ground in a vain effort to melt it, and Evgeny Stepanovich kept pouring vodka for the workmen, who crawled back blind drunk to their digging while the car headlamps blazed away and finally ran the battery flat.

Evgeny Stepanovich was terrified that they would give up, or drink themselves into a stupor and go off shouting, 'Fuck your mother, old man, and fuck your money . . .!' What did they care for his good name? What did this drunken riff-raff care about anything? Yet there was no one else he could possibly find to do the job, so he kept handing them more money and pouring them more vodka. Money and vodka, money and vodka . . . When they had got down about seventy or eighty centimetres, they yelled out to him that the grave was already a metre deep, and the shorter of the two jumped in to show him.

'There you are! Measure it against me! Where does it come to! How are we supposed to go deeper?'

Just as the coffin was being lowered into the ground and their drunken hands could hold it no longer and let it go, the black-garbed crones reappeared out of the darkness and advanced like cawing crows, their twisted hands reaching out and scattering handfuls of frozen earth into the grave. They could not be sent away, of course, that would only intensify the slanders. They must have been watching and listening in the cold all this time, because afterwards they told the whole village that she had been shoved in her coffin and under the earth to avoid a proper funeral, and that her grave was not even a metre deep . . . Evgeny Stepanovich felt as though all the stares and whispers fed the hatred within him and turned it to stone.

Elena once again went to church to light a candle, and he sacked his driver, unable to bear his face any longer. The man was demoted to an ordinary driving job, while Evgeny Stepanovich acquired a tall sporting young man in dark glasses named Victor.

The dust was finally beginning to settle when Galina Timofeevna entered at the end of one working day to tell him that a strange young woman was waiting to see him but would not give her name. 'Tell him it's his namesake,' was all she would say. 'He'll see me.'

Evgeny Stepanovich was in a good mood. The apparatus lives on rumours, and he had just been told in confidence that a certain important person had referred to him favourably, and this joyful news had later been confirmed.

'Namesake? That sounds interesting. Is she young? Nice looking?'

Galina Timofeevna pursed her lips. 'Really, Evgeny Stepanovich . . . !'

The centre light was dimmed, the table lamp was lit and the innumerable gifts and goblets gleamed behind their glass-fronted cabinets. She came in. It was odd that he experienced so little sense of threat. She wore a neat speckled suit with a white collar. A tiny woman, like a small grey guinea-fowl, with thick black hair like an Armenian's and huge grey eyes, she had good breasts, nice legs and hips, and a certain dignity of bearing. She was nervous too, he sensed that at once. Her face seemed slightly familiar; he had definitely seen her some-where before. She must be an actress he had seen on tele-vision. He was in high spirits, and felt the physical attraction ageing men feel for younger women. If she was an actress with a favour to ask him . . .

'Sit down, sit down. How can I help?' Evgeny Stepanovich, chivalrously moving the chair from behind the little desk for her and wondering whether to offer her tea. She remained standing, and smiled. She had lovely white teeth.

'I have come to tell you . . . Don't you recognize me? No, I can see you don't.'

He knew her now all right. But this striking woman seemed worlds away from the person he had seen at his son's funeral, her life finished, blind to all around her.

'I have come to tell you that you are a swine. And you will never see your grandson again. Never, do you understand!'

She looked around the room, seeming to measure him against his own office. He was so bewildered that he stood rooted to the spot, his hospitable smile glued to his lips.

'In this huge office – '

At that moment Panchikhin entered with a worried look on his ace and a telegram in his hand. Galina Timofeevna always sent him to extricate her boss from unwanted or unexpected visitors, and the rest of the conversation took place in his presence.

'. . . In this huge office, you sit in that huge armchair like a little toad. Let your subordinates know that. You can take me to court for insulting you – do it, I'd be glad.' And she quietly left the room.

'Don't let her get away with it! Find out who she is, where she's from! You can't leave it at that!'

One of Evgeny Stepanovich's cheeks was blazing, as though he had been slapped. 'Just another hysterical actress.' He waved his hand languidly. 'She's no good, I'm afraid. God gave her no talent. She comes to Moscow demanding that I help her. As though it were in my power to turn her into a decent actress . . . She may be a patient at some mental hospital for all I know . . .'

Panchikhin was furious, and Galina Timofeevna was even more so. It was appalling what Evgeny Stepanovich had to put up with – he should get a medal! With these two people he found sympathy and a common language, yet a cold weight lay upon his heart and made him gasp for breath. She was full of energy, she had pulled herself together and come back to life. She had probably got herself a new lover – you could always tell with a woman – and the son she had stolen from them lay dead in the ground.

SIXTEEN

Evgeny Stepanovich's problems were compounded by a new play, which was to open in the new Tverskoy Boulevard building of the Moscow Arts Theatre on 21 January, the anniversary of Lenin's death. According to rumours which were soon confirmed, the opening night was to be attended by Leonid Ilich Brezhnev himself, together with the entire top leadership, ordained by protocol to accompany him on such occasions. Evgeny Stepanovich had not been invited, however. He tried numerous times to find out why. His rank and position positively demanded his presence that night at the theatre, at the epicentre of events, seeing it all for himself, observing the reactions at first hand, hearing what was said and how it was said, catching all the nuances. More importantly, people would know who was invited, and where they sat, and who was behind and in front of whom; seeing he was not there, they would draw their own conclusions and the next day they would look at him differently. You can have all the medals in the world, but fail to be invited to one or two events and they will turn to dust; those who considered it an honour to be your friend will look upon you as a doomed man, an invalid, and the emptiness will open up around you.

Evgeny Stepanovich could not possibly be mistaken; his years in office told him that his position was precarious. He went through every conceivable channel to discover what had gone wrong, and at which level. But he drew a blank. People knew nothing – or, more worryingly, they would not talk. He sensed a new coolness in the way they addressed him, as though they were trying to keep him at a distance. It was like an organism rejecting a foreign body. That was it, he had become a foreign body!

Strange, panic-filled thoughts entered his head. A word, a gesture, could decide one's fate. One word and you're out. An old man whom people neither need nor care about. Doors which once flew open at your approach now slam shut in your face. Remarks which people once listened to with fascination are now taken as utter nonsense, of no possible relevance to anyone.

He had long ago realized that there was always a third, invisible force present in relationships between government officials, and that was the power of the state. If this third force was behind you, people would bow down before you. But the moment you lost that support, people knew it. He had experienced this simple truth many times in his years in office. One had only to think of Comrade M., the former minister of culture, who strode into his office one morning feeling fit and cheerful and full of the joys of spring, his coat unbuttoned and his hat at a jaunty angle, completely unaware that he was no longer minister of culture or even Comrade M. His waiting-room, which by the time he arrived was generally crowded with people bearing documents, or just introducing themselves and murmuring greetings to make sure he knew how they were, was now deserted. No one pushed forward to hand him a report or make an appointment, and someone actually brushed past without even greeting him. They did not notice their minister!

Evgeny Stepanovich had witnessed all this at first hand, and he remembered his own feelings of almost morbid curiosity at the time. He thought of the fall of Ekaterina Furtseva, Khrushchev's now forgotten but then all-powerful minister of culture. Rumour had it that they had come to Furtseva's office and unscrewed from the door the special lock that had been one of the perks of the job, to which she was suddenly no longer entitled. Had they not taken the lock, it would presumably have been something else equally precious.

Even before that, when Evgeny Stepanovich was a mere nobody, the struggle with the 'bourgeois cosmopolitans' and the 'toadies to the West' was at its height (in the Soviet Union, as in China, you call someone a toady and that is what they become). One of the 'cosmopolitans' under attack had been the great writer Ilya Ehrenburg. Ehrenburg had actually been on the presidium of the meeting at which it was cooked up, and although Evgeny Stepanovich had been too lowly to attend, he had heard all about it from those who did. There had been tremendous tension in the hall as the attack was mounted. The revered and hitherto untouchable Ehrenburg sat there as they hurled him off his pedestal and trampled him in the mud. Then he went up to the podium. Everyone sat in a numb silence, waiting for him to recant. Finally he opened his pendulous lips and rumbled in a putrid, sepulchral voice ('putrid' was the word he himself used in one of his stories) that a few comrades had described his last book and his work in general as such and such, but that a Certain Reader had written him a note. (At this part of the story witnesses differed on the details, some asserting that Ehrenburg had brought out a folder, from which he produced the note, some that he produced the note from a notebook, others that he had simply taken the note out of his pocket.) In the ensuing silence Ehrenburg read out this Reader's two-line judgment on his book, which had just been subjected to such abuse. (The Reader was always brief and to the point.) He read out this safe-conduct pass of his, and then, to everyone's consternation, put it back. (Here too people disagreed on the details: some maintained that he slipped the note into a folder; others, who were more experienced, insisted that it was common knowledge that Ehrenburg never carried a folder and placed the note between the pages of his notebook; and still others said that he simply put the note back in his pocket.) He did all this unhurriedly, then walked back from the podium to the seat in which he had just listened to all the insults with that trump card up his sleeve.

163

He swept the hall with a sleepy gaze, and people fell silent and the stormy sea of critics was quelled.

Others would have been carted straight off to the cemetery with heart attacks or strokes after such a reprimand, with only the most devoted of their friends daring to accompany them on their final journey. But Ehrenburg had stepped out, said what he had to say and rejoined the presidium. Ehrenburg had spoken, that was an end to it.

Yet the words which are unspoken often carry just as much weight. Such as the ominous silence which greets one's nomination at the approach of an election. Evgeny Stepanovich could think of nothing else these days, and after mentally running through various versions of events he had finally come to the conclusion that he had probably got as far as he was likely to get in this job, that his nomination would be turned down and that no one would feel able to second him. He knew exactly how these things happened. He himself, when someone handed him a document to sign, would occasionally look up coldly and say, 'Didn't you read the weather forecast yesterday?' and, returning the document unsigned, would pick up the next one. The official would then go out, kicking himself and praying that he had not incurred the boss's rage . . . A movement of the white hand could decide one's fate and dash one's hopes. Power intoxicates; it is a sweet sensation to capsize another's fate.

Evgeny Stepanovich spent a terrible night, dozing fitfully, his heartbeat slow and his pulse sluggish, so that Elena was even tempted to call out the emergency ambulance service. This was in fact the very night that the old woman was lying on the frozen veranda, and the dog she had had since a puppy was howling over her corpse. Evgeny Stepanovich later said he had sensed that something was amiss, and Elena backed him up. 'He couldn't stop fretting! I sensed nothing and I'm her daughter, but it was uncanny the way he knew . . .'

The next morning, washed and dressed and fortified with strong coffee, Evgeny Stepanovich climbed into his black

164

Volga at the usual hour. He had noticed recently that two important officials who lived in the adjacent buildings had taken to leaving their cars at the corner, out of sight of the windows. This was a sinister development. Not so long ago their cars used to wait outside the building for an hour or so while one of the drivers took his master's dog for a walk. The dog would waddle along on its decrepit old legs, trembling with exertion, and the driver would wait patiently while it did its business under a bush. Now they waited at the corner . . . There was definitely something funny going on. Evgeny Stepanovich felt the other residents' hate-filled stares as he arrived and left, and he found himself longing powerfully for the old days, when people dared not think, let alone give each other funny looks, and everyone knew exactly where they stood.

All that day at the Committee, in his vast office which had recently seemed so insultingly small but now seemed friendly and comfortable again, he kept himself busy listening to reports, calling people in, sending people out and burying his problems in work. Yet every so often the memory that he had not been invited would fill him with anxiety, and fear gnawed at his entrails . . . Old E.S. (those at the top of the apparatus were generally known by their initials) was observed to be more than usually friendly that day, and people began to think he wasn't such a bad sort after all. He just had to loosen up a bit with those beneath him, and he became delightfully human. The only problem was that his subordinates actually far preferred a strict hand at the top.

Evgeny Stepanovich kept going to the mirror inside the cupboard to peer at his face and smooth out the bags under his eyes. How they had swollen during the night! Maybe he had something wrong with his kidneys.

As he went through mental contortions trying to work out what he had done wrong, he remembered how he had opened his arms to the author of the odious play which had caused such problems.

'What an honour this is!' he had said, striding into the middle of his office and clasping the man's hand with both of his. 'So we haven't managed to shut you up yet, eh, ho-ho!'

He never stood on ceremony with writers of this stature, knowing that frankness would be taken as a sign of trust. The two men had a long discussion about the play, and tea was served, brewed especially by Galina Timofeevna, with slices of lemon on a dish and three kinds of biscuit. Everything was of the best. The man obviously had some powerful backers – that must be the secret of his immunity. If only one knew who they were. Evgeny Stepanovich had nothing but praise for his new play; it had struck him on first reading as an extraordinary literary achievement; he was impressed by the vast range of colours and the sharp pen, which might irritate some, but which he personally found most congenial ... His one regret was that he would have to send it off to the Marx-Engels-Lenin Institute for their opinion. The play was about Lenin, after all.

The people at the MELI knew the writer well, and his plays had all had a fairly rough passage. Like mine-layers entering a field with mine-detectors, they would comb his work, checking each line and reading the invisible thoughts which lay in between. It would then make its way through the various departments, and their collective work would finally bear fruit in the Conclusion, printed out on a blank form and signed by two or three people well known in such circles. If the Conclusion was favourable, Evgeny Stepanovich would be the first to say, 'There, I told you so!' But he was always careful to hedge his bets, like the doctor who assures his patient, 'You'll have a boy', and writes in his diary, 'It will be a girl', thus being right whatever the outcome.

But this playwright turned out not to be so straightforward. He drank his tea and listened to what Evgeny Stepanovich had to say, knowing full well, because of some sort of leak, that his play had already been sent off and that the Conclusion was at that very moment being written. Suddenly he began to shout. He was a large man, and although he was not yet fifty, his hair was white and he had recently suffered a minor stroke. His florid face now made his hair look even whiter, and as he went on bawling at the top of his voice, Evgeny Stepanovich grew worried: if the man crashed to the floor in his study, tongues would certainly wag. He poured him a glass of water, which he refused . . .

In the cold light of day Evgeny Stepanovich had concluded that he had only shouted from a position of weakness: the man with real power behind him does not shout, the man with power speaks calmly. But Evgeny Stepanovich was evidently wrong. The scene in his office had been acted out according to the best rules of the theatre, with the writer playing both roles, and the end result was that Evgeny Stepanovich was not invited to the opening night. His presence was not required, his name had been struck off the list, and there could be absolutely no doubt that the decision had been taken at the highest possible level.

The most extraordinary thing was that the play had gone into rehearsal despite the fact that M. A. (in other words Mikhail Andreevich Suslov himself) had spoken out against it. Suslov had not read the play, of course, but people had given him various adverse reports, and Evgeny Stepanovich had used one of his officials to bring several more to Suslov's attention. Yet the rehearsals went ahead all the same. Such things never happen by chance. Someone was obviously pushing the play.

They called Suslov the 'Grey Cardinal'. As Brezhnev's ideology supremo, he was always second in command, always in the shadows, but he never put a foot wrong, and his opinions often carried more weight than those of the great man himself. True, he had once slipped up, and maybe that was what people were now exploiting. But it was immediately after this that he had pulled off his boldest masterstroke. Evgeny Stepanovich would not have put his neck on the line about it, but he had heard the backstage version from people close to the centre. Apparently M. A. had proposed to the seventy-year-old Leonid Ilich that he be awarded a fourth Hero of the Soviet Union medal and a fifth Gold Star (Brezhnev was already a Hero of Socialist Labour). One of the General Secretary's closest assistants, who obviously knew Brezhnev well, protested that since it was not even a special date, people might get the wrong impression. Not one soldier in the whole of the Second World War had received *four* Hero of the Soviet Union awards, and a second such medal had been awarded only to a couple of men in the artillery, one of whom was unable to take it in his hands since he had none, and had led an entire artillery regiment into battle without them. But Leonid Ilich had apparently said, 'Let the comrades decide.' And so the comrades had decided.

The nation switched on their television sets to watch M. A. (who himself had two Hero awards) pin a fifth Gold Star to Brezhnev's chest. Being a head taller than the General Secretary, Suslov had to bend his knees. His powerful spectacles were perched on top of his beaky nose; as usual, his trousers refused to stay up and fell into his shoes while Leonid Ilich stood waiting, his chest thrown out in eager anticipation. The two men kissed, and the semicircle of important people behind them applauded approvingly.

So what had happened this time?

Worrying rumours had circulated. The 'voices' reported that M. A. was ill, that the diagnosis was bad and that he had two tubes sticking out of his body. With these two tubes he stood in his place of honour at the podium (it must have been terribly painful) and sat in his office wielding infinite power in his withered hands. But none of this was ever confirmed or denied, since the most closely guarded of all government secrets is the health of its ministers. Amid all this alarm and uncertainty the only hope one could cling to was that the 'voices' were lying; they would think nothing of this, since their sole purpose was to destabilize the country and spread panic. Leonid Ilich had only to miss one or two public appearances or fail to attend some meeting for rumours to fly. At such moments Evgeny Stepanovich would switch on his Japanese radio set and tune in to the 'voices' through the howls of the jamming. More and more people were tuning in these days. The story even went that the entire top leadership had once met behind locked doors to prevent news of their discussion from getting out, and had turned on the radio to hear one of the 'voices' announcing that they had met behind locked doors to discuss . . .

It was on that fateful day, when Evgeny Stepanovich's life appeared to be in ruins, that the village warden telephoned to say that his mother-in-law's body was lying on the veranda and the dog was standing by the porch howling over the corpse. Only when they had rushed out to the country and seen her there did he realize the full extent of the shame which would now fall upon him, and he knew that this was the end. They would never be able to live it down; people would denounce them, disown them and flee, to avoid the contamination of their disgrace.

The old woman was eventually buried on the night of 20 January. As Evgeny Stepanovich watched the smoking sparks of the bonfire, its sooty red flames illuminating the trees in the cemetery, he imagined the whole of literary Moscow drawing up to the theatre the following evening in their warm cars, the women sweeping down to the cloakrooms in clouds of French perfume and throwing off their fur coats to reveal their bare shoulders – while here he stood in the cold with these drunken oafs on the edge of the grave which they appeared incapable of digging.

Yet there was light at the end of the tunnel. Just then the driver remembered to pass on a note which Galina Timofeevna had handed him earlier in the day. After removing his gloves Evgeny Stepanovich read the note in the cold. The smooth paper burnt his fingers as he read, afraid to believe the words before his eyes. He read it through again in the light of the car headlamps, bending down towards the radiator, while

169

the men hacked at the grave and steam hung heavy in the black air.

Galina Timofeevna, the loyal soul – tears of gratitude sprang to his eyes – had sorted out the whole story, even details which he himself had been unable to discover at a higher level. What she had found out through her own more lowly contacts was that he had been on the list all the time and no snub had been intended; some secretary had merely omitted his name through a typing error. To think that some little typist could decide a person's fate! Evgeny Stepanovich had always said the country needed the very latest western technology. It was criminal to scrimp merely in order to save on hard currency. They needed computers, printers, lasers . . .

Those with experience of such things will know the difficulties involved in issuing an extra invitation after the lists have been proofread, checked and passed. But Galina Timofeevna went along and talked to those in charge, and she was finally promised an invitation for him.

Exhausted and chilled to the marrow, Evgeny Stepanovich went virtually straight from the burial to the theatre, having shut up the dacha. The dog was locked in the yard, but he bolted, he was seen beside the grave, and eventually disappeared. There was a fashion then for dog-fur hats – the papers reported the trial of a group of knackers – so maybe he was fated to end up on somebody's head.

As soon as they got back to town, Elena fell ill. Delayed reactions are always more worrying, and they twice had to call out the doctor, who administered various drops and injections. Evgeny Stepanovich and Irina took it in turns to sit with her all through that dark winter's day. The lights were permanently switched on and evening descended early, and as he dozed fitfully, he had the most horrific dream. He dreamed that he was naked – nakedness in dreams always means something bad, he must find out what – and was being thrown out of a church. He could see and feel everything vividly; the heat of the burning candles, the faces, the voices of the choir under the vaulted ceiling, the richness of the vestments, the waving of the censor, the smell of the incense. Stark naked among these crowds of people, he stood covering himself with his hand and felt deathly cold fingers on his plump, pimply back as they threw him out of the church. Evgeny Stepanovich woke in horror, and for some reason his first thought was of his back: he had a clean back, with no pimples . . . As he shaved in the bathroom, he saw his anguished lathery face in the mirror, and was unable to shake off the chilling sense of foreboding left by this dream.

When the car approached the Nikitin Gates, Evgeny Stepanovich felt in his pocket for his pass so he could show it to the policeman through the window instead of rummaging about for it. But he was somewhat surprised to see that the boulevard was not closed to traffic. This was very odd indeed. A special pass was normally required for far less important occasions than this. By the wide, brightly lit entrance of the theatre, where thick snow whirled out of the darkness into the light of the headlamps and on to the steps of the building, two warmly dressed police captains in felt boots and galoshes waved their striped batons directing the cars. But where were the gleaming ranks of black Zil limousines? Presumably they would all roll up at the last moment.

Evgeny Stepanovich left his coat at the cloakroom and re-entered the milieu he felt he had been starved of for so long. As he was combing his hair in the mirror, he greeted a minister of his acquaintance who wore his thin wisps of hair plastered across his head from ear to ear. Fragrant women tossed fur coats into their husbands' arms and hurried to the mirrors, enveloped in clouds of scent. As always, there were plenty of soldiers with large stars on their epaulettes and stripes of shiny medals on their high-collared jackets. Literary awards glittered on civilian jackets too, and medals were pinned diagonally along several lapels. It was only then that Evgeny Stepanovich noticed that he had forgotten to wear his. Several people in this medal-wearing crowd cast severe glances at his

171

jacket and, feeling naked and ashamed of his undistinguished presence, he suddenly realized the significance of his dream . . .

After joining the leisurely crowds moving upstairs and thronging the foyer he greeted numerous people, and they acknowledged him and saw that he was there, one of the invited, not one of the banished. Having escaped the horror of being cast to the bottom of the pit from which there is no return, he breathed freely in this select society. In just one night his chilled, wind-burnt face seemed to have coarsened and now blazed in the heat. He had also picked up the habit of involuntarily twitching his neck and looking anxiously behind him, as though he were being followed.

The auditorium was empty, as was the main box, on which all eyes would fixed; it hung in the darkness above the upholstered seats, the subdued hum of voices and the faint, mysterious breathing of the stage. Wanting as many people as possible to see him, Evgeny Stepanovich was in no hurry to go in. He felt humiliated because since his ticket was a spare one from the reserve pile, his seat was not where it should have been but in the circle, right near the wall at the back. He decided to slip forward quietly to a better one as soon as the lights went down.

A sudden stir of activity was followed by a concerted rush into the hall. The main box was lit up now but still empty. Everyone hurriedly took their seats. The voices grew hushed. People looked at their watches and waited. The waiting dragged on, it was time for the curtain to rise . . .

Suddenly a group of people stepped into the light of the main box. They were not the people who had been expected, however, the ones whose presence would have given a special lustre to this crowded event. The hands of the audience, which had been poised to clap their leaders, fell apart in dismay; the scattered applause spread to the far corner of the balcony from where it was just about impossible to see and almost immediately ceased.

172

Those in the box cheerfully made themselves at home in their usurped seats and behaved in an extremely free-and-easy manner. Thinking about it later, Evgeny Stepanovich realized that they were behaving like this because they knew how disappointed people were by their appearance. They were only the Moscow leaders, and not even the top Moscow leaders at that. A hum passed down the rows, and the entire first act was drowned in whispers. What did the play matter, if something was going on at the top! The anxious whispering did not stop even when the actor playing Lenin appeared on the stage. The theatre seethed with speculations, some of them too frightening even to be mentioned. On sober reflection, however, Evgeny Stepanovich decided that if something really important had happened, the performance would certainly have been cancelled. Although who knows, the play was not a comic operetta, but a play about a most serious subject . . .

When it was over, a few women ran up to the stage to throw bunches of flowers, but most of the audience rushed down to the cloakroom and straight out to their cars: something had been going on somewhere while they had been sitting there, cut off from all sources of information.

Evgeny Stepanovich never discovered exactly what had occurred, but one or two things gradually seeped out, and soon a general picture emerged. M. A. had stood his ground, and at the last moment he had found the necessary formulas to convince the General Secretary to put off his attendance until later, rather than honouring the illustrious night of 21 January with his presence, as some people had been hoping he would.

'But I've already postponed the Spartak-Red Army ice-hockey match . . .' Leonid Ilich complained, and various sources confirmed that these were indeed his words.

SEVENTEEN

It was only when the old woman was gone that they realized how much they needed her. Elena was efficient and, like the wives of many important officials, she had picked up various tricks and short cuts needed to keep things going domestically. But she had not learned from her mother the things her mother in turn had taught her, and so on, back through the generations. She could whisk up a snack in the blender, put together a light meal and polish and tidy a room, but as for baking a cake . . . 'I have never in my life baked a cake, thank God!' she would laugh to her friends. Meals were bought or delivered to the house ready cooked, so all she had to do was to reheat them; one dish generally did for two or even three people, and it was cheap. There were always plenty of snacks around; they had only to open the fridge, unwrap something and put it on a plate.

Evgeny Stepanovich had his mid-morning meal at the Committee, at the special buffet. Some places (but not the Committee) even had separate lifts. When these lifts were waiting on the ground floor with the doors open, their rich depths shone with mirrors and red wood, and those who passed by on their way to the ordinary lifts would see themselves reflected in the polished glass.

Of course, his mother-in-law had had some exasperating habits. When she was sitting on the sofa darning or knitting or looking at the newspaper, for instance, she would invariably perch at one end, near the armrest. Evgeny Stepanovich would feel obliged to point this out to her, at which she would jump up, terrified, and go into the kitchen to sit on a stool. 'Come now, there's no need to make out we're robbing you of your seat and driving you into the kitchen,' he would say, following her in. 'It's quite simple. The weight must be evenly distributed, don't you see? Why are you so stubborn?'

Elena frequently told her off too. Yet they would keep finding her in the same place; she was clearly not amenable to reason. Since they had not done anything with the furniture since her death, the mark she had left on the sofa was still visible, and the springs were quite damaged.

Everything was the same, everything was in its place, precooked meals were still delivered to the door, yet a bleak and lifeless atmosphere settled upon the flat. They no longer went to the dacha to ski and enjoy the fresh air. They managed to find a woman to keep the boiler stoked, but it was so cheerless to arrive there with nothing organized and no food on the table that they decided to drain the radiators until the spring. They had enough worries anyway in town, where Irina, who had finally married her young diplomat, was frantically preparing to leave for Thailand with him. Poor Panchikhin was now retired. He had no idea why it had suddenly become necessary to pack him off to a 'well-earned rest', and replace him with a totally green young man who had been trained in a totally different system. Even his long experience had not taught him to work out that this young man was merely a pawn in a complex manoeuvre whose ultimate goal was Thailand. Evgeny Stepanovich, once again secure in his own position, had naturally pulled out all the stops to get Panchikhin a special pension, and since the state paid for it, he lost nothing. He was obliged to Panchikhin for that priceless information which no books can impart, which had been honed and polished within these institutions for centuries, and brought to a high lustre during the last few decades. But it was hardly surprising that the students in this art were now surpassing their teachers.

One of Elena's friends advised her to get a dog to keep her company in the flat, and she was given the phone number of someone who could provide her with one. And so they acquired Dick. This puppy was no mongrel stray but an extremely rare breed which, like so much else in Russia, had all but died out and was only just beginning to come back again. These dogs were completely black and grew to an emormous size. They also had a fairly long history, and were said to trace their pedigree back to the days of Julius Caesar. The woman who came to clean the flat used to say 'You should rub its nose in it' as she cleaned up its messes in the corner. But Elena would kiss his nose and touchingly spring to his defence. 'He's only a baby. He doesn't understand. But we will, won't we? The poor darling must have a nasty operation soon. He has to have the tips of his ears snipped.'

As always with pedigrees, the puppy caught every conceivable disease. He had to be fed special food and taken to the vet, and vets had to be called out. One night when his life hung in the balance, they both sat up with him, sleeping in shifts. And in the course of nursing him through all these illnesses they became as fond of him as of a baby – perhaps even more so, since the poor creature was unable even to tell them what was wrong.

Every evening after a hot dinner and several cups of tea Evgeny Stepanovich would put on his musquash hat and his comfortable three-quarter length Finnish sheepskin coat and, after tucking his woollen track-suit trousers with the white piping into his tall fur boots, he would take Dick out for a walk. He would carry the coiled lead in his leather-gloved hand while Dick shambled along in the snow, sniffing out his special tree. When he found it, he would cock his leg, relieve himself and scratch the earth, invariably yapping at one particular neighbour if he happened to pass, so that Evgeny Stepanovich would have to apologize for him. There was a dog run nearby, but someone would always sidle up to Evgeny Stepanovich and force him into conversation, as though the miracle of their dogs' friendship bestowed some sort of spiritual kinship on the owners. Evgeny Stepanovich would smile the formal, affable smile he reserved for times when a request was about to be turned down. He much preferred walking on his own with Dick. He was not yet thinking ahead to the time when the pup was grown into a healthy guard dog, but he would certainly have to soon.

And then Suslov died. On that day Evgeny Stepanovich and Elena had been invited to a banquet in honour of a very important official. The timing was dreadful. Elena had had a new dress made specially for the occasion, and because of this dress they arrived late. Some damn thing was wrong – the shoulder-straps had slipped, or the bodice did not fit, or the hooks and fastenings were loose. Evgeny Stepanovich fretted and the car waited, while Elena stood around fussing with her dress and finally, after a huge row, they drove off in an angry silence.

'There, you see!' He jabbed his finger at the restaurant's cloakroom, where they were surprised to find nobody to meet them. The banquet had obviously already started.

Evgeny Stepanovich with his gift and Elena with her fixed smile and bouquet of flowers hurried down the corridor past wedding parties and flushed, tipsy young men and painted girls who had stepped outside for a smoke. From the other end of the corridor they could see the open doors of the Winter Fairy Tale hall, and when they entered, they found the hall deserted and the tables being cleared. It was only then that they learned of Suslov's death. Apparently the banquet had not been cancelled until the very last minute. A modified version of it had been considered, minus music or noisy speeches – the man had gone to enormous expense, after all . . . But no, things which might be forgiven in the ordinary citizen would be unforgivable in a public servant; he would be judged harshly for throwing a party on such a day, and it would cost him more than mere money.

Three large tables, each consisting of several smaller tables under one cloth, had been moved next to the presidium table with its two microphones. Everything was now being dismantled, the hors-d'œuvres were being removed, the tablecloths bundled up and the microphone wires reeled in. Some buffoon, seeing the two of them standing bewildered at the door with their bouquet, shouted 'Cuckoo!' through the still connected microphone, and the empty hall resounded to his inane laughter.

They drove home as from a funeral. It was not just the banquet that was ruined. Their entire future faced ruin, all that they had built up over the years, in which everything and everyone was connected. A bitter sense of injustice welled up within Evgeny Stepanovich; he had given his life to the Cause, he had sacrificed everything, and now some new man would take over, and this new man would decide whether the sun rose or the earth remained in darkness. All those so-called freelance artists could still sleep easy in their beds. He might have created something of eternal beauty – people had remarked on his artistic talent when he was at school. Yet this too he had sacrificed!

Evgeny Stepanovich listened to the 'voices' until late that night, clutching his little Japanese radio to his ear, twisting it this way and that and cursing the howls of the jammers. He heard the swine say in so many words that Suslov's disappearance from the political scene meant more in terms of the changes inexorably sweeping across the Soviet Union than would the death of Leonid Ilich himself. Evgeny Stepanovich did not want anything to change, the very idea filled him with terror. Oh, he would be trampled on all right, and the first to vent their fury on him would be those who had grovelled the most and appeared to be the most loyal.

He went on listening with mounting rage as they calculated the average age of the remaining members of the Politburo. As if he needed them to tell him how old they all were, and which of them had pacemakers! It was Kirilenko who had joyfully announced (a major mistake, this) that the average age on the Politburo was now seventy. The entire press had obediently picked up on this happy news. But ordinary people greeted the information with rude stories and scurrilous anecdotes.

How could the government have so misjudged their own people? There were no public opinion polls then, of course, but there were other age-old methods for gauging what people thought. There was the technology for it too. It was in the open press, not a private official document, that Evgeny Stepanovich had read that when talking to a friend in a crowd of people it would be wrong to assume that your voice will be lost in the surrounding hubbub, since there are receivers which can pick out and record every word. Evgeny Stepanovich had realized then that there must be some reason for publishing this; it was obviously a way of warning people not to let their tongues run away with them.

If someone knew something and what sort of reaction it would provoke, they ought to report it. Yet long experience had taught Evgeny Stepanovich that 'ought' was one thing, but few would actually risk it. Who would voluntarily put his neck on the line when throughout history the messenger who bears bad news has been put to death? They hear only what they want to hear – anything to avoid censure! The worse things are, the more glowing your report must be, and the more glowing your report, the more you will be praised. Why, he himself had frequently found it to his advantage to tell them what they wanted to hear, and had been well received. Now, when everything appeared to be imminent danger of collapse, one had to do something. No more revolutions were needed. Things were perfectly well set up as they were. One had connections and could rely on them for support.

After much sad and bitter reflection Evgeny Stepanovich decided upon the time-honoured solution of sitting things out in hospital. First he would have a thorough check-up, then a period of convalescence at some sanatorium-type holiday home, by which time everything should be much clearer. Especially since modern communications enabled people to keep in touch even from a distance. But his clever idea was pre-empted by the President, the old rhinoceros himself, whose post Usvatov had long since had his eye on. For the whole of his life the rhinoceros had sat at his vast empty desk in his vast empty office on the fifth floor, while Evgeny Stepanovich sat on the floor below quietly chipping away at the foundations which kept him there. Although it was hard to know if it really made any difference when the average age was seventy . . . Evgeny Stepanovich had always been quite frank about this. According to him, the limits of socialism did not lie in its failure to realize its second postulate, 'to each according to his labour;' its tragedy was in its refusal to take from each according to his abilities. It is a terrible thing when talent finds no outlet, when the work one does is beneath one's ability. The brain atrophies, the nerve cells die and the process is irreversible . . .

Since he was talking about himself here, he would speak with special pathos. He had observed that a certain ponderous sentimentality on these occasions always went down well, not only with the ladies. The more hazily expressed one's thoughts, the more profound people felt they must be. No one would dream that a man of Evgeny Stepanovich's stature would say anything he did not understand. When people do not understand something, they generally feel it must be too profound for them, and they would rather pretend they understood than appear foolish.

On the very next day Evgeny Stepanovich decided to tell the rhinoceros that he was going into hospital, the rhinoceros himself telephoned from a call-box in the hospital grounds, saying the quacks were keeping him in for a bit. He was just interrupting a little stroll to give Evgeny Stepanovich urgent instructions to mind the shop, and to let him know if there were any problems. So that was that.

Whenever Evgeny Stepanovich had been left in charge in the past, he had been extraordinarily efficient and people had immediately noticed the difference. Now, however, the opportunity gave him no joy. He felt like a broken man. His heart-beat was irregular, his liver troubled him, even at night, even though he had long since cut out fats, and he had a perma-

180

nently unpleasant flavour in his mouth, a sort of coppery aftertaste. But, worst of all, he completely lost his appetite for life. Nothing interested him any more and, instead of the usual apple-pie order on his desk, unsigned papers piled up, he forgot vital tasks and telephone calls and he kept remembered a saying he had heard somewhere: 'If I don't get to heaven, the donkey will kick.'

Seeing him like this, Elena anxiously telephoned the doctor, and he set off one morning for the polyclinic. They gave him little jars to fill with samples which were sent away for analysis. They opened a vein and took one and a half test-tubes of black blood, which the nurse said contained a lot of carbon dioxide. (He was too frightened to ask what this meant, but immediately feared the worst.) After that he went from one doctor to another, while they tapped and listened and peered into his pupils and took his blood pressure. He undressed to the waist and below the waist, got dressed, did up his tie, took his clothes off all over again in the next room, dropped his trousers and obediently adopted the most unseemly postures (thank God none of his underlings or the anxious petitioners outside his office could see him now!). As they looked and poked around his body with their rubber gloves, his gloomy premonitions cast everything in the worst possible light.

While he sat in the corridor waiting to be seen by the next doctor, shades of the past flitted across his vision. The decrepit old men shuffling over the parquet floor, some held up by their equally decrepit wives, he recognized as figures who had once been all-powerful. Those men had held people's fates in their hands, and now the white lifeless faces, the baggy skin, the dull gaze, and death peering out of their eyes, death and fear ... Had he glimpsed one of these men before, he would have jumped up and moved off as fast as his legs could carry him. Now he stayed put and turned his face to the wall. Huge time-darkened portraits of eminent bearded doctors gazed sternly down at those sitting in the chairs or shuffling down the corridors, as though to say you disobeyed us and broke our rules, now you must accept the consequences. Evgeny Stepanovich strained to read the brass labels bearing the doctors' names. Botkin, Sechyonv, Skilfosovsky . . . They looked just like governor-generals.

Hurrying down the corridors past the invalids, outnumbering them and filling the place with new life, went strong young men. Their shoes, their faces, their garish pink or yellow shirts and wide flamboyant ties marked them as out-of-towners, recently arrived in the capital. They had acquired none of the greatness which had formed their forebears, yet they were evidently on their way up, and their steps were firm with a sense of common purpose and their own power and importance. Evgeny Stepanovich remembered the awe with which he himself had once entered this building for the first time. Now he felt caught between the past and the future, and the men of the future were striding past him, ready for anything. Yet they simply did not compare with their predecessors. Their predecessors had had greatness, yes, they had proclaimed the greatness of their age. This new generation proclaimed nothing at all but a willingness to serve. He felt as though they might turn to him and say, 'You old men have eaten, now it's our turn at the table.' Their whole demeanour proclaimed this – and such vast numbers of them were infiltrating the system.

The clinic seemed old and shabby now. The parquet was worn and dirty, and here and there the wooden wall panels had been replaced with varnished plywood which looked badly out of place. Before, they would not have dreamed of using this sort of cheap substitute. Even the staff in their hygienic blue gowns, and the nurses with name-tags on their chests like delegates at a congress, appeared different now, less obliging: they no longer cared, standards had slipped.

In his quiet spot he peeled and ate an orange, segment by segment, to make up for the blood he had lost. He felt terribly thirsty. As he ate, his eyes on the floor, he remembered hearing that priests conducted church services on an empty stomach, without even a sip of water, so their souls would be pure when offered up to God. At that moment he felt as weak as if his own soul was about to be borne up to God.

He was finally told that he would have to come back for a layered X-ray of his liver. So there *was* something wrong: all his worst fears were confirmed.

Colourless days followed. Morning and night slid together, the snow would fall, then stop, the winter sky loomed low over the buildings, the sun seemed never to rise, the lights would be on for days on end, and as soon as you looked up, it was evening again.

On the day of the X-ray Evgeny Stepanovich sat in a chair in the ground-floor lobby awaiting his turn. Huge doors lined the corridor and mighty machines whirred in the silence amid the rarefied smell of ozone, and in a large aquarium filled with green plants tiny black fish swam about, opening and shutting their mouths. The face of the man sitting in the chair opposite had been turned green by the illuminated plants. He too had probably once stepped into this building for the first time looking fit and well – now his body was emaciated, his temples hollow and the whites of his eyes glistened in the light of the aquarium. The thin fingers of his large hands drummed anxiously on the arms of his chair, and every so often he would jump up on his thin legs, as though trying to escape the fate which traps us all like fish swimming endlessly around their aquarium . . .

Evgeny Stepanovich was called in first. He was made to lie on a table which was wheeled up to a machine, then a voice from a loudspeaker above him in the darkness ordered him to take a deep breath and hold it. The machine whirred. He could see two white doctors' caps bending over something behind the glass partition in the next room, but he could not make out their faces. He was wheeled out, wheeled back, raised up, and as he lay sprawled there on the table, he felt more and more hopeless.

183

Eventually the light was switched on, the voice told him to dress and a nurse came in saying, 'It's all right.'

He looked sternly at her. 'Why did it take so long, then?'

'It's a tomograph; we photograph different parts, a layer at a time . . .'

To remove all possible doubt he said, 'Was it a Japanese machine?'

'No, American.'

He walked out. The green man sprang from his chair, but Evgeny Stepanovich walked past without meeting his eyes. Each to his own fate. He collected his outdoor clothes from the cloakroom, put his coat on and went out without doing it up. Rows of cars were parked beneath the steps of the clinic, and it was snowing. Evgeny Stepanovich took the cold air deep into his lungs. As he absorbed the soft, bright day, and the delicious air, and the large snowflakes lying in the ground like the first fall of the winter, he felt he was seeing the world about him for the first time. He stood there breathing, as if he had been born again, and, strange to say, he no longer felt any pain. He walked off, buttoning his coat. He was not ill. He would live. And he ran lightly down the steps to his car, which had been waiting for him.

From the mound of paperwork which had built up at the Committee he selected only the most urgent items. This included the membership list of a theatre group which was to travel abroad. Evgeny Stepanovich's eye was caught by one name, but he could not for the life of him work out why. He sat there with his eyes closed while the young man who had replaced Panchikhin waited obediently to the right of Evgeny Stepanovich's desk, just as Panchikhin used to do. Then suddenly he remembered. About eight years ago he had seen Ostrovksy's *Lively Spot* at the Theatre of Satire, and this actor, then still a young man, had become so carried away in his diatribe against such 'lively spots' that beads of sweat had appeared on his face, and when he shook his hair he threatened to splash the second row where Evgeny

Stepanovich was sitting. Evgeny Stepanovich had thought then that there was no knowing what young men like this might do if given their heads. Now he took the list and with a steady hand full of renewed vigour firmly crossed out the man's name.

That evening he took Dick out for a walk. The combination on the landing did not work, and the lift button on the floor below was black where boys had been trying to set fire to it with matches. It's appalling! I must remind Elena to tell them to fix it, he thought. The day before he had noticed that a small pane of glass had been smashed in the door. Yesterday he had crunched the glass underfoot with weary indifference. Today everything had acquired a fresh purpose in his mind.

Behind a high fence on the ice-hockey rink in the middle of the yard boys with hockey-sticks skated under garlands of lights. When the puck shot through the goalposts, Dick dashed in terror behind his master's fur boots. As the dog lunged back and forth, Evgeny Stepanovich whirled around, tangling himself up in the lead, and he knew at last that he was cured in both mind and body.

EIGHTEEN

It was especially significant that the première was scheduled for 21 January: the play's Leninist theme made it an appropriate offering for the date. This was what they had originally used to lure Leonid Ilich to the theatre, and the inveterate ice-hockey fan, forced to sacrifice his Spartak-Red Army match, had actually cancelled the game television viewers and ticket holders had been so eagerly looking forward to. The supreme presence at the theatre on such a day could be compared only to laying wreaths at Lenin's Mausoleum, and this in itself would have guaranteed the play's success, if not a state prize, or even something greater . . . It was on a Leninist theme, after all.

Evgeny Stepanovich had only the haziest notion of the forces which had induced the deaf and physically infirm General Secretary to honour with his presence a play in which he himself had a role, and he wished someone could explain it all to him. But after giving the matter serious attention and realizing that if you can't beat them it's best to join them, he had signalled to the writer and director that they could count on his support; he had always predicted the play's success.

On 3 March the Tverskoy Boulevard was closed to traffic by what appeared to be police captains and KGB men in police uniforms. As they waved their striped batons to divert the cars up Herzen Street and Vorovskovo Street to the Sadovoe Koltso ring road, several army majors, and even some colonels, patrolled up and down keeping an eye on things.

An obscure ambassadorial car swept past, its little tricolour flag fluttering from the roof. Then Evgeny Stepanovich's car was allowed through. He ascended the snow-covered steps to the theatre tugging his leather glove off his hand, his confidence growing by the minute. In the cold below police detachments blocked off the entire area of Moscow from the Nikitsky Gates to Pushkin Square, cars rolled up and departed and doors opened and slammed for this vast invited gathering. As in January, there was a large number of high-ranking military men with their medals and ladies with strings of pearls at their throats, as well as various prosperous civilians. He greeted people, people greeted him. Here with his peers and superiors was his home, his milieu, where he could always air some grievance, discuss some urgent matter or quickly sort out some problem which might otherwise take months of fruitless official correspondence to settle. These informal contacts also offered the opportunity to make a favourable impression; when the powerful of this world got together, new possibilities always arose.

Among the crowds in the lobby Evgeny Stepanovich noticed half a dozen men standing in a semicircle. One of them, evidently something of a wit, took his place in the centre with a flourish, and a press photographer clicked and flashed, dazzling the genial faces. Evgeny Stepanovich felt drawn to this group, but his way was barred by the massive bust of Maslakova, a huge ministry official from one of the republics. She pranced about before him, prattling on about some nonsense and not letting him go, and it was only when the group had dispersed and the photographer had left that Evgeny Stepanovich noticed the badge, a tiny two-coloured book, on her breast. So she had been trying to tell him she was now a deputy to the District Soviet Deputy! Heavens above, fancy a woman with such natural endowments flaunting her wretched little badge at him!

People were already taking their seats in the auditorium. The fluttering programmes and restrained hubbub of voices were pregnant with the gravity of the occasion, and when the lights went up in the main box and he appeared, followed by his entourage, the audience rose to its feet and applauded, just as in the old days. Five Gold Stars on the left and three civilian gold medals on the right – these were his only marks of distinction. Looming out of the darkness behind his shoulder were the crooked Mongolian cheekbones of Chernenko, the austere countenance of Grishin, who appeared to be nourished exclusively on curd cheese, the eyeless Solomentsev and the rest of them, all pushing him forward to greet his people, smiling, clapping encouragingly at his back and playing up to their tsar.

Evgeny Stepanovich's seat was close to the stage this time, and he had never had a better view of Brezhnev; he saw the huge, mask-like face, the famous eyebrows, the bleary, sightless eyes, the flabby jowls and the mouth champing on its dentures. Yet through a rosy golden haze he saw too the former splendour he so longed for, and caught up in the emotion of the audience, he put his hands together with the rest of them. Deeply moved, he even had to blink back a tear.

Long after those in the box and the audience were seated and the play had started people continued to point their binoculars upwards, handing them round, asking questions and passing whispered information down the rows about who was sitting where. Even when Lenin appeared on stage with his familiar gestures and gleaming bald head, the disrespectful whispers could still be heard.

It was then that a hollow voice boomed out from the box, as though issuing from a barrel, 'There's Lenin. Let's give him a big hand . . .'

Evgeny Stephanovich felt a chill run down his spine. As he sat there, afraid to turn his head, he saw out of the corner of his eye a pair of white hands slowly rise from the box to give a couple of desultory, silent claps. From the back of the theatre another pair of hands met and parted, and Evgeny Stepanovich's corpulent neighbour in her bright-blue sequinned gown obediently joined in, rings flashing, until her husband grabbed her arm to stop her.

An eerie silence descended, and in the stillness the hollow voice boomed forth again. 'It's talking about our problems . . .'

A timid laugh came from somewhere. Evgeny Stepanovich looked round. The insane idea occurred to him that someone might be imitating Brezhnev's voice. This could not be happening, it could not be true. His neighbours faces were lifeless and official, seeing and hearing nothing, as if they were not there. Only a general in front, with his red, wind-blown soldier's face, naïvely peered around him. The rest of the audience sat absolutely still, waiting for further amusement, no longer watching the stage but the drama unfolding up in the box.

More inarticulate mumbling could be heard. 'She's nice. Must be Khammer. Let's give her a big hand . . .'

Laughter rang out, real, open laughter now.

Too deaf to hear his own voice, he boomed on to the amusement of the audience: 'Hey, Kolya, is there much more of this? When can we go home?'

Gripped by horror, as though the skin were being peeled off his head, Evgeny Stepanovich braced himself to look around. In the box a terrible sight met his eyes. Sitting there was a row of masks, living parodies of faces: the twisted mouth of what appeared to be Gromyko, the flattened face and senile protruding eyes of Tikhonov, and that huge mouth, excreting inarticulate sounds . . . God Almighty!

He could not remember how he sat through to the end. He gripped his knees and ground his fingers against his forehead, waiting for more sounds to issue from the box and more laughter from the audience. As soon as he could, he slipped inconspicuously from his seat to the cloakroom, threw his coat over his shoulder, grabbed his hat and emerged on to the street, feeling utterly crushed. For the first time in years he dismissed his car and chose instead to walk back himself, heading up Tverskoy Boulevard to Pushkin Square underground. But it was too bright under the street-lamps and, afraid that someone might come up and engage him in conversation, he decided to walk the other way, towards the Nikitsky Gates. In spite of his long years of public exposure, he could have been any ordinary solid citizen, with the sparkling snow falling under lights on to his soft musquash hat and the back and shoulders of his Finnish coat. A young couple ran past. She slipped on the ice and fell, and he tumbled after her and pulled her up, kissing her loudly, then they ran on. He glanced at people's faces as they walked towards him talking, the cold steam billowing from their mouths. Everything was the same. Poor wretches, they knew nothing. It would probably be like this just before the end of the world, with people laughing and talking on the verge of extinction . . .

The dark, starless sky stretched above into the black, fathomless cosmos. The white branches of the snow-covered lime-trees lining the boulevard floated upwards, closing over his head. These old trees suddenly carried him back to the old times, the old Moscow, and he yearned for the past. He longed to dive head first back to the old life, as far back in time as he could get. How quietly they had lived in those days, how good things had been. There had been order and security then, and time had moved at a slower pace.

Never before had he envied all the little people passing him on the street. What did they have to worry about? They went home, ate supper, drank tea and went to bed, and if anything happened, they would read about it next morning in the paper.

Three people, talking loudly, brushed his shoulder as they passed. He glared after them. Two men were walking on either side of a girl, and as Evgeny Stepanovich was watching them, one of the men looked back. There was something vaguely familiar about the cheerful bespectacled face but Evgeny Stepanovich could not place it. The man took another few steps, then turned and walked towards him. He wore a long black fur coat, now quite out of fashion, with a grey lambskin collar and grey rabbit-fur hat, and his empty right sleeve was stuffed into his pocket . . . It was then that Evgeny

Stepanovich recognized him. The man, coming closer, peered uncertainly at him through his powerful spectacles.

'Usvatov? Zhenya? Well, bless my soul . . .!'

'Why bless my soul?'

'Have we really grown so old? Well, fortunately nothing disappears from this earth, one life merely flows into another.' He beckoned to the other two who were waiting for him a little distance away.

'This is Masha, my daughter.' He gave the girl an adoring look. 'And this is Misha. Masha and Misha.'

Evgeny Stepanovich nodded briskly, his hands behind his back. It was quite obvious. The daughter and her boyfriend. You can always tell when two people are in love.

'And you . . . I don't even know how to introduce you now. Once we were at university together, and now . . .' He lifted his one arm to the grey rabbit hat and gave it a little flourish. 'And now . . . Hey, you aren't a minister or something, are you?'

That 'or something' grated on Evgeny Stepanovich's ears, as did the familiarity and affectation of his manner. Then a breeze wafted the smell of alcohol to his nose: he had clearly been drinking.

This old man standing before him with glasses on his nose was Lenya. Leonid Oksman. For three years they had sat next to each other at university. In those days Leonid used to carry himself erectly in his cotton army tunic, his empty sleeve tucked into his military belt. Stitched to the front of his tunic were one red stripe and two yellow ones, indicating one minor and two serious injuries. There was also one small medal, for victory over Germany. In those days his face had not been such a stereotype, or perhaps it had just not been so obvious. And now he was an old man, and the girl standing beside him looked like his granddaughter.

'Hello, Leonid,' said Evgeny Stepanovich evenly. 'Usvatov's the name,' he went on, turning to Lenya's daughter, unhur-

191

riedly removing his glove and offering his hand first to the lady, as etiquette required.

She was indeed a lovely girl, young and in love. He offered his hand to Oksman, who squeezed it with his twisted left hand, then he gave a curt nod to the boyfriend.

'We've just been enjoying a real comedy show,' Leonid said in an obliviously loud voice. 'What a comedy act! What a laugh we had!'

'At the Pushkin, was it?' Evgeny Stepanovich said, hoping that his dry tone would put some distance between himself and all this emotion. He knew that the Pushkin Theatre, formerly the Kamerny, was also on the Tverskoy. It was not in the same class as the Moscow Arts, of course; in fact it was a fairly second-rate establishment. This must be where they had been.

'No, no, it was the Moscow Arts! Our Leonid laid on a real show for us! You should have heard him giving the cues. The audience was in stitches, waiting to hear what he'd say next!'

'Papa!' His daughter touched his arm, noticing the way Evgeny Stepanovich jerked his head at this reference to 'our Leonid'.

'So you were invited too?' demanded Evgeny Stepanovich, even more coldly.

'Not invited, we had to pay through the nose. We wanted tickets for something else, but we ended up going to this – cost a fortune.'

Somehow it had not occurred to Evgeny Stepanovich that the public would be allowed into the theatre on such a day. He had naturally seen plenty of ordinary people there, but as he moved exclusively with his own kind, everything else lay outside his field of vision, and it was so long since he had bought his own ticket for something that he had forgotten how it was done. It was physically impossible for him to attend everything he was invited to anyway. He would be told that his presence was indispensable at some preview, then pressure of work would forbid it and somebody else would go in his place. But there were also plays like the one today, to which one was specially invited, and what counted was the invitation itself.

'Look here, children,' said Leonid firmly. 'Why don't you two walk on? I'm sure you don't need me.'

Evgeny Stepanovich regretted that he had not made his excuses and left before allowing himself to be drawn into this. Yet he was in such low spirits that even Oksman's company was better than nothing.

'Don't worry, we won't go anywhere,' Lenya said in response to his daughter's anxious look. 'To be honest, I wouldn't mind. But rest assured, I'm in safe hands.' And he nodded at Evgeny Stepanovich.

Evgeny Stepanovich too could have done with a drink, but not in present company. He disliked people who got drunk quickly.

They walked side by side, gradually falling further and further behind the young people. The odd thing was, he realized, they had bumped into each other in exactly the same spot before, in the mid-fifties, when Lenya had just been released from prison. The ground had been covered in slush, and wet snow had clung to their coats and dripped off Lenya's glasses. His daughter had not even been born then, and now here she was with half her life behind her.

They strolled through the back streets away from the crowds, re-emerging every so often on to either Malaya or Bolshaya Bronnaya Street, then circling again.

'What I don't understand,' said Leonid, 'is why you're so upset. What was so shocking about it?'

You wouldn't understand. You don't care,' Evgeny Stepanovich thought, conscious of the heavy burden placed upon him. Then he looked Leonid straight in the eye. 'The government is falling. Didn't you hear people laughing?'

'Sure. So what's new? We've been laughing at him for years. Everyone mimics him.' And he said in a passable imitation of Brezhnev's voice, 'During the current Five-Year Plan we shall be short of meat. We are making gigantic steps forward, and cattle cannot keep up with us . . .'

'Stop it!' snapped Evgeny Stepanovich with a sharp twinge of hostility.

'When they put him in power, they said it was just temporary. But with us temporary means for ever. People are still living in the barracks and prefabs we put up at the beginning of the thirties. Generations have been born and grown old in them. And on the horizon the shining heights of communism grow ever more distant the closer we get to them.'

Yes, those who were there at the front will never forget or forgive, thought Evgeny Stepanovich. Stalin was right.

'Don't worry, it won't fall quickly,' Lenya went on. 'Masses of people have everything to gain from propping up the rot for as long as possible. The system is riddled from top to bottom with millions of favourites, each of them out to grab their share while they're still alive. I looked at them in the theatre tonight. It's something very strong, based on the most primitive instincts. And in nature the most primitive organisms survive the longest.'

'For your information, I am not afraid,' said Evgeny Stepanovich with a growing animosity, which was more than purely personal. 'Presumably you *want* it to fall, then?'

'Not really, no. It's a sad fact of our history that the first victims are always the ones who did nothing wrong. It's always the innocent who pay. But whatever happens, you won't lose. Comrade Usvatov, vessel of God, you are destined to prosper!'

'What you should know' – Evgeny Stepanovich shook his head gravely – 'is that I have no desire to prosper. I wish only to be set free to devote myself to my work. Did you see my last play?'

'So you also write plays?'

'It's a pity you didn't. It got a good press, people talked a lot about it. They were even selling tickets at the underground.'

'I don't know about the play, as they say in Odessa, but

194

you'll do all right. Everything reaches for the sun, but the sun is different for each of us.'

'And what is yours?'

'Mine? My daughter, of course. I could never have realized at the front that if they killed her, they'd be killing me too. After I was wounded the second time, I believed like a fool that they wouldn't kill me. Every day of her life I worry about her future. What I had to endure in the camps with one arm . . . ! For me it's a miracle she's alive. That whole generation is a miracle. I suppose every family must feel that. But, do tell me, you must know: are they really pushing Chernenko? They say he holds God by the beard. I saw them all together close up today for the first time. God, it was frightening!'

'He has the second seal,' said Evgeny Stepanovich significantly.'

'What's that?'

'It would take too long to explain.'

'I know the scribes of the Zaporozhian Cossacks carried a bronze ink-pot on their belts. But the second seal . . .' said Lenya, with a puzzled shrug which jerked up his right shoulder without the arm. 'I saw his photograph in the paper recently, with a group of soldiers. He apparently served at some remote outpost in the war. His country needed him to be in the rear, naturally. God forbid Comrade Chernenko should die at the front . . . ! What would we have done without our dear Konstantin Ustinovich? And you know who are the most grey and faceless of them was in that picture? He was, of course! Some of them looked really striking too. One sat there as proud as an eagle, with his legs crossed and his rifle on his knee. First they wiped out the Nazis, then they were wiped out themselves. Did we have to destroy all that and debase the value of human life, just so people like Chernenko could rise to the top? Was the point of all that toil and sweat just to let him and his cronies swap seats?'

'Kindly keep your voice down!' snapped Evgeny Step-anovich.

They walked on in silence for a bit.

'Do you remember the three of us standing by the embank-ment, you, Kulikov and me? And you suddenly started talk-ing about Goering? It came back to me yesterday for some reason.' Leonid smiled, and for an instant he resembled the boy he had been all those years ago. 'You said if we could give you a leg up, you could pull us after you . . . Well, I laughed.'

'Stop talking rubbish! You're drunk . . . !'

'I remember the sun setting behind the chimneys of the Thermoelectric Power Station. We stood with our backs to the parapet, and you were in front, and the sun shone in your face. You can't have forgotten. But it's Kulikov I can't forgive you for.'

'Me? Kulikov? I don't get it!'

'During the war we were older than him. He was just a boy, and that was how we treated him. He was the brightest of us all. He was so clever . . . He had real talent, you know. I was jealous of your friendship with him at university. Now his book's finally coming out. Not in this country, of course – over *there*. I read it in manuscript. He was afraid to send it out of the country while he was alive – he was afraid for Irina. He loved her all his life. There was some sort of tragedy there, I could never piece it together. They kept splitting up and coming back together . . . To think he died without seeing his book published, or even holding it in his hand . . . And his poems! I haven't been able to memorize poems since I was shell-shocked at the front. His old woman was so happy when our first Sputnik went up. She was out in the cowshed clear-ing dung with a pitchfork, and she looked up through the holes in the straw roof – they fed the straw to the cows. "It will be good for her to look out from there . . ." he wrote. It's terrible to recite poetry. But he wrote that when everyone else was rejoicing. There's a whole economics dissertation con-tained in those two lines.'

'So you can't forgive me for Kulikov. That's interesting,' said Evgeny Stepanovich with a sour smile. 'Very interesting. Even though he was the one who informed on you. I don't judge him, he must have been under enormous pressure at the time, but the fact is he was the one who betrayed you.'

'How do you know?' asked Lenya quickly.

Evgeny Stepanovich proceeded with even tread, his hands behind his back. There was a lengthy pause as he adjusted his spectacles.

'How? Since he is no longer with us, I shall not mention how bitterly he regretted it afterwards. He was in torment. But you must have lost your memory – it was you who told me. And I might remind you, incidentally, that it was not far from here, on almost exactly the same spot on the Tverskoy, that we met that first time. You asked me then to forgive you, and you apologized for suspecting me. Must I remind you of that too?'

'I know that's what I said then . . . But I want you to know it wasn't Kulikov. Yes, I know, they told me it was. They repeated information which only the three of us could have known. He, you and I. Nobody else. It destroyed him, you know, it sent him to an early grave. They told him I'd think he had betrayed me whether he had or not. It's a form of refined sadism. Yet there were also facts and phrases which were known only to you and me. Nobody else. They quoted them to me on several occasions. They kept repeating them.'

'Why, you bloody little . . .' Evgeny Stepanovich swore, his gold-capped canines flashing.

'You should have lost your temper then,' said Leonid. 'Anyway, who cares now? It was all so long ago. Ask all these people walking by if they care. If it hadn't been you, it would have been someone else. So you betrayed me. People get upset when they're threatened . . . There's a time to throw stones, and a time to gather them up. And there's a time to betray. Of course, it hurts that you were a friend. But it always *is* a friend. I expect it was forced out of you, you probably couldn't hold out . . . I actually felt sorry for you when I realized. For the

197

Zhenya you used to be, for the Zhenya I used to love. But friends are blind, like lovers, and what I've only just discovered is that you've always served power – not ideas, but power, *any* power. You longed to be a part of that power, and now you *are* a part of it. Deep down you're not an anti-Semite, I'm sure. At least you weren't then. But it goes with the job, and now you sincerely believe all those things, for people like you put your heart where the main chance lies. Your position requires it. Nowadays you're your own man – one of the chosen.'

Evgeny Stepanovich gave an angry, tight-lipped smile. Long ago, in his student days, his lips had been thick and full and the girls had loved them; now his mouth was like a hard slit. 'Lovers are blind . . . But you're not. I can't understand why you were so pleased to see me. I was walking along, and you rushed up to me.'

'I know, I don't understand either. I really *was* pleased to see you. You're part of my past. I must have grown sentimental in my old age.'

'If you want something, just ask for it!'

Leonid ignored him. 'Before the war there was a German film called *Professor Mamlock*. It was before the pact with the Nazis – afterwards they banned it. Mamlock is a doctor, and they bring him a high-ranking SS man who needs an operation. Mamlock saves the man's life on the operating-table. But he knows the man will kill him, and the man does. That film was talking about something I don't understand. Something that makes people powerless. Yet without it, the human race would have died out long ago. It's something people repeat time and time again, at the cost of terrible sacrifices. A baffling contradiction – '

Evgeny Stepanovich stopped and glanced at his watch. They had just stepped out on to the bright lights of Pushkin Square.

'I am indeed my own man!' he said decisively and without ambiguity, interrupting the failed philosopher mid-flow.

'People understand me, and I understand them. That's the way it is.'

He looked about him, trying to work out where the underground station was – it was so long since he had used public transport. At that moment the lights turned green, the cars raced forward and he raised his arm with an imperious gesture, as if giving orders to present arms. A black Volga, recognizing it's master's signal, braked and drew in at the kerb, and he climbed in and slammed the door without a backward glance, leaving Lenya standing on the corner in his cheap rabbit hat and his ancient, ankle-length black coat with its grey collar. Lenya belonged to his past, and that past was gone. Done with. Like the innumerable forms which Evgeny Stepanovich had had to complete with each new promotion, writing with the assurance of one whose record is already known: not there, no connection, not a member . . .

At home Elena already knew about the events at the theatre from her friends, who had not been there but were better informed than most who had, and had evidently reported everything over the telephone in the usual vocabulary of hints, half-speak and evasion. All Elena was interested in was whether the men had brought their wives.

'I told you before – only ministers and upwards could take their wives. This was work, not pleasure! People's futures were at stake!'

He drank a glass of lemon vodka with his supper, chewing angrily and messily, dropping the food from his mouth on to the plate and the tablecloth, and mentally rehearsing all the things he should have said to Lenya which would have won him the argument. Only after taking the edge of his hunger and drinking a second glass of vodka did his tension ease, leaving a dull ache in his temples.

'What an insult!' he said, removing a piece of meat from his plate and plopping it into the red, slobbering jaws of the black dog, who was rubbing himself against his chair. 'What mockery!' And, after dropping another piece of meat into Dick's mouth and wiping his fingers, he told Elena all about his recent encounter on the street.

'I should think so too! Serves you right!' she said angrily. 'You're much too soft with all these people you were at pioneer camp and university with years ago. Call up everyone who shared a potty with you at kindergarten, and they'll come running. But what do *you* get out of it, I'd like to know? I know what's in it for them! Isn't he that man you once did such a lot for?'

Evgeny Stepanovich mumbled noncommittally and drank some strong sweet tea. The silver-plated spoon at the bottom of the heavy crystal glass flashed in the light. He always drank from this glass in its silver holder. Each object in this flat was a part of his life, every single thing meant something to him. Would it really have helped anyone if he had lived his life differently and sacrificed all this?

Someone had told him a long time ago (he had forgotten the precise details) that during a chase the young 'Soso' Stalin had escaped with his pal, and his pal had helped him on to a wall; but instead of then giving him a hand up, Stalin had jumped over and run away. Some time later they met again. The other man had either been wounded or in jail, but they met anyway. 'Why didn't you give me a hand?' he said. 'I helped you . . .'

And Stalin replied, 'I was needed for greater things.'

Evgeny Stepanovich would not dream of making comparisons, yet he had never doubted that he too was needed for great things. You can't make a revolution in kid gloves; this was an undeniable fact which he was wont to repeat.

As Elena and Evgeny Stepanovich lay side by side in their twin beds of Romanian walnut wood, each with its own bedside table and lamp, he said in a weak voice, his stomach heavy from eating too much and too fast, 'I wonder why this always happens. You help people, and they return it with stark ingratitude. Take my play . . . The director couldn't deal properly with such a big subject, of course, but people could always read into it what they dared not say on stage. If just

200

one of those literary big shots had said one kind word about it in the papers . . .'

'It's pure jealousy!'

'Then all these people come to me with their requests. They're the élite, the upper crust, whereas I . . . Perhaps I have no talent?'

'You?' Elena waxed indignant. 'Bless you, you've done more than *they* ever could – that's all there is to it! I myself am the target of so much envy. People can't imagine what a responsibility it is to be the wife of a great man!'

As she showered curses on the detractors who constantly tried to block his path and were not worth his little finger, his heart softened. Then she threw back the corner of the satin quilt which had been warmed by her body, and said, 'Come to me.'

He fell asleep immediately afterwards, forgetting even to switch off the light. Elena watched over him and cradled him with the hanging flesh of her plump arm. If at that moment his mother had seen him asleep, his peace still undisturbed by dreams, she would have pitied him. His downturned mouth had lost the hard, ruthless lines which had appeared when they spoke of envy and jealousy, and his hanging lips dribbled saliva on to the pillow. It was an old face, and it is painful for a mother to see her child grown old. He slept so quietly that Elena became worried and thought he had stopped breathing. Then he sensed her eyes on him and stirred and sighed, and she reached over and switched off the light.

A few days later on Saturday evening Evgeny Stepanovich was in his armchair in front of the television, watching a large orchestra of well-dressed musicians raising and lowering their bows (various decisions were to be taken on Monday regarding this ensemble). As he munched a juicy Caucasus pear, holding a plate under his chin to catch the drips, and warmed his slippered feet against Dick, who lay sprawled out on the floor, he had a sudden flash of insight inspired by the music. What a magnificent idea for his next play! All of a sudden he was in a fever of creativity, as though gentle hands were caressing his cheek and filling his soul with warmth. He must get hold of that boy who worked with him these days, and tell him that their new theme was to be a friend's betrayal. The times demanded treachery, and he is betrayed. Eight years later they meet again. It is a wet day, and wet snow drips from his glasses . . . It would be all the more vivid as a film, of course. It would even have something about the camps . . .

The unfinished pear stood on its plate on the table. Since the music interfered with his concentration, Evgeny Stepanovich wiped his fingers on a napkin and turned down the sound, leaving the violinists to bow silently on the big screen. Perhaps he could set it way back during the war? Say he was a company commander, and his friend was a commander somewhere else and lost his nerve and betrayed him . . . There would be a lot of details to get right, of course, and he would need another co-author. But maybe people were sick to death of the war.

He stopped. Staring intently ahead of him and chewing quickly, he finished the pear. Perhaps it could simply be a crime story. Something about forgeries, or bribes . . . An old one-armed convict, an inveterate speculator, sly and sharp faced, who deliberately dresses like a pauper and lies in wait for his friend on a street corner. A colourful figure, big nose, glasses, a real stereotype . . . He started pushing ideas around, and images slowly began to form in his brain. Now that his mind was working on it, he merely had to commission someone to dig out the facts and knock them into shape.

It was suddenly as though he were released from the burden which had been oppressing him, and his heart felt lighter.

NINETEEN

Several months passed. One night Evgeny Stepanovich quarrelled with Elena and went off to sleep alone in his study. There was no real reason for their argument other than her frightful stubbornness. Seething with irritation and mulling over all the wounding remarks he had not thought to say to her at the time, he was unable to sleep, first picking up a book, then switching off the light and finally dropping off into dark, troubled dreams. When the events of the following day had burst upon them and they remembered everything from a completely different perspective, he was amazed that they had created a tragedy out of such trivia. Of course, it might have been no coincidence; perhaps some premonition of disaster had strained their nerves, and he had reacted to this during the night. Perhaps there had even been something in the air – some sort of atmospheric emanations . . .

But these things only occurred to him later. When he eventually fell asleep that night, he dreamed that the telephone was squeaking above his head. His telephone was just a handset with buttons, a frightful piece of Taiwanese rubbish which someone had brought back from America for him, and which squeaked rather than rung. He heard the squeak in his sleep, and at first thought he was dreaming. Then he leaped up. It was pitch dark. The squeak stopped, then started again. His head muzzy with sleep, he grasped the handset. 'Yes?'

A hoarse, drunken voice drawled, 'Hey, Commander, what are you playing at? Kurashov the loader here. We arranged to meet, remember?'

'Commander? Loader? What are you talking about, you

drunken oaf! How dare you phone me at this time of night . . . !'

All the anger from the quarrel exploded within him, and after slamming down the handset he went back to bed. His pulse beat wildly, then slowed right down. He clutched his throat, feeling for a heart attack, and switched on the light, momentarily blinding himself. He looked at his watch. A quarter to five. 'The bastard!' he groaned. 'I'll give him a load he won't forget!'

His heart pounded with rage and his body was soaked in sweat; smelling his own sour odour, he wiped himself with a corner of the quilt-cover. His sleep was ruined now, and no sooner had he managed to doze off again than the phone squeaked once more above his head. He sat bolt upright, his whole being braced to snap like a mousetrap.

'Yes?' he said in a quiet, even voice, determined not to put the phone down but to demand who was calling, and from where. Mentally he was already penning an article on telephone hooliganism.

'Evgeny Stepanovich, switch on your radio,' said a quiet voice.

'Who's that?'

'Panchikhin here, Panchikhin. Switch on your radio.'

Peering through the gloom, he saw the light through the open tops of the closed shutters. It was morning already. That early call . . . And the familiar way Panchikhin had addressed him, like an equal . . . Something must have happened. He switched on his Japanese radio, which was still tuned to the Voice of America, and twiddled the dial to get Moscow. Living virtually at the centre of things in the capital, he had never discovered the wavelength for Moscow, and these days he always used the television for the news.

Every so often he caught the strains of some familiar classical music on long wave – Tchaikovsky, perhaps, or Bach. Evgeny Stepanovich knew very little about music, even though his work forced him to sit through many a concert and he often went backstage afterwards to say a few heartfelt words if the performer was particularly well known.

The music came to an end, and a voice announced that he had been listening to the Sixth Symphony of Pyotr Ilich Tchaikovsky. Tchaikovsky's Sixth, at this time in the morning? There was definitely something wrong. Clutching the gap at the front of his pyjama trousers (he had asked Elena to take in the elastic at the waist, but she must have forgotten), he slipped barefoot into the dining-room, switched on the television and stood in the middle of the room waiting for it to warm up. He could still smell the musty odour of his sweat-soaked pyjamas, which had dried on his body. Before the picture appeared, more heart-rendering classical music rang out. Then from the murky grey of the screen a picture glimmered into focus, and he saw an orchestra of black-suited musicians with their conductor waving his rippling black sleeves.

Not having his spectacles on, Evgeny Stepanovich peered short-sightedly at the broadcast times in the newspaper. It should have been the daily gymnastics, but instead these violinists, black suits and funeral-white faces, were scraping away at their instruments.

Elena entered the room belting her dressing-gown, and found him in an extraordinary stare, standing barefoot before the television, one hand clutching his trousers, the other clasping his radio to his ear. Both radio and television were playing the same music.

'Something's happened,' he said, last night's quarrel forgotten.

Elena, however, had not forgotten. 'What on earth's the matter with you?' Her face, creased from sleep and stripped of make-up, was a muddy-yellow colour. 'What's the radio on for? Isn't the TV enough for you at this time of the morning . . .?'

Only then did he notice that he was holding the radio to his ear. 'Don't you understand? Every disaster, here and in

Europe, has happened to music. When they don't know how to break it, they play us classical music. When war started . . .'

The musicians came into close-up, and suddenly he recognized the face of the first violin. The man had been dead for over six months, and Evgeny Stepanovich had recently had to sign some papers for his widow about his pension rights and so on. Yet here he was, alive and well, gripping his violin under his chin and bowing away. The entire orchestra, all white and black, seemed like something from beyond the grave. Presumably they had been in a hurry, and this old recording was the first thing they could dig up.

The phone rang again. It was Panchikhin. 'Switch on the radio, Evgeny Stepanovich.' he said. 'Switch it on . . .' Then silence and mounting suspense, as the classical music continued to pour out.

Victor, his driver, was the first to tell him. 'Everyone at the garage is saying Brezhnev's dead. They've rounded up all the police, or rather KGB men with police uniforms and radios. We'd better be off, Evgeny Stepanovich, before they block off the centre.'

Showered and shaved and smelling of aftershave, with his hair brushed and clean clothes on, Evgeny Stepanovich sank into the depths of the back seat on the passenger side, so he could talk to Victor.

'Turn on the radio,' he said.

The radio was still pouring forth an endless stream of heart-rending music. There was indeed a fair number of police around, and one with a radio beneath every lamppost.

At the Committee it was finally confirmed that Brezhnev was dead. Evgeny Stepanovich's initial response was a groan of despair; if only he could have hung on for another month or two. His promotion had already been confirmed, Brezhnev's assistant had been told and had said, 'Fine!' Evgeny Stepanovich had imagined himself one day in the not so distant future entering his office and aiming the toe of is boot at this entire decrepit Committee and its old rhinoceros, who had spent all

206

his life at his empty desk on the fifth floor, as though someone had once jabbed him in the back of the head and left him hunched there for ever more. People were not appointed to this Committee, they were banished here. Towards the end of Stalin's life he had threatened to send Molotov to the Ministry of Culture, because there was nowhere for him to go from there but the camps.

The General Secretary's assistant had merely been waiting for the right moment to tell Brezhnev about Evgeny Stepanovich. Picking the right moment is a fine art. The story went that Bolshakov, then minister of cinematography, had carried some boxes of film around in his car boot for several weeks, waiting for exactly the right moment. One day the films had been shown to Stalin in his absence, and Stalin was in a bad mood and had wrought such havoc upon the film-makers that their lives were ruined. Not only them either: from that time a dark cloud hung over the entire film industry.

Ultimately it all came down to the assistant himself. All he had to do was to make a couple of calls and drop a word in the ear of the relevant person. It was never clear if he was acting in his own capacity or that of the Boss. It was reported in great confidence that in the last months of Suslov's life an assistant had decided which questions visitors were to ask him, and had prepared the answers Suslov was to give. It wasn't just his assistant, in fact. There was a certain army commander who read out vital top-secret international telegrams to the sick man and sorted out various life and death matters for him.

That day at the Committee people were too busy clutching at the latest rumours to do any work. There was the appearance of activity. Everyone bustled around, the typing pool clattered like machine-gun fire, documents were typed, papers were taken from office to office, signed and returned. But the thinking section of this little community speculated tirelessly on the crucial matter of who would head the Funeral Commission. Lenin had been buried by Stalin. Stalin had been buried by Khrushchev, and Khrushchev had been in charge of the Funeral Commission, for that was how things had always worked. But then Khrushchev had been buried by . . . Well, everything had changed then. If Chernenko now led the Commission, he would certainly assume the reigns of government.

Long before it was announced on the radio word of mouth had it that Andropov was to head the Commission. At once many people's mental calculators, including Evgeny Stepanovich's, started working out the repercussions of this appointment. Long lists of names passed before his eyes. One of them was about to be moved to the front, and it was vital that he guess who it would be. Some would inevitably be downgraded and packed off as ambassadors to foreign lands, some close to home, others further away. But, of course, the most tormenting uncertainty was how everything would affect him. What could uneducated folk know of these anxieties, which turn people old before their time?

He remembered that March evening in 1953, standing under the loudspeakers on Trubnaya Square, where vast crowds had later gathered for Stalin's funeral. (Or had it been at the Kirov Gates?) Anyway, it had thawed that morning, then frozen again, and the steam from people's breath rose above them into the black air. All faces were raised to the loudspeaker, as the voice of the great radio announcer Levitan solemnly described how Stalin's legacy was to be divided, and which posts the leaders were to inherit. When it was stated that Beria would head the newly merged NKVD and Ministry of Internal Affairs, the Colonel standing next to Evgeny Stepanovich with the blue stripes on his epaulettes nodded his peaked cap vigorously and looked around him joyfully as though he were about to soar into the air.

On the day of Brezhnev's funeral Dick's frantic barking at the door heralded the arrival of Panchikhin. He came totally unannounced, without so much as a telephone call, and this struck Evgeny Stepanovich as an extremely bad omen, as though his former subordinate were trying to reduce him too to a mere pensioner. Panchikhin's appearance, however, was living proof that Soviet pensioners don't do so badly: he had put on weight, his cheeks were pink, he had changed his spectacles for a pair of gold-rimmed Zeiss lenses, and the eyes behind them were no longer faded in obscurity and regret but were those of a spruce, rather severe old gentleman. They watched the entire funeral on television together, Panchikhin sitting in an armchair with his legs crossed and wearing a pair of Evgeny Stepanovich's slippers.

As the funeral music played, endless crowds of grey mourners poured into the Hall of Columns and were directed past the high rostrum before filing off. The previous day the Committee had drawn up lists of the people who were to join the procession, including various 'workers' representatives'. One of these 'representatives' had refused, saying his mother-in-law, his wife and his children were ill, and the stupid idiot who was permanent secretary of the party organization, and who should have been given the boot long ago, blurted out. 'Well, mind it doesn't happen next time . . .'

Evgeny Stepanovich peered closely at those passing through. There was not a trace of grief on their faces, merely interest. As they walked past, they whispered among themselves, looked around curiously and even smiled. Only one woman was wiping her eyes. Could these really be the masses, he wondered with angry foreboding. Why, they were savages! Cattle!

A row of nameless sentries with naked rifles flanked the coffin, their identical faces as stony as if they had always been thus, carved out of the same rock for all eternity. The hall's famous chandeliers were draped in black; little men had scurried up to the ceiling like ants and covered them in crêpe. And there on top of the high rostrum, surrounded by strips of red and black cloth, mounds of flowers and innumerable wreaths, lay the body, its chest piled high with flowers. The camera panned in for a close-up of the eyebrows, looking even darker on the dead face, and the sunken eye-sockets, and the nostrils, and the collapsed mouth which seemed even hollower without its dentures in. The sounds recently issuing from that mouth might have been inarticulate rubbish, but at least they were something. The top of the pyramid might have been rotten, but at least it was there. This pyramid consisted of countless smaller pyramids, the very smallest of which had its own pinnacle and foundations. And each was sustained by a single force, each was joined firmly to the other and welded into a single monolithic unit. This brilliant construction had lasted for thousands of years. It was immortal, it answered to the deepest needs of the human spirit. Each aspires to move up, to create a stable basis beneath himself and to move on. And now what lay ahead?

A lieutenant-general, with the slow step befitting a funeral, led on a guard of honour. This was his moment of glory, the moment which his grandsons would remember with pride. He stepped out in front, a mere pawn in comparison with those who followed him. Standing now beside the coffin, in their black suits and black armbands, were Grishin, Ustinov, Gromyko, Chernenko and Tikhonov. The camera showed their faces in close-up. No, they certainly weren't young, Evgeny Stepanovich sighed to himself, they too hadn't much longer to go. There had already gone in short order: Kosygin, Suslov and now Brezhnev. Suddenly, unbidden, he remembered a joke he had heard from some scoundrel: what was the leaders' new sport? Coffin races... Nowadays people laughed at everything that had once been sacred. One tried to stop it, of course, but the extraordinary thing about Russian jokes was the lightning speed at which they spread.

On the other side of the rostrum the camera panned slowly over the faces of Andropov, Shcherbitsky, Kunaev and Romanov. What secret plans must be passing through their minds! Each was deep in his own thoughts. Soon they would announce details of the collective leadership which must inevitably follow. Perhaps Romanov would fit the bill; he was the shortest of them, to be sure, but little men always had big dreams. He had icy, inhuman eyes, watery and colourless.

He would not waste time talking, he would establish iron discipline ... Then Evgeny Stepanovich recalled the time when Romanov had visited Lenin's house in Finland and had tried to lay a bunch of flowers beneath Ilich's bust. He had climbed on to the plinth and stood on tiptoe but was unable to reach, even though the bust was only the height of an average man. Before, this information would have remained locked within a tiny circle of people. Nowadays, with television, everyone could see him struggling and lifting his leg and finally giving up, jacket stretched tight across his back with the strain. No, it was impossible to imagine Romanov leading Russia ...

Stepping forward even more magnificently and inspiring a whole new host of family legends, the Lieutenant-General brought in a new guard of honour, leading out the first one with him as he left. The new group lining up with bowed heads included Aliev, Rashidov, Demichev, Solomentsev and Dolgikh. Once again Evgeny Stepanovich sought solace by scrutinizing the faces of these comrades-in-arms paying their last respects. Dolgikh's face was long, expressionless and utterly unremarkable; according to Evgeny Stepanovich's information, he used the same brand of American hair dye. Pyotr Nilich Demichev was like a white-haired old woman, which was why everyone called him by the female version of his name. As for Aliev, no one knew what he was up to. His face was unctuous and evasive, as though anointed in lies. He also tried too hard to please, which was unforgivable. The last time Brezhnev had visited Baku the ferocious heat had withered the bushes, and Aliev had apparently had them sprayed with green paint to make them look fresher. He had also had the bright idea of constructing a platform on the main square which was so high that when the General Secretary had reached its pedestal, it was completely beyond his strength to climb up to it. Then there was that fishy business with the diamond ring. Whatever the truth of the episode, the factory director had ended up hanging himself, and there's no smoke without fire . . .

'What are you so down in the mouth about!' Elena interrupted his thoughts indignantly. 'You look awful. I've been beside myself all morning too, but I know where to draw the line. You're not young, the anxiety's bad for you.'

She brought in a folding table and laid out tea and snacks. Evgeny Stepanovich could have shouted at her for thinking of food at a time when the whole country was holding his breath, but Panchikhin perked up at once. 'Ah, Elena Vasilevna, how very timely, a proper Russian funeral feast! That's the female mind for you!'

'Aren't we being a little hasty?' Evgeny Stepanovich found it hard to reconcile his austere subordinate with this cheerful old man. 'Surely we should wait till he's been buried.'

'Excessive enthusiasm is no crime – what matters is the feelings behind it. You know, I've taken to reading the Bible before going to sleep. I never had time for it when I was working – I never read anything then but bad plays. The interesting thing is that it turns out the world was planned! It's a heavy bible, an old edition, and I drop it as I nod off, so the corners are bent . . .'

Elena fetched a bottle of lemon vodka from the fridge, and Panchikhin cheerfully played host, pouring out three glasses and screwing in the cork, then raising his and waiting for them to follow suit.

Evgeny Stepanovich tried to think of something solemn to say, but instead found himself blurting out, 'What's to become of us all, Vasily Egorovich!'

'What indeed, Evgeny Stepanovich, I quite agree! We shall not see his like again.'

They drank without clinking glasses. Evgeny Stepanovich wondered whether it would have been possible to talk and drink like this during Stalin's funeral. He remembered everyone standing to attention, hardly daring to breathe, and the women sobbing, and the hostile looks directed at the only one who did not. She had blushed crimson under their gaze, but her eyes were dry, and she would have had no recourse against the people's anger had it not been for subsequent events. 'Just think, Evgeny Stepanovich...' Panchikhin's cheeks had flushed even more after his second glass, and his whole appearance seemed suddenly more youthful and relaxed, as though he were inviting Evgeny Stepanovich to join him. Evgeny Stepanovich felt a growing sense of distaste.

'You know,' – Panchikhn balanced a sliver of cold smoked sturgeon on his white fingers and nibbled at it with his incisors – 'it was quite wrong to attack Stalin when he was alive. Drivers used to stick pictures of him on the windscreens of their trucks and he certainly never chopped anyone's head off. I am of the firm opinion that we enjoyed the best years of our lives under him. We shall always remember him. Remember that spy –' At this point a piece of sturgeon gristle got caught in the precarious bridgework in his mouth, threatening to dislodge it. Testing the construction with two fingers, he cautiously moved it around and finally recovered the gristle, then said the first thing that came into his head. 'Remember that spineless little playwright Sukhovo-Kobylin! When I was working at the Committee, we didn't allow a single one of his plays to be performed. I warn you, there was nothing that scoundrel wouldn't have stooped to. The Tartars used to hold processions in old Russia, he said, and now it's the bureaucrats' turn! Well, no wonder they tried him for murder! Only a murderer would say something like that. It's people like us who keep the government united and strong. As long as we remain, it will be invincible ...!'

And in Panchikhin's flushed face, with its porous nose, angry eyes and flashing Zeiss lenses, Evgeny Stepanovich suddenly saw not just one government official, or two, but generation upon generation of Russian functionaries, their honour insulted. Panchikhin was right, he thought with emotion, they must not abandon their country to its ruin.

In the Hall of Columns people were taking it in turns to

bend over the coffin and pay their final respects. First was Andropov. Brezhnev's widow rose to her feet, and he kissed her, then her son. Chernenko kissed her next; according to Evgeny Stepanovich, that must mean he would be in charge of ideology. But the two men's kisses meant quite different thing. When Andropov kissed the widow of the dead leader, it was in the name of the country and the party, whereas Chernenko did so merely as an old family friend. He's blown it, thought Evgeny Stepanovich with a mixture of irritation and contempt. He didn't have it in him. He used to follow half a step behind when Brezhnev went on to the stage, virtually holding on to his jacket. Everyone knew he was ready to take power from him – but he's blown it. . . .

Lining up behind them, a long queue of people awaited their turn to go to the widow and shake her hand. There was a clear hierarchy of seniority here. But only two had kissed her.

A cameraman hoisted his camera on to his shoulder and recorded for posterity the dead man's numerous medals on display at the rostrum. Finally, when all the leaders had passed, Kirilenko slipped in furtively from the side, like a bystander. For a horrible moment Evgeny Stepanovich thought he was wearing his bedroom slippers, but after standing up to peer at the screen he saw that all was well. Yet Kirilenko seemed suddenly to have shrunk to such insignificance that there was virtually nothing there; he was small anyway, and now he looked even smaller, and his face seemed older and flatter. Not so long ago people had hung on this man's every word and gesture, and here he was, cast aside as though he had never existed. In a little while no one would remember his name. 'Kirilenko? Who was he?' they would say. He would not even be allowed to die in dignity. Had he died in the course of duty and been raced through Moscow in a black limousine, with black escort cars front and back and two-way radios blared 'He's coming! He's coming!' and clearing all the traffic off the road – had he died then, crowds of people would have come to pay their last respects, and there

214

would have been funeral marches, and the coffin would have been borne through Moscow on a gun-carriage . . . But what awaited him now? As Evgeny Stepanovich looked at him, he pondered his own fate. What had been the purpose of all his labours? For what had he sacrificed his entire life to the Cause?

He was briefly consoled by the sight of the empty square before the Hall of Columns, with its freshly painted white lines and the immovable rows of solemn-faced officers in their white belts, sword-straps and caps. There was perfect order, there was security and stability . . .

'Moscow is sad and stern,' the announcer's voice rang out over the capital. 'The flags are lowered. Leonid Ilich's whole life was an example of his selfless love for communism and his people. He loved his country . . .'

Through the doors of the Hall of Columns the white-belted officers with ribbons on their shoulders bore out portraits of the deceased: a youthful face, five Gold Stars on the left, four medals on the right. Senior officers carried out wreath after wreath. They were followed by innumerable generals – lieutenant-generals, major-generals and admirals – each holding a satin cushion bearing the dead man's decorations and medals. Suddenly a wholly inappropriate memory came into Evgeny Stepanovich's mind, which seemed to mock the sadness of the occasion. He and Elena had been holidaying in a delightful socialist country with warm seas and golden sandy beaches, and one evening they had had a drink with a journalist who was working there for one of the major Soviet newspapers. The man had casually told them that this country shipped abroad, without unloading it, over half the oil it received on the cheap from the Soviet Union and sold it for dollars, at inflated world-market prices. The Soviet Union also lent it billions of roubles. Apparently Leonid Brezhnev had once paid a visit to this country, where they received him with much pomp and ceremony and awarded him their old Gold Star of Socialist Labour – and hey presto, the entire debt was written off. Among the dead man's 150 decorations this totally worthless Gold Star was borne aloft on its satin cushion by a general, anyone of a lower rank being naturally unworthy of the honour.

'Ever conscious of the depth and complexity of party work,' the voice boomed over Moscow, 'Leonid Ilich served as a commissar in the Great Patriotic War . . . His name is linked with the glorious victory at Malaya Zemlya . . .'

Grishin wearing his large hat stood crouched on the empty square as though driving out an invader. To one side of him some civilians strode briskly past and a group of officers presented arms.

'With tears in their eyes, the men of Malaya Zemlya stand by the grave of their former comrade as our armed forces bid farewell to the Marshal of the Soviet Union . . .'

The red coffin was placed on a gun-carriage, which was hooked up to an armoured troop-carrier headed by a machine-gun, and Evgeny Stepanovich and Panchikhin peered again at the screen to see exactly where everyone stood, their fates already decided. The rejected Kirilenko waddled forward among the relatives, finally relegated from comrade-in-arms to mere family. By the side of the gun-carriage young soldiers stepped out like automata, carbines clasped in their bent arms, legs suspended in mid-air, toes pointed, raised faces white with strain.

'A heavy loss has befallen us, the party, the people and the whole of enlightened humanity . . .'

Panchikhin refilled the glasses with a bitter sigh, and they drank in silence as the coffin was removed from the gun-carriage and placed before the Mausoleum by the Kremlin wall, which contains the ashes of murderers and victims alike, their names shining in gold. There followed the final farewells. He lay face upwards, his body covered in red calico, as people took it in turns to go up to the podium facing the Mausoleum. Standing among the innumerable portraits, they read prepared speeches written on pieces of paper. The bare head of Academician Alexandrov, a worker, a student . . .

The neatly dug grave waited, lined with red calico, strips of black mourning cloth at the corners. Then the coffin was lowered in on white silk cords. There was a shudder, something snapped, the coffin paused . . . Planting their legs wide apart to take the strain, the coffin-bearers stood motionless, holding the coffin suspended in mid-air. The salvoes waited. The camera soared up to the roof of the Kremlin Palace, where a red flag, lit by the sun, flapped and fluttered in the wind. Then a mighty thunder rang out into the air, and a black crow zigzagged across the red flag.

'His spirit has flown!' murmured Elena superstitiously.

Later, after handfuls of earth had been scattered over the coffin (Andropov the first, and the rest followed in order of seniority), the grave was filled in with professional speed, leaving a little mound topped with the deceased's portrait. Then the army moved off in a slow and solemn march. With the severe expression young soldiers wear when bearing arms, they paid their last respects to a man who after the war had appropriated the title of marshal and awarded himself the supreme military order of Victory, the man under whom their country had been corrupted, plundered and sold off. Faces uplifted, ready for battle and victory, row upon row of soldiers marched past, sons and grandsons of those who had saved their country in the Great Patriotic War.

The leaders, like the leaders before them, stood on the podium of the Mausoleum. The moment between the past and the future stretched on, an interminable moment. The future is not ours to know.